Addicted to a Dirty South Thug

Shan

www.urbanbooks.net

Urban Books, LLC
300 Farmingdale Road, NY-Route 109
Farmingdale, NY 11735

ISBN 13: 978-1-945855-00-9
ISBN 10: 1-945855-00-2

First Trade Paperback Printing August 2018
Printed in the United States of America

10 9 8 7 6 5 4 3 2 1

Distributed by Kensington Publishing Corp.
Submit Orders to:
Customer Service
400 Hahn Road
Westminster, MD 21157-4627
Phone: 1-800-733-3000
Fax: 1-800-659-2436

OCT 2018

Addicted to a Dirty South Thug

Shan

Follow me on IG and Twitter @myss_shan
Add me on facebook www.facebook.com/myss.shan.7
Or like my page www.facebook.com/authorshan

Prologue

When It All Fell Apart

October 2009

Baby, you're my everything; you're all I ever wanted.
We could do it real big, bigger than you ever done it.
You be up on everything; other hoes ain't never on it.

"Nigga, that was the lick of the fuckin' century. We for sure 'bout to come up off them birds we just copped. This may could be the last time we have to hit a lick, though, for real," my bae Rue yelled over Drake's "Best I Ever Had" as it blasted over the radio.

I was sure he thought that my sister and I would be too busy jamming to the music and couldn't hear him, but my ass was always eavesdropping. Shit, I knew what my nigga did for a living, and he kept it dirty. Anytime he talked about his *business* in front of me, I was sure to keep my ears open. I never knew when some shit he did would come back on him, and if and when it did, I wanted to be ready. That nigga wasn't about shit and was always taking somebody's stuff for a come up, but I loved that nigga. He was my nigga. We had been together for four years since I was fourteen years old, and since then, Rue had become my everything. I couldn't imagine my life without him.

My parents had tried everything to keep us apart, but you know love ain't never steered a bitch clear from danger and only lured her right in. I was addicted to Rue. Everything about him screamed that he was a bad boy, and my parents knew that, but I just had to have him. His thug persona was what made it so easy for him to talk me out my drawers at such a young age and have me going against everything my parents told me. I would sneak out at night, skip school, lie, and steal just to be with Rue. It was only right, because if I didn't, another bitch would, and that I wasn't having.

Everything was cool, though, now that I had turned eighteen. My parents told me I could no longer stay with them being that I was grown, and I understood and wasn't going to dare fight them over it. Rue quickly opened up his two-bedroom apartment to me, and life was grand for us. No matter how he got his money, he made sure we didn't struggle or want for anything, and I couldn't do nothing but respect him for that.

"Cuba, bitch, I have something to tell you," my sister Alaska said as she whispered into my ear, only loud enough for me to hear her over the music. I looked over at her light brown skin, and even in the night light, I could see that she was flushed. Whenever she was nervous or stressed about something, her cheeks would turn red, and right about now, they looked like they were burning with fire.

Alaska was a year older than me, and even though she was old enough to make her own damn decisions, my parents blamed me for her dating Bry, who was Rue's best friend. True, if it hadn't been for me dating Rue, Alaska and Bry wouldn't have met, but Alaska did what the fuck she wanted to do. Shit, to be honest, she was nowhere near as innocent as my parents believed her to be. She was a bad girl and had always been that way.

I was the good girl that fucked around and fell in love with a thug, and it fucked me up how they were always in my shit about turning Alaska and making her become rebellious.

How the fuck is that my fault? I thought as my face involuntarily scrunched up into a frown. I quickly shook that shit off. No matter how hard they tried to make me out to be the villain and tear my sister and me apart, we wasn't having that. I loved her to the death of me, and I knew she felt the same.

I brought my attention back to Alaska. She was looking like she was struggling to get whatever it was off her mind. She looked ahead to make sure Bry couldn't hear her, and then brought her attention back to me. We had just left the State Fair of Texas on some double-date-type shit and were now cruising through the South. Everything had been good between all of us, so I couldn't imagine what could be wrong with Alaska. It was around ten or eleven at night, and the streets were wet from the light drizzle that fell from the sky. I had a bad feeling in my gut, but I couldn't tell if it was because I felt like Alaska was about to deliver me some bad news or something else. I guess maybe Alaska felt the tension radiating off my skin, because she reached in her purse and pulled out a fat-ass blunt. Just looking at how much weed Alaska had packed into that 'rillo had me rolling my eyes. That bitch loved to get high. If my parents only knew that it was Alaska that got me started on smoking that purple, they would have a fit.

"Alaska," I said as I scooted across the back seat, leaving her with practically no room to breathe. "What, bitch? Tell me what the fuck is up already. You looking all nervous and got me scared over here."

She swallowed hard before she took a pull off the hay and handed it over to me. I did the same, but only I didn't take in as much. It was some good, too, because it had me in a coughing fit the minute it penetrated my lungs.

"Got damn, bitch," I said, choking, and decided to hit it again.

"I'm pregnant," she said, and my eyes bucked wide as hell. I looked up toward the front, and the fellas were too busy whispering about their own problems to be concerned with what was going on back here. I looked back over at Alaska, and she looked so damn scared.

There goes that feeling again, I thought as I looked through the back window. Nothing seemed to be out of the ordinary, but I just didn't feel right. I pulled at my shirt, suddenly feeling hot.

"Cuba, did you hear me?" Alaska said a little too loud, because Rue's nosy ass was now looking dead at us through the rearview mirror as he drove. As soon as he took his eyes back to the road, I looked over at Alaska, and she had tears running down her face.

"Damn, I know Bry be fucking up, but I didn't know it was that bad," I said to her, and she shook her head.

"Remember the guy I started telling you about the other day? The one I said I was falling in love with—" Alaska started, but her words were cut off when the glass from my window shattered. It seemed that every time she brought dude up, we were somehow rudely interrupted. We all ducked down, shielding our heads, but for Bry, it was too late. I briefly looked up as his head bounced forward, hitting the dashboard, and then to the side before it rested against the passenger's side window.

I saw the blood, but I didn't even have time to completely process what was going on before I felt the car nicking something in the road and flipping over. Both Alaska and I were jerked around a few times before the car finally came to a stop.

"Fuck! Y'all okay? Cuba!" Rue called out from the front of the car, but I was slow to come to. My head was spinning, and my leg was on fire. It didn't feel like it was broken or anything like that, but I was too out of it to tell.

"Aye, yo, Bry! My nigga, you good?" Rue asked him, and although I knew that he was no longer with us, I held onto my breath and waited, hoping that he would say something.

"Bryson!" Alaska screamed. Her voice was jittery, but for the most part, she seemed okay. I grabbed at her hand, and she squeezed mine and held it inside of hers. "Bryson!"

"My nigga! Say something, bro!" Rue yelled, his voice shaky. He reached over to shake Bryson, causing his whole body to fall forward.

Screechhhh!

"Get out the car! Get out the car!" Rue barked, panicky, just as bullets began to rain our way.

"Alaska, get out!" I screamed at her, but she didn't budge.

We were posted up in the middle of the damn street, but we weren't dead, and I wasn't about to lay down without putting up a fight. Luckily, we had landed back on all four wheels and wouldn't have any issues getting out this muthafucka. I climbed over Alaska, quickly pushed the door open, and brought her ass along with me. I could tell she was in a state of shock, but we had to get the fuck up outta there before we were all dead.

As soon as I looked up, Rue was running around the car toward us, but the bullets that hit his back took him down to the ground. My eyes bucked as I let Alaska go and ran toward him. I could feel the tears as they ran from my eyes and down my cheeks. I couldn't believe this shit was happening to us, but this was how it was in the streets. That good bullshit never came without a good dose of karma.

"Rue, get up!" I yelled at him just as the gunfire seemed to cease. Once I made it over to Rue, I rolled him onto his back, and immediately, he looked into my eyes. I could see that he was scared, and I didn't know if I should be too. I didn't know if he would make it, but I knew one thing was for certain, and that was I was willing to die with him. Shit, what was life without Rue in it? I no longer gave a fuck about anything going on around me at that point. Fuck ducking and dodging bullets; they needed to take me, too.

"Rue!"

"Cuba, help me get him out of the car," Alaska cried, snapping me out of my reverie. It seemed that she had come to and was finally aware that shit was going down, but what she was fighting for no longer mattered. I loved Bry like a brother, but that nigga was dead, and my Rue was all I was concerned about.

"Cuba, baby, I love you . . . and . . . I know you love your nigga, but you and Alaska . . . need to go. Sounds like them boys is close," Rue breathed out, and I looked around, because he was right.

I could hear the sirens, Alaska crying over Bry's dead body that she had managed to drag out of the car, and the music from the shooters' car. Although I was ready to die if I had to, I was starting to second guess that thought when the shooters' car came to a halt and the muthafucka in the back seat jumped out and barged in our direction. I thought maybe he was coming to finish Rue off, but when he headed for Alaska, my heart stopped. He grabbed her by her hair and dragged her away from Bry.

I didn't know what the fuck was going on. Slowly, I crept away from Rue to try to get to Alaska, but I was quickly grabbed up by another nigga that I didn't even see coming.

The one that had grabbed Alaska left her sitting where she was and made his way over to Bry. When he pointed his pistol at my nigga, I knew he was about to do him dirty. Shit was fucked up, 'cause Bry was already gone. What was the point of that? When he pulled the trigger, Alaska jumped up and ran at him. The shooter turned toward her, forcing her to stop and back away from him. I panicked. His face was fully covered, but . . . the way his eyes bored into Alaska made me rethink what this was all about. I had assumed this was on some payback shit for something Rue and Bry had done. They stayed ganking some dope boy's shit, and Rue had always told me that one day, his time would come. For that reason alone, I tried to stay ready, but shit, I wasn't prepared for this—especially not anything that involved my sister.

What the hell did Alaska have do with this shit? I pondered as I watched the shooter stare at her like he was hurt about something.

"Yo, nigga, hurry up and let's go! I know you hear them sirens," the one holding me yelled as he loosened his grip and finally let me go.

"Alaska!" I yelled out and made my way in her direction. Momentarily, she turned her head to look back at me. Fear was written in her eyes. I reached my arms out for her to run to me, but instead, she turned away and took her attention back to the shooter that was near her.

He brought his pistol up and aimed it at Alaska. I was only a few feet away from her, but that little distance seemed so far away when he pulled the trigger and bodied my sister right before my very eyes.

12 hours later

"Cuba Lance," a short, fat, and wide white dude said, slamming a stack of papers right next to my head as I rested it against the table. I picked my head up and looked at him with a frown smeared across my face. I could smell the bullshit seeping through his pores. "My Cuba, my Cuba . . . what a pretty name for such a pretty young lady. How are you feeling, Ms. Lance?"

"I'm ready to go home. I've been here for hours already. Did they say anything about my sister . . . about Rue?" I questioned, already halfway knowing their fate. Another detective walked in and came and sat beside his partner, but I ignored him and continued asking the questions that I needed some answers to. "Can you tell me why y'all still got me here? Have you talked to my parents? What are they saying about Rue and Alaska?"

"Cuba, I'm Detective Jameson with homicide and major crimes, and this is my partner, Detective Madison. How are you feeling?" the second detective asked me as he pulled out a pen and pad.

"I'm fine. Damn, man, just tell me what's going on. What's going on with my sister and Rue? They're dead, right?" I panicked and began to cry again. It seemed like that was all I had done since everything had gone down. I didn't even know why I was asking. I knew they were gone and suddenly became mad that they had left me there all alone. How was I supposed to deal with shit if they were no longer around? I would be so lost without Rue and my sister there to hold me down. I needed them.

"Rue's going to be fine. His condition was critical, but doctors updated him to stable a few hours ago," Detective Jameson told me, and I sighed.

"My sister?" I quickly asked.

"She's . . . well, she's not as good. She's hooked up to machines right now that are breathing for her. Did you know that she was four months pregnant?" Detective Jameson asked, and my eyes dropped to the table as I went deep in thought.

Alaska four months? That can't be possible, I thought as I wondered why, if she was that far along, that night was the first time she was telling me.

"I knew . . . she didn't tell . . . I knew," I stuttered. "Is she going to be okay, though?"

"Crazy thing is, the baby survived, and the doctors convinced your parents that Alaska has a slight chance of surviving, and as long as there is oxygen being pumped into her body, her baby has a chance at surviving as well. I guess we shall see," Detective Madison, said nonchalantly.

"Okay," I said sadly, not sure how to take any of what he'd just said.

"But we have a problem, little lady, that we need you to clear up for us," Detective Madison said.

"Rue is saying that the dope stuffed under the seat belonged to you," Detective Jameson bluntly stated.

"What?" I questioned. "What dope? Rue would never say that. I don't know anything about no dope."

"He also said that he believes you're responsible for everything that happened out there last night, which would explain why you're the only one that escaped everything with just a few scratches," Detective Madison said before lighting the tip of a cigarette.

I laughed, but nervously. They had to be fucking with me. I had been with Rue far too long for him to do me dirty like this. We were each other's heart, or at least he was mine. I would never set him up, or let alone my damn sister, and Rue knew that. Nah, these muthafuckas had to be playing with me. This had to be their way to try to get me to give up Rue and Bry, and shit, I just wasn't about to do that.

"Rue would never say anything like that. I know what the fuck you're trying to do, but it ain't gonna work with me."

"Cuba, you're young. Still a baby. You have your whole life ahead of you, and I would hate to see you get caught behind trying to protect some young punk who don't care about you like maybe you thought he did," Detective Madison said to me.

"I'm not protecting anyone. I don't know anything about any dope, and I didn't set nobody up to be killed."

"I believe you, Cuba. I don't see you as doing anything like this," Detective Jameson said.

"Well, if you believe me, then why are you even questioning me as if I did?"

"Because Rue said that he believes that you planted those kilos of cocaine under that seat, and it was all because you were jealous and mad. He said that the two of you had just fought a few days prior over him and your sister Alaska. You found out that he was sleeping with Alaska and that the child she was carrying may have been his. He showed us text messages between you two where you said you would kill him and her for what they had done to you."

"Wait, what?" I asked in disbelief.

Rue and Alaska? The baby might be Rue's? What the fuck? I tried to process everything that was happening. Tears ran down my face, but I still felt like they were playing with me. Alaska would never betray me in such a way, would she? I wasn't sure about shit now.

"Yo, y'all lying to me! Look, just let me call my parents. Y'all ain't gonna charge me with nothing, then I should be able to go home, right?"

"We're gonna charge you with a count of murder, two counts of conspiracy to commit murder, and possession of a narcotic with intent to distribute if you don't start talking. If what Rue said isn't true, then tell us what is true. Where did that amount of cocaine come from, and who would want to kill Bryson, Rue, and your sister?"

I shook my head and brought my stare down to the floor beside me. I didn't know what to do or what to say. I just knew that I wasn't about to snitch on Rue. I knew the dope had to have come from somebody they robbed, because they had gone out to hit a lick earlier that day before taking us to the fair, but I didn't know who it had come from. Rue never mentioned names whenever he talked about the dirt he had done. He always said the less I knew, the better for me, and now that I was sitting there faced with a load of phony-ass charges, I understood what he meant by that. If I didn't know shit, I couldn't say shit. Not that if I knew anything I would snitch, but still, I understood.

Before I could say anything, Detective Madison set a tape recorder in between us and pressed play. Rue's voice was groggy and stressed, and he almost didn't sound like himself, but it was him. I knew my man's voice anywhere. Everything that they'd told me Rue had said, I heard him repeat himself in that recording, but for some reason, I was still in disbelief.

"We had a fight, and I threatened to kill him and a chick, but it wasn't my fucking sister we were fighting over. The ho's name was saved as Brielle in his phone. I saw text messages between the two of them going back and forth about hooking up again, and I clowned Rue for it. We broke up for a couple of days, but as usual, he found a way to make me forgive him. He bought me this brace-let," I said as I held up my arm. "Told me it was over, and that it would never happen again. I didn't know anything about my sister, man. Not about them keys . . . and nothing about why somebody would want to kill them. No matter what, I wouldn't do that to my sister. They killed her right in front of me. I wouldn't do that to her. You gotta believe me," I cried as the pain I felt watching my sister being gunned down tore at my heart all over again.

"It's not about what we believe, Ms. Lance. It's about what you can convince that jury to believe. Those messages alone are a hard piece to walk away from without you giving yourself a leg to stand on," Detective Jameson said.

"But I don't know anything. You said you believed I hadn't done anything."

"And again, it's not about what I believe. It's about what you can convince the jury that is set to convict you to believe. We're gonna give you some time to sit here and think this through."

I nodded my head as the detectives got up and left me sitting alone. I thought about everything and how shit just wasn't adding up to me. I had held Rue down through thick and thin, and no matter how many times he'd cheated on me, I had always taken him back. It wasn't because I was a weak bitch, but the fact that I loved him and was scared to see what life was like without him, and that alone had always kept me coming back. The addiction I had to Rue was strong. It was something that I just couldn't break if I wanted to, and I never felt like I was wrong for feeling that way until now. My parents had tried to warn me that falling in love with a thug was going to lead me down a path of destruction, and it had always gone in one ear and out the other.

Damn! I wish I had listened. I wish I could turn back the hands of time. I wish I could do things all over again and that Alaska and I could choose better. I wish . . .

But it was too late to wish now. Not one of those wishes would ever come true.

Chapter 1

Khian Prince

3 Years Later . . .

"Khi—" Selena started, but I cut her off.

"Man, bitch, get your muthafuckin' ass in the car," I yelled as I loosened my tie and unarmed the alarm on my cocaine-colored Maserati. "Sick of your ass always fuckin' embarrassing me with your bullshit."

I pulled the door open and fell down into the front seat. Quickly starting the car, I pulled off the minute Selena's ass touched her seat. I didn't even wait for her to close her door before I was racing out of the parking lot of the movie theater.

Selena sighed and flipped her long, brown hair over her shoulder. Selena was half black and half Mexican with pouty, thick lips that she always kept poked out. Her green eyes made her peanut butter-colored skin stand out. When we met, I was mesmerized just like any other nigga by her thick-ass hips and fat ass. Shorty had that video-vixen-type shape, looking like she did time in the gym. I just had to have my way with her, but shit went too far. My dumb ass just had to get her ass pregnant, knowing damn well I wasn't beat for no long-term relationship with her; but even then, I tried to make it work.

I shook my head as I glanced over at her, while she placed her hand over her small but round belly and moved it in a circular motion. She was pregnant with my second child, and we weren't sure what we were having yet. I was hoping for a junior, being that I already had a little princess.

"What the fuck is wrong with you, man?"

"You don't have to keep disrespecting me and calling me out my name, Khi. All I did was ask you a question," Selena whined.

I leaned back into my seat and gripped my hand tightly around the steering wheel. I was getting mad all over again with the way her ass had just clowned me in front of a bunch of muthafuckas I didn't even much know. We had just come from dinner and seeing a movie— my attempt to spend some time with her big-headed, ungrateful ass. But shit, it was never enough for a bitch like Selena. She was always complaining and nagging about some shit.

"'Cause I'm getting sick of your shit, Lena. You doing childish-ass bullshit, and I swea' to God you pushing me to the point where I'm about to give up!"

"You're the one that got mad at me because I called up one of your little groupie bitches and put that ass in her place! The fuck is the bitch calling you all hours of the night for? We can't even enjoy a night out without hoes calling you, Khi! I took your word when you told me Bri was always blowing you up just to be petty, but now I don't know. It seems like bitch after bitch is always dialing your phone. Something has to be going on."

"Your ass is fuckin' stupid, yo! I walk off to go to the damn bathroom and come back with you in a full-blown argument with a bitch, You don't fuckin' listen. Listen, Lena!" I said as I mocked the little boy from the *Listen, Linda* video meme. "I'm not fucking that bitch you talked to, or any other bitch! She fuckin' works for me just like any other ho calling my phone. If I gotta go out and fuck these other hoes, then why the fuck am I coming home to you every night? I might as well be single. Don't you give me the pussy every time I fuckin' want it?"

"Whatever, Khi. That's not what she was saying. She sure didn't say she was just your worker."

"Yeah, because she was fucking with your goofy ass. You calling her up and checking her over some shit she ain't e'en much doing. What the fuck you think she gonna say?"

"Khi, we have a child on the way! I'm pregnant with your daughter, and you out here fuckin' these nasty bitches. Especially Bri's junky ass! What if I catch something?"

I sighed but was relieved when I pulled up in front of our home. I pressed down on the button on my keypad that opened my gate and erratically drove inside before it could even fully open. As much as I cared for Selena, I was getting sick of her constantly accusing me of cheating when all I was doing 90 percent of the time was working. Of course, bitches came at me left and right, trying to throw themselves on me, and I ain't gonna even lie. Every now and then, I sampled a few, but them bitches knew not to go running their mouths, and it wasn't like I was gonna tell Selena shit. I wasn't sloppy about nothing I did in the streets, and Selena's ass was just being fuckin' crazy. Every accusation she made wasn't based on shit but her own fuckin' insecurities.

Even though I wasn't trying to fuck with Selena like that in the beginning, I treated her good—just like I did with any chick that I made mine. I moved her ass up in my house, bought her a car, and paid all the damn bills. She didn't have to do shit but sit on her pretty little pregnant ass, but I guess being that her mind was always idle, she found shit to come at me about. I had put a ring on her finger and told her one day we would be married, but it would be a cold day in hell before I walked down the aisle with Selena. She was too insecure, always throwing a tantrum whenever I left the house, and constantly calling my phone and asking me a thousand muthafuckin' questions while I was working. Fuck I look like marrying her ass knowing the shit wasn't going to change? I wanted to blame it on her raging hormones due to her being pregnant, but Selena had always been that way. No matter how much love I tried to show her, she always found room to say that it wasn't enough. I was just tired of her shit.

"Let me guess: you're about to leave again?" Selena let out a frustrated chuckle.

"Yeah, you know I got shit to do. Mrs. Davis called me, too, talking about some shit is going down at Briana's crib, and I need to get over there to check on Skylarr. After that, I got this business to handle with Tramell, but I'ma be back after that," I told her, just trying to dead the tension so when I did come back, I would feel comfortable in my own damn home. She hated when I spent more time in the basement than I did with her, so she needed to just dead that shit now.

"Chmmp, some shit always going down at Briana's. Damn! Why won't you just admit it that you're fucking around on me? That you're sleeping with her," Selena yelled as she aggressively reached for the handle of the door.

I grabbed her arm to stop her. "Lena, I'm not cheating on you. Damn, what I gotta do to make you believe that?"

"Let me see your phone."

"Are you fuckin' serious?"

"Yes, give it to me." Selena held her hand out to me, and I wouldn't hand her the phone. She reached over to grab it out of my lap. I grabbed my iPhone just in time, and that only seemed to make Selena angrier. She backhanded me in my mouth, drawing blood with the eight-carat diamond ring that she wore on her finger. "Oh my God. I'm so sorry, Khi. I don't—"

"Bitch, get the fuck out of my car. I'm done with your ass," I said without even looking in Selena's direction. I ran my tongue across my bottom lip, and then reached over in the center console to search for a napkin for the blood that was pooling inside my mouth. I then slid my hands into my pocket and gritted down on my teeth.

This was another reason why I would never walk down the aisle with her. Selena had a serious problem with her hands, and although I had never hit her back, it was becoming harder and harder each time for me not to. This was the final straw for her. My relationship with Selena was becoming toxic, and me sticking around would only bring out a side of me that would possibly land her in a grave. She just wasn't worth it.

I hated to have another baby mama out there caring for my seed but not carrying my last name. I had made the same mistake with my first baby mama, Briana, but it was what it was. I wasn't going to force this shit with Selena. I was going about shit with her for the wrong muthafuckin' reasons anyway, and hell, maybe she acted this way because she could feel it. Either way, I knew when it was time to let shit go. Bitches like Selena, and even my first baby mama Briana, were bad for business.

My brothers and I had finally gotten our drug operation off the ground after putting in years of hard work, and I wasn't about to let anyone bring us down—no muthafuckin' body. Everybody knew us in the streets as the Prince brothers. It was five of us total. We grew up in East Dallas and had later moved to the South in our early teens when our father, Cain, had gotten thrown in jail and our mother, Angela, couldn't afford to take care of us on her own. She moved us in with our grandmother in a small-ass four-bedroom house where my mother's brother, our uncle, also lived.

Shit, we knew all about the struggle then. All five of us had to sleep in one bedroom with only two twin beds available to us. And at that time, we shared everything from our clothes to our shoes. The oldest of us, KaeDee and Cassidy, were the only two that got the new shit, and they had to pass down their old stuff to us. It was fucked up and sometimes depressing as hell, but it made us all have a bond that could never be broken. We respected our grams and our moms so much for the sacrifices and all the hard work they put in just to feed us. Having five hardheaded li'l niggas to take care of wasn't no joke, and they did that shit making sure not one of us got out of line.

Even then, they couldn't stop the fact that we were some born hustlers. The minute we got our feet wet in the game and made a little dough, there was no stopping us. KaeDee was the first one to hustle when he got in contact with a goonie named Moe, who our father used to get money with back in the day. He fronted KaeDee some weed, and it was get money ever since.

Them niggas Cassidy and KaeDee tried their best to keep us young ones off the block, but I wasn't having that shit. I was sick of fuckin' hand-me-downs, and I needed to have my own bread in my pocket. They protested for the longest, but they ended up finding out the hard way how beneficial I was to have around when I had to pop some nigga with sticky fingers when he tried to roll up on my fam. Murking that nigga was how I got my name, Killa Khi, and was crowned to be the thorough-ass nigga that I was known as today. I was the one that made sure we were known out there. I was the one that would never stop beating down the block until we had made enough to cop our first brick, and then, our second. I was so muthafuckin' hungry back then, and I had promised my brothers that we were gonna be some muthafuckin' kings. 'Til this day, I was still making good on that promise.

Things had changed a little bit, like KaeDee going off to school to become a lawyer, and Cassidy and our youngin', Emon, being locked away. That made it just really me and the young one, Daelan, out there putting in that work until them niggas came home. KaeDee got his feet wet still from time to time, but we tried to make sure he never really got down and dirty. We needed his smart ass to keep shit legal for us.

"Khian, did you hear me?" Selena yelled, snapping me out of my thoughts. I glanced at her, and then took my attention out the window. "I said I'm sorry. Baby, just talk to me. Don't make that decision right now while you're angry," Selena pleaded.

She tried to grab for my arm, but I pulled it away and turned to face her. I had so much disgust and hatred in my eyes for her, and I could tell by the pain written in hers that she could see it. She knew that it was best for her to back the fuck down and leave me alone. "Okay, I will see you when you come home. Hopefully, by then you would have changed your mind."

I waited until Selena got out of the car, and I quickly sped back down the driveway. I didn't even wait to see if she got in safely. That's how mad I was. I just didn't care anymore. Glancing at the digital clock on the stereo, I realized that I was running fifteen minutes behind for my meeting, and I still had to stop by Briana's to see what was up with her and my shorty. I had promised my goonies that I would meet them at the factory, help them with the count, and even planned to surprise them with a bonus.

The crew had been working hard to help me and my brothers get our drug operation just where we needed it to be, and shit, I just wasn't the type to let hard work go unnoticed. I believed in honoring those that gave their loyalty, because then it was more than likely that they would never betray us. As long as we showed our appreciation, they would, in turn, do the same for us.

I reached over and turned the knob of the stereo up to the max and began to bob my head to Rich Homie Quan's "They Don't Know" as the music blasted through the speakers. Just as I leaned back in my seat and prepared for the ride across the city to Briana's, the flashing light of the gas signal and the beeping sound alerted me that I was almost out of gas. I shook my head and pulled into the first gas station I spotted. Before getting out of the car to pump the gas, I shot the li'l homie Tramell a text:

Running late, but I'ma be on my way after I check on Skylarr. Don't let nobody leave til I fall through.

It was a little after midnight when I finally pulled up to Briana's house. I grabbed my .380 that sat inside the center console and tucked it inside of my slacks before turning off the car and stepping out. I looked up and down the dark-ass block, noticing a few of Briana's nosey neighbors outside lurking and watching her crib like a hawk. I didn't know exactly what had gone down but knew it had to be interesting enough that muthafuckas was still hanging around outside. I had gotten a call from Briana's neighbor saying that Briana may have been in trouble, but that was all that she'd told me.

But when is Briana not in any trouble? I thought before I loosened the first couple of buttons around my shirt. I had gotten all dressed up, suit-and-tie-type shit for Selena's ass, which was something I hardly ever did, and that birdbrain bitch had fucked up my entire night.

"I heard the baby crying, and when I tried to knock on the door, no one would open it. I figured I'd call you to come check it out. It stinks, and I hope she's not in there dead," Mrs. Davis said as she stood out on her porch with her robe pulled tightly against her body.

"A'ight 'preciate it, Mrs. Davis. I'ma go up in here and see what's going on," I told her.

Briana still lived in the hood due to her refusal to let her Section 8 go. We butted heads over it all the damn time, and I had even purchased her a three-bedroom home right outside of DeSoto where my mama lived, but Briana had declined. She wanted and felt like she deserved me and the world, and if she couldn't have all of that, she didn't want any of it. She knew that it killed me to have our one-and-a-half-year-old daughter, Skylarr, still living right next to the projects, when I had worked so hard to give her better. But Briana always bitched about how she was the one that wanted better. Everything that I was giving to Selena, Briana had felt like was hers, but we were far beyond that. Briana had long ago fucked up our relationship, and after all the ups and downs we had gone through, the downs outweighed the good far too much for me to ever give that broad another chance.

"Why is my fuckin' daughter screaming like that?" I questioned as I grabbed the pistol from my back and held it down by my side. The closer I got to the house, the louder Skylarr's cries had become. My jaws tensed, and I could feel the anger ripping through my veins. I hurried and put my key in the lock, unlocked it, and rushed inside to find my daughter huddled over her mother and screaming at the top of her lungs. The stench in the air hit me so hard that it caused tears to form in my eyes. My daughter ran for me and wrapped her little arms around my legs as she fought to catch her breath from crying so hard.

"My Sky baby. You okay?" I asked as I reached down to pull her into my arms. I shook my head at the smell coming from her soiled diaper that made it damn near impossible for me to breathe. "This bitch gonna make me wring her fucking neck! Briana, get your bitch ass up!"

"Hmmm," Briana moaned.

"Why the fuck you got my daughter sitting around this bitch in this nasty-ass diaper? Man, get your ass up before I beat the fuck outta you!"

"You . . . you don't care . . . about me, Khi."

The slur in Briana's voice made me even angrier. *Is this bitch drunk*? I thought as I charged through the house and made my way to Skylarr's room. Once I flipped the switch, my heart skipped a beat just looking at the condition of her room. There were dirty diapers, soiled clothing, food containers, and toys all over the place. It had been months since I had stepped foot inside of Briana's home. We would either meet up whenever I picked Skylarr up, or Briana would bring her outside to my car when I came through. Either way, seeing how badly my daughter was being cared for had made me regret every day that I hadn't been more attentive.

I searched around the room for clean diapers and clean clothes, and when I couldn't find any, I stormed out of the room and down the hall to Briana's room. There was a naked man lying across the center of Briana's bed, and it took everything in me not to pull my pistol and murder that nigga. I bit down on my bottom lip, backed out of the room, and headed back down the hall where Briana was now sitting up. Her face was swollen, with dried-up blood that rested against the opening of her mouth. She had two black eyes and what looked to be a huge knot on her forehead, but the one thing that really caught my attention was the belt that was loosely tied around her right arm. The track marks were fresh, and I knew that all the money I'd spent on rehab to get Briana clean had gone down the drain.

Briana had started using heroin four years ago, unbeknownst to me. It was a secret that she had kept well and one that she had apparently never planned to reveal. I first met her at a going away party that I was throwing for Cassidy for the shit that he got knocked for. She was a bad-ass yella bone with a fat ass, and her sexy-ass eyes had me in a trance when I first met her. Right off the bat, we clicked with a real strong-ass chemistry. Briana and I were like the modern-day Bonnie and Clyde, and I could always count on her to ride for a nigga whenever I needed her to. She was the type to take a charge, beat a bitch down, and even body a nigga if I ever asked her to. Our shit was tight, and no lie, I had fallen madly in love with Briana. We were on some us-against-the-world-type shit, and I was ready to propose to Briana, give her my last name and whatever else she asked for. That is, until about a year or so into our relationship, when a dark side of her emerged.

Her erratic and spontaneous behavior had never alerted me that shit was as bad as it was with her, but the problem was nothing I could ever put my finger on. Not even the many times that my money would come up missing, the goonies that had always hung close to home, and Briana always being sick and sleeping had ever told me anything. It wasn't until I found Briana passed out with a needle sticking out of her arm on our bathroom floor that I knew that I'd fucked up when I laid down with her. Briana was already four or five months pregnant with our child, and it was too late to terminate the pregnancy. I had immediately placed Briana in rehab, and she had gotten clean just in time to give birth to Skylarr. By then, we had already broken up.

After time to sit back and think about shit, I realized I was in fucking denial. All the signs had been there, and I just flat out ignored them. Briana had really hurt and fucked a nigga up with that one. It was the first and last time I would ever let a bitch break my heart. She had turned me completely cold to these hoes. Even with Selena, I wouldn't open all the way up. I loved Selena, but that was only conditional, and I could easily put my feelings in my pocket when it came to what he had.

When it was time for Briana to come home with our daughter from the hospital, she had convinced me that she was well enough to care for Skylarr, and she had up until now. Looking at the condition Skylarr was in was eating me up inside. I didn't understand how Briana could let almost two years of her being clean go like this.

"I'm taking Sky with me, and I swea' to God you bet not contact me! Got my fucking daughter up in here with some bitch-ass nigga getting high and shit! You lucky I don't fuckin' kill you, Bri!" I roared. I brought my foot up and kicked Briana in the leg, causing her and my daughter to yelp out. I didn't care that her ass was already bruised and broken. The only thing that mattered to me at this moment was my daughter.

"You better not take my baby, Khi . . . She's the only thing I have left of you," Briana slurred as she rubbed the spot where I had kicked her. Once she noticed that I was serious about taking our daughter, she rolled over onto all fours and slowly picked herself up off the floor. "Khi, bring me back my baby! Give her to me!"

"Get the fuck off of me!" I pushed Briana as she grabbed my arm, causing her to stumble back onto the floor. I glanced over my shoulder just in time to see her grabbing a hold of her stomach and doubling over in pain. I shook my head in disgust. That monkey was on Briana's back now that she was up and alert, and I knew that she would no longer give a fuck about fighting for our daughter.

I raced out of the house, quickly placed Skylarr inside the front seat of the car, and wrapped the seatbelt around her little body as best I could. She had tiny tears falling from her eyes when I looked down at her. I wondered when was the last time she had been cleaned or the last time she had eaten.

"You hungry?" I asked Skylarr, and she nodded her head. "Daddy gonna get that baby something to eat, all right? Just hang on."

Khian: Bruh, I'm a kill Briana. This bitch is really trying me. Where the fuck you at? Meet me at the Wal-Mart on Wheatland.

I hit send.

"I'm saying, though, little girl, what kinda diapers ya mama be buying you?" I asked Skylarr as I held onto her. She smiled and pointed at a juice that sat nearby.

"This," she told me, getting slob all over me.

"Oh, you want some juice. You can't help your daddy out on these diapers first, though?" I reached over and grabbed the fruit juice and pulled the plastic tie away from the cap. I handed it to Skylarr, and she quickly brought it up to her mouth and started to suck the liquid down her throat. I figured she probably was thirsty as hell and no longer wanted to wait until I could stop to get her something to eat.

I shook my head and sighed as I watched her down that sweet-ass juice in damn near less than a minute. We had been in Wal-Mart for the past twenty minutes, trying to figure out the size and brand of diapers that I needed to buy. I was so embarrassed. Skylarr looked and smelled a mess, but this whole situation brought light to an issue that I didn't even realize existed. I had to and needed to do better when it came to being a father. I was young, though, only twenty-three years old, and Sky was my first kid; but even then, that wasn't an excuse. It was all good, though, because I had quickly learned from the mistakes I had been making with Sky and already learned what not to do when Selena gave birth to our child.

I was so used to handing Briana money for everything that she'd needed for Skylarr that I didn't even realize that I knew absolutely nothing when it came to her. I didn't know what size clothes she wore, shoes, diapers, or anything like that. Going forward, I promised myself that I was going to get more involved when it came to my kids.

"Aye, aye, li'l mama, can you help me?" I asked a woman that stood nearby with her back turned to me. I figured a nigga might as well ask for some help; otherwise, I'd be there all fucking night.

"With?" she asked and turned around to face me.

Damn, I thought as I stared into her brown eyes. I couldn't help the attraction I suddenly felt for her. It was hard for me to even understand this shit, 'cause it wasn't like she was bad or no shit like that. She actually wasn't shit to talk about. She stood about five foot three, thin, with barely any titties or a waist. She had mocha-colored skin, thick lips, and her hair was scattered all over her head. The clothes she had on were dingy, making her look completely busted, but damn . . . it was something about her eyes that made me overlook all that shit. My mama had always told me that what lies behind a woman's eyes is all a man needs to see in order to know if she is the one for him, and her eyes told me everything. I had previously thought the same thing with Briana, but I had never even felt like *this* when I first met her.

I stepped closer to her, and my six-foot-two frame towered over her as she looked up at me. I watched as she looked me over for a few, and then frowned a little when she brought her eyes to Skylarr. I couldn't even blame her, though. Briana had my daughter looking pretty fucked up. Her hair was all over her head, too, not to mention the fucking smell of urine and feces coming from her overly soiled diaper. The shit was fucked up, and my jaws clenched tightly just thinking about it.

"With?" she asked me again.

"I'm embarrassed like a muthafucka to admit this, but I'm trying to figure out what kind of diapers to buy my daughter and . . . shit, what size," I told her as I licked my lips and continued to stare down at her. This chick had a nigga all the way in a trance.

"How much does she weigh?"

"Damn," I sighed and said under my breath. "I don't even know, shorty. She's a year old. She'll be two in March."

"But when's the last time you changed her diaper? Not trying to be funny, but it looks like you ran out days ago."

I bit down on my bottom lip in frustration as she moved around me and grabbed a small pack of Huggies from the shelf. She then grabbed another pack in a smaller size and handed them to me.

"Either one of these look like they should work, but hell, I don't know. I ain't got no damn kids," she said and began to walk away from me.

"Aye, aye, hol' up, ma," I called after her. "You can't tell a nigga your name? Let me take you to eat or something for helping me out."

"Nah, I'm good, babe. You go home and take care of your seed."

"Don't be up in here acting like you a super model type or something, shorty."

"Nah, I ain't acting, nor am I tryna be a super model. I just do this shit with no effort. I saw you staring though, nigga. Don't get mad. You cute or whatever, just not my type," she called over her shoulder as she headed out of the store with her thieving ass.

I headed toward the register to pay for Skylarr's diapers, a rag that I had picked up when I first got yhere, a bar of soap, and some pajamas that I hoped she could fit. When I got done, I took Skylarr to the Wal-Mart bathroom, placed her in the small sink, and cleaned her up as best I could. Once I placed the pajamas over her body, I placed a kiss on her cheek and headed out of the store.

My brother KaeDee had finally made it up there and was parked right next to my car. He stepped out, dressed down in a white T-shirt and some sweatpants, with flip-flops on his feet.

"What the fuck you want, nigga, and what did Briana do now?" he asked as he walked up on me. I shoved Skylarr into his hands and walked around to my car. "What the fuck you doing?"

"Take her to Deonna, and I'll be over there to get her tomorrow. I was supposed to meet up with Tramell and them almost two fuckin' hours ago, and I *gotta* go out there to pick this bread up."

"Where the hell is her mama, bruh?" KaeDee asked, and I angrily shook my head.

"Man, Briana gonna make me snap her fuckin' neck. She got me so got-damn mad, bruh, I can kill that bitch. She back on that shit again and had my fuckin' daughter in a nasty-ass diaper for I don't know how long."

"Damn!" KaeDee sighed and rubbed his fingers through his thick and long-ass goatee. He kissed Skylarr on the cheek and looked at me with sympathy in his eyes. "You a'ight?"

"I'm good now that I got my shorty cleaned up. It broke my heart to see her like that, bruh. I can't believe Briana would let this shit happen to her."

"So, what you gonna do?"

"I'm not gonna do a muthafuckin' thing. Briana is dead to me, bruh. Ain't shit to me. Sky is gonna be good with her daddy. Ain't that right, baby?" I said as I gently pulled at her hair. She looked at me and smiled before resting her head into my brother's chest. "But look, bruh, I met my soul mate just a minute ago, and that bitch don't even know she belong to me."

"What-the-fuck-ever." KaeDee laughed and shook his head. "That ho must've had a fat ass. The last bitch you thought was your soul mate running around with a baby in her stomach, and that ho stay mad. Half-breed-ass bitch always calling me, speaking Spanish and shit. She called me right before you did, nigga, talking about you gone mad."

"Fuck that bitch. And nah, my soul mate is ugly as fuck, and she ain't have a fat ass . . . but I know for a fact shorty is for me, nigga. It's just something about her, and you ain't never heard me say Selena was my soul mate. I said she was perfect for a nigga, but that was at-the-moment-type shit. She was an I-was-in-my-feelings-type fuck, and shit just went kinda too far. Shit sometimes changes, though, you know. Just never did with her."

"So, who is this chick then, bruh?"

"I don't know."

"What you mean you don't know? What's her name? Where she live at?"

"Why the fuck you gotta ask so many questions, bitch? I don't know none of that shit, but I'm the nigga that's gonna change her life. I promise you that," I said just as my phone buzzed in my pocket.

KaeDee laughed at me as he placed Skylarr in the back seat of his car and strapped the seatbelt around her. I reached into my pocket and pulled out my phone only to see a text from Tramell that made my heart drop. I could feel the sweat forming on my forehead as I went to slide the bar across the screen and open the message.

Tramell: Bruh . . . Twelve did us dirty my nigga. Everything is gone. Everybody gone. I'm fucked up.

"What's wrong?" KaeDee asked, noticing the change in my demeanor.

I showed him the text, but he showed no emotion. KaeDee was cool like that. He had always been that way, though. Growing up, didn't too much piss him off, but when it did, he was not a nigga that you wanted to fuck with. KaeDee was a beast with his muthafuckin' hands. He was the biggest of us all, standing at six foot four and weighing about 240 pounds. Niggas that didn't know him was often misled by the fact that he preferred the suit-and-tie look and had a muthafuckin' degree that he received from Howard University. He was a smart-ass nigga, but ruthless nonetheless. He only got down when he absolutely had no other choice. For the most part, I fought his battles because I knew that if it ever came down to that, he would get me out of whatever charge I caught. He was important in the scope of what we was trying to build, and the last thing we wanted was him in anything that we could handle ourselves.

"I'll go drop her off with Deonna and catch up with you. Keep yo' shit open, nigga, and make sure you watch your fuckin' back," KaeDee told me, and we dapped each other and hugged before I walked off to the Mazi, got in, and peeled out of the Wal-Mart parking lot.

Chapter 2

Cuba

It had only been three days and a few hours since I walked out of that tiny cell with a bunk bed that I shared with my cellmate, Tiffany. I had spent the last three years of my life locked up and told what to do damn near every second of the day. It was no place for a chick like me, but I had made my bed, so I had to lie in it. Jail was the hardest thing that I had ever had to do in my young life, but I did it, day for day. Some days were harder than others, and most times, it seemed like I wouldn't make it, but I pulled through that bid feeling stronger than I ever had.

Them pigs had charged me with two counts of attempted murder, one count of murder, and one count of possession with the intent to distribute for that coke that Rue and Bry had lifted off some niggas that night. I had to count my blessings, though, because the only thing that they were able to stick was the possession with the intent to distribute charge. The DA didn't have enough evidence to prove their case against me for those murder charges, and I knew that that wasn't nobody but God on my side. I had tried my hardest to get out of that drug charge too, but with Rue pointing the finger at me, they wasn't having it any other way.

When I had finally came to my senses and realized that that nigga didn't love me, it was too late. They had given me chance after chance to give him up, but love had completely blinded me and made me a damn fool. For some reason, I felt the need to be loyal to Rue, and just in case he was testing me, show him that I was down for him. I was so fucking dumb for Rue; so dumb that I ended up having to plead guilty and taking the five years they offered me. With good behavior, I only had to do three years out of the five.

Five months into my sentence, I got a call from my mother that had only added to my stress. My sister, Alaska, had made it through to give birth to my first and only nephew, but unfortunately, shortly after, she passed away. Her death had been ruled a homicide, and the person that killed her was still out there. I didn't have any idea of who had done my people that way. It was something that I thought about every day that I was down, but not once could I come up with something that made sense. I wanted to blame Rue since he was so quick to put the blame on me, but that didn't make any sense either. He took six bullets to the back, damn near lost his life, and was inches away from being paralyzed. I couldn't see him taking that much of a risk, and I felt like, if anything, he was just a fuckin' coward for the shit he did to me.

He tried writing me a few times when I was locked up, but I didn't have anything to say to him. His actions and the way he handled the entire situation spoke to me loud and clear. He was a sucka-ass nigga, and there wasn't shit that either of us had to say to one another. I could sit there all day long and say what I could've done differently, like listen to my parents when they tried to warn me, but it was too late for all that. I knew better now, and although the last thing on my mind was a nigga, I knew for sure what type I was going to steer clear of.

I sighed as I walked into the She is Beauty shop. It was packed to capacity, with ladies and children sitting in every available chair. I looked around for my cousin,

Tangie, the only person who had my back and held me down while I did that bid. I don't know what I would've done if it had not been for her. Just like always, my parents blamed me for what happened to Alaska. After sending me a picture of my nephew with a note attached saying: *Look at what Alaska can't enjoy because of you*, I knew that I would never hear from them again, and I didn't. They didn't write, answer any of my phone calls, or pay me any visits, but Tangie did. She did it all. I saw her one or two times a month, and she put money on my books and sent me letters and books to hold me over.

Tangie was my cousin on my father's side. We were never close before me getting locked up, and we really only saw each other at family gatherings and a few outings, so it surprised me how down she was for me. She owned She is Beauty and promised me that when I came home she had a job for me at her shop. She even allowed me to stay with her and her boyfriend, Camp, so you know she was a real-ass bitch, because wasn't no chicks out there letting females stay with them and their man, family or not. Tangie had already given me the talk before I came home about staying away from Camp, but that shit went in one ear and out the other. Not that I didn't care; I just wasn't trying to hear that shit, 'cause I wasn't that type of bitch. I was more than capable, when I was ready, of getting my own man. Didn't want or need hers. Plus, I would never fuck over anyone that was there for me like Tangie had been for me.

"Hey, cuz, welcome to She is Beauty," Tangie said with a huge smile on her face.

I returned the smile as I looked around. Tangie definitely wasn't missing a meal. Business was good, and I was happy for her. She talked about this shop so much, from the time it was just an idea to its building stages, and her hope that it would be successful. I could definitely see that everything she had wished for had come to fruition.

"Girl, look at you," I told her as I admired the whole setup. It was chill and classy at the same time. Just at first glance, she had about six stylists working for her and a few girls that worked the shampoo bowls. She had already told me beforehand that I would be stocking and keeping up with the inventory and also scheduling appointments for the ladies. I was cool with whatever. Although this wasn't my dream job or anything that I ever saw myself doing, I was more than thankful. Tangie had afforded me the opportunity to put some cheddar in my pocket, and she was allowing me to stay with her rent free. All I had to do was stack my paper and figure some things out later on down the line. I wasn't gonna complain at all.

"So, what you think?"

"I'm proud of you, cuz. It's everything you said you was gonna do. I'm glad that it's working out for you."

"Me too, girl. Me too. So, you ready to work? 'Cause these phones are ringing off the hook, and between that, these clients, and their bad-ass kids, I can't keep up."

"Yes, just show me what I'm going to be doing. I'm ready," I said with a laugh and followed behind Tangie as she showed me to my workstation. It was a cute little desk that held a phone, computer, and a cash register. I started to feel a little overwhelmed thinking I wasn't going to be able to do this shit. I had never held down a job before in my life. My parents had always taken care of me, and when I was with Rue, I never had to work, because although he was a coward to me now, he was a great provider to me then. I never wanted for anything.

"It's okay, Cuba. I'ma make sure you become a pro at this. Don't worry," Tangie said to me, noticing my apprehension.

I looked at her and shook my head before taking a seat in the soft leather chair. Tangie was so damn sweet.

I looked at my guardian angel and admired her beauty. She stood at exactly five feet, and she wore her hair in a short 'do that was neatly tapered around her pretty brown skin. She had dark brown, Chinese-cut eyes and thick lips. She had a small frame just like me, except for Tangie had a nice little ass back there. I smirked, because all the women on my father's side were small as hell.

It took Tangie about two-and-a-half hours to show me around and to teach me how to use the computer and phones in order to do my job correctly. She didn't schedule her first appointment until after the lunch hour to ensure that she had enough time to work with me. My first day was going cool, and for the first time in a long time, a sincere smile was etched onto my face. I felt a little bit of happiness, something that I had not thought possible after everything that I had gone through over the last few years. Tangie just didn't know how much I appreciated her and everything she was doing for me. I felt myself getting emotional just thinking about it. When I stood up to tell Tangie everything that was on my mind, the door chimed, and it seemed like all eyes were suddenly on me.

Once I brought my attention toward the entrance of the shop, I could swear I felt my blood run cold. The smile I wore was completely wiped off my face, and my heart raced inside my chest. I didn't know how I should feel or even react to seeing him, but I couldn't stop the anger that had suddenly built up so intensely inside of me. My chest began to heave up and down as our eyes locked with one another. He had the nerve to be rocking a smirk. He loosened the grip that he had around the red-head chick that he was with, who just so happened to be Tangie's best friend, Anastasia. I looked at Tangie and rolled my eyes, because I knew this wasn't some shit that had just happened the night before. All the times I had talked to her, and not once did she mention that Rue and Anastasia were dating.

I didn't want to seem hurt, but I was. I bit down on my bottom lip as it trembled—my attempt to stop the tears that I felt threatening to slide down my face. Everybody had their damn eyes on me, waiting to see how I was going to react, and part of me wanted to be cool, but there was this fire in me that burned so bad with hurt and anger that I just fuckin' snapped.

"So, you knew this nigga was fucking with this bitch, and not once did you mention that shit to me, Tangie?" I yelled as I walked up to her and got in her face.

"Cuba . . ."

"Nigga, don't you say one muthafuckin' word to me," I said to Rue, cutting him off. I wasn't trying to hear nothing that he had to say. He said it all three years ago when he pointed the finger at me for some shit he knew wasn't on me. My life, my young life, had been ruined all because of him. Fuck him!

"Now, Cuba, that's their business. I don't have anything to do with who Tasia dates. Besides, that's not some shit you needed on your mind while trying to do that time, baby girl. I didn't say anything, because I knew it would mess with you. Now, Tasia is my best friend, but trust me when I say, she knows that I don't agree with her dating Rue's ass," Tangie told me, and although I was mad, I could feel the sincerity in her voice and knew that she would never do anything to hurt me. I also understood what she was saying. So much was already on my shoulders, and the last thing I needed to know was that Rue was out there doing him, and with someone I knew, at that. "Now, take a deep breath and let's walk outside."

I nodded my head and took a deep breath just like Tangie suggested. When I looked up, Rue's eyes were planted on me, and I could feel the damn room heating up. Anastasia was also looking at me, but she had the nerve to be rocking a smirk.

Is this bitch getting satisfaction from this? I thought as I followed Tangie out the front of her shop.

"I'm sorry, Tangie, but damn!" I exhaled the breath I had been holding and also the tears that had built up in the corners of my eyes. Tangie wrapped her arms around me and held me until I finally stopped crying. I wiped my face with the back of my hand and let out an embarrassed chuckle. "I'm sorry. The last thing I want is to bring drama to your shop."

"No, it's okay. If I had known that Rue's bitch ass was going to show up here with Tasia, I would've told you. He never ever comes here, because Tasia always claims that she doesn't want him around too many women. I can betcha that he found a reason to come today, because he knew you were going to be here, and for some reason, Tasia's dumb ass think being with him after what he did to you is cute. I tried to tell that sick bitch not to fuck with him, but she wouldn't listen. I don't know what makes her think that he wouldn't do her the same way he did you. She's one dumb bitch. Best friend or not, she's a dummy, and I told her exactly that."

"It's cool, Tangie. I don't give a fuck about Rue no more. It's just that I would've given my life for that man, and he did me so wrong. To see him walking around free as a bird like nothing happened kills me. My sister died, my parents disowned me, and I don't even know what my nephew looks like. I lost so much because of his shit, and the least he could've done was ride for me like I would've done for him."

"Rue ain't shit, girl. You might have lost three years, honey, but trust me, that was a minor setback for a major comeback. You gonna be everything and then some. Us Lances are nothing to play with, girl. Don't you ever forget that."

I laughed and pulled a pack of cigarettes from my back pocket. Smoking these cancer sticks was a nasty habit that I picked up when I was locked up, and I promised myself when I got out that I was going to quit, but not that day. I slid my lighter from my pocket, lit the tip of the square, and leaned back against the wall.

I looked over at Tangie as she looked me up and down. I knew she was taking in my appearance. My hair was halfway combed, and I was rocking a white T-shirt and a pair of loose-fitting sweats with my rundown jailhouse tennis shoes. I shrugged my shoulders, not really giving a damn how I looked. I was just happy to be free and happy that I wasn't going to be out there starving like I knew most chicks I was locked up with were.

"I was about to tell you thank you for everything, Tangie. I know I've said it a hundred times before, but you know it means the world to me that you held me down like that," I told Tangie, feeling emotional all over again. She hugged me once again, and I tightly hugged her back, holding the cigarette behind my back so the smoke wouldn't get in her clothes.

"That's what family is for, boo. You know I got you. My client will be on her way soon. I'll clock you out for lunch, so go on and get your head together, and I'll see you in an hour."

I nodded my head and began to walk down the block while puffing on the Newport. I was in deep thought when I spotted a gas station across the street from where Tangie's shop was located. I figured I would grab me a few snacks and something to drink while trying to get Rue off my mind, but I guess the muthafucka was reading my mind. He pulled up in front of me just as I made my way across the street, and he hopped out of the car. I can't lie . . . he looked good. He had grown up so much since the last time I saw him. His baby face was now covered with facial hair that was neatly trimmed around his face. Rue was around five foot eleven, with a high-yellow-ass skin tone and dimpled cheeks, with an innocent smile. Before he had been a little on the frail side, but now, I could see his muscular frame as it poked through his clothing.

I tried to walk around him, but Rue grabbed at my arm and pulled me toward him. Snatching away from him, I frowned, ready to spit in his face; but I had to remember that this nigga was a fuckin' snitch bitch, and I was on probation for the next two years.

"A'ight, I'm sorry, but damn, ma, you can't talk to a nigga?" he had the nerve to ask me as if I owed him time.

"Talk to you for what? You said everything you had to say three years ago, nigga, when you sat down at that police station and lied through your damn teeth. And let's not forget the fact that you were fuckin' my sister behind my back."

"It's not even like that, Cuba. Them muthafuckin'—"

"Look, I don't even care, Rue. Whatever explanation that you thought up in your head to give me, save it. It's over and done with now. I took that L for you, nigga."

"Man, that fuckin' night, Cuba, I told you to get Alaska and get out of there before twelve ran down on us. Do you think I would get down there and snitch on you like that?"

"Do I think? Do I fuckin' think? Nah, I fuckin' know! I heard you on the tape loud and clear saying I put them bricks in that car and that I set y'all up to be killed. You said that shit, not me, so what the hell do you mean, do I think?"

"Those cops twisted—"

"Save it, Rue. I don't care, man. For real, I don't care."

"Cuba, come on, baby. You know I love you," Rue said, causing me to shake my head and laugh.

"Love me? If what you showed me was love, then I don't ever—and I mean ever—wanna be in love again."

Chapter 3

Daelan

"Aye, I'm saying it's only a few niggas that got that kinda fire power to do some shit like that. My man, we lost fam and shit up in that bitch last night. Start talking," I told this Arab muthafucka as he separated brown paper bags with his nasty-ass fingers. I was standing inside of the local food mart in my hood that was owned by these got-damn Arabs. They wasn't paying taxes to the government, nor were they paying taxes on that bullshit-ass dope they were pushing in my streets. I was sick of these clowns, and I knew that they had to be responsible for that loss we took the night before at the factory. I had been telling Khi and KaeDee for the past year that we needed to take these dudes out, but they were always talking about I was a hothead and never thought shit through.

My bro Tramell lost his baby mama, Cocoa, in the chaos when six dudes came through dressed from head-to-toe in military gear and packing assault rifles, claiming to be the DEA. They shot everything moving, taking all the dope, money, and the lives of men and women that I fuckin' cared about. Tramell was one lucky nigga, 'cause he only caught a couple of bullets that were through and through and didn't do any damage.

"I don't know anything about that, *Dylan*," he said, and I sighed, hiking my pants up a couple of inches, and then pulled my dreads from my face.

"You tryna be funny, huh? You think this shit is a game?" I clasped my hands together and looked at him before I grabbed him by the collar of his shirt and pulled him over the counter. Dragging his ass outside, I punched him in the face as I kept my grip tight around his neckline. Blood squirted from his mouth, and he yelped a few times before the red liquid filled his mouth and prevented him from speaking.

I pulled my pistol out the back of my pants and shoved it in between his teeth, causing a few of them to shatter. He choked, and his arms flailed while I laughed. Fuck Khi and fuck KaeDee. I was going to start listening to my gut when it came to matters that fucked with my money and fucked with my fam.

Damn. Cocoa and Rhamin. I thought about two of the people I messed with the most. Two of the people that grew up on the same block as me was gone and never coming back. Tramell and Cocoa's kid would never get a chance to see their mother again, and that agony alone was enough to body the muthafuckas I thought were responsible. If I was wrong, then so what? Fuckin' Arabs already had the game fucked up by pumping that poison they were selling into the streets that didn't even come from the coalition. Not only that, that shit was quickly killing my people, and these niggas was turning a blind eye to it like they couldn't even see it.

Yeah, I moved that dope, pushed that crack to damn near whoever would buy it, but even then, I had a heart. I didn't want shit with my name on it going into the hands of pregnant chicks and kids. The Arabs didn't give a damn about that. I had seen far too many deaths from the neighborhood that was marked by that shit that they called *Allah*. These cats were just straight up with that disrespect, and I was a low-tolerance-ass dude.

"Nigga, what's my muthafuckin' name? Call me Dylan again, bitch. Say that shit again!" I told him as he looked up at me with desperate eyes. By now, a small crowd had formed, and instead of me backing down, it only made me go harder. I wanted anybody who even thought about testing my gangsta to see this shit. I gave no fucks about no witnesses. I was a real live goonie out there, the type that had no fucks to give. Khi be hollerin' all the time that he put us on the map and that he was the one that made us gain the respect from the streets, but after the night before, that nigga ain't do shit. But it wasn't shit, though. I was about to show everybody not to fuck with the Prince brothers.

Screechhhh!

Just as I was about to murder this clown, I see my brother pull up in his dusty-ass Maserati and hop out the car. He casually walked over to me like he was stepping out of *GQ* magazine or something. I laughed at this nigga the closer he got to me, because in reality, no matter how hard he tried, he wasn't shit but a street nigga just like the rest of us. He low-key thought he was Mafia affiliated or some shit. Shit was just going too far.

"What the fuck is wrong with you? Get in the fuckin' car," Khi said, and I frowned at him before I shoved the gun further down the Arab's throat. Of course, his bitch ass wanted to flex as usual. He grabbed me by my throat and shoved me back. The gun fell out of my hand and onto the ground, firing off a round that didn't do shit but skid across the pavement.

I pushed Khi off me and went to pick up my pistol, but he shoved me toward his car. I pushed my dreads back, ready to square up with that nigga, until KaeDee hopped out the passenger's seat and came in our direction. I wanted no parts of that fool 'cause I knew he would knock me out and take pride in that shit. I looked at Khi and shot his ass the bird before I walked off toward my whip that was parked across the street from the local food mart.

"Dae! Get your ass in the car, nigga!" KaeDee yelled, sounding like a big-ass bear. I shook my head and turned to walk back to the Maserati.

"I drove myself here; I can drive myself back," I told him and frowned as he casually pulled that long-ass beard of his.

"You out here on that drank?" KaeDee asked as he grabbed me from the back of my head and pulled me closer to him. I always felt like a little kid under scrutiny when dealing with KaeDee. He and Cassidy stepped up and took on the father role when our father got knocked and went down with that all-day-and-a-night sentence. He was the only one of my brothers that I didn't test when he was getting in my shit. With Khi and the rest, I would play all day, but no matter how much shit I gave them niggas, I loved them 'til the death of me. They were my brothers, forever and always.

"When is he not on that drank? Man, get your ass in the car before we be late. You supposed to be on your way to the fuckin' meeting, and we get a call about your ass out here fooling," Khi said as he flopped down into the driver's side.

Damn, I thought, forgetting all about the meeting we had with our connect. I hit the alarm on my car and got in the back seat of the Mazi.

"Yo, Dae, is you stupid, nigga? You out here with a crowd of muthafuckas ready to murk Amin like that. What the hell is you thinkin'?" KaeDee asked the moment he got inside the car.

I shrugged my shoulders and took my attention outside of the window, watching a few of the onlookers help that Arab fool to his feet. I smirked and thought about coming back to body the nigga during closing.

"You really ready to go to war with them, mane?" KaeDee continued.

"Shittt, them niggas declared war when they popped our people and got our shit last night. I know it was them. Who else riding through the hood with them ARs, nigga? Tell me a nigga you know in the hood that got that kinda firepower? They took our fam away from us. Nigga Cocoa died in that muthafucka last night," I said, and both of them fools sat in the front seat all quiet and shit.

Thinking of Cocoa had me thinking of the wifey, Amber. I didn't know what I would do if someone were to take her away from me and the kid. I used to have her out there trapping with a nigga, but the minute she got pregnant with our shorty back when we were young as hell, I made her get off the block. I couldn't have the both of us out there risking our lives when we had a mouth to feed. Somebody had to be there to care for the kid in case shit got bad out there.

"Bruh, even if that's the case, what you going after Amin for? Fuck that's gonna do? Make them niggas madder so they can get at more of our people . . . more of our shit? We can't be out here on no slick, dumb shit 'cause we angry, bruh. Come on now, Dae. I'm always telling you we ain't on the block no more. We can't be out here like that," Khi preached, and I yawned, letting him know I ain't give a fuck about nothing he was saying.

"Yeah, whatever, nigga," I said as I leaned back in the seat and tried to sleep off some of this drank. Khi turned the music to the max, and minutes later, I had drifted into a slumber.

"So, y'all don't know of anybody that could've did this shit? My nigga, that's a big-ass loss," Tamar said as I fought to keep my eyes open.

Tamar was known nationwide in this underworld drug game. He had the game on lock and was the reason we were seeing the kinda paper that we were now. I heard all kinds of stories about how this cat stumbled upon some coca fields and had somehow taken over the Mexican Cartel, but I didn't know what exactly was the truth. What I did know was that he had the best product we had ever seen, and he had invited us to be a part of the coalition that he had formed under his drug cartel that he called United Nations. It was supposed to stop the beefs in the street over territory and ensure that everybody was getting paper. The shit had its ups and downs, 'cause a nigga always felt like he could be getting it from everywhere, but it was what it was. I wasn't missing no meals, and my pockets had been far from shy as of late. The only muthafuckas that acted like they missed the meeting and refused to get on board was them damn Arabs. They were fucking the game all the way up.

"I mean, we got a few possibilities, but I ain't ready to jump on shit just yet. We just ready to put that work back out there like nothing ever happened," Khi said, and I let out a big yawn that had everybody in the room looking over at me like I did something wrong. I shrugged my shoulders and sat up in my seat.

Suddenly, I felt sick to my stomach like I had to throw up. I jumped up from my seat and shot out the first door that I came to, which led to the back yard. I kneeled over the grass and dry heaved until what seemed like everything I had eaten over the past few days came up. I started getting all hot and shit, so I pulled off the T-shirt I was rocking and used it to wipe the sweat from my forehead.

"Shit," I said as I spit into the grass and took a few steps back.

"Here," I heard someone say from behind me. I turned around to see a short, brown-skinned female with some pretty, hazel brown eyes. I ran my eyes over her body, admiring the way her hips filled out her jeans.

"Figured you might need this," she said, handing me a bottle of a water.

"Thanks, li'l mama. I appreciate it." I took the top off the water and downed a couple of gulps before I looked back over at shorty. She smiled as she stepped a little closer to me and held out her hand.

"I'm Taylana, Tamar's sister."

"Dae," I told her as I took her hand into mine and brought it to my mouth to kiss. She flashed me another pretty smile, this time bigger, showing off a set of perfect white teeth. I knew I was flirting with danger, but shorty had approached me, and a nigga like me loved new pussy. Yeah, I had Amber at home taking care of the kid, but that was that and this was this. I shot shorty a smirk before I let her hand go and took another sip of the water.

"You get drunk like this in the middle of the day often . . . Dae?" she asked me.

"Leanin' a li'l bit, that's all."

"Look like more than a little bit. You out here sweating and shit. I got scared looking at you from my bedroom window, thinking you were gonna pass out."

"You was gonna save me if I did?"

"Yeah, but no lie, you still look like you need a little saving. I want you to take me out."

"Damn, shorty, you always this bold?"

"Not unless I'm going after something I want . . . and I want you."

I chuckled, and then looked up to see my brothers wrapping things up with Tamar. I slightly nodded my head so that Taylana could see. I already knew that more than likely, her brother didn't approve of her talking to niggas like me, because if I had a little sister that looked like her, I would feel the same way.

"Give me your phone real quick," she said and held out her hand. I reached into my pocket and pulled my phone out. Unlocking it, I handed it over to her and watched as she quickly typed her number inside and handed it back to me. She walked off just as KaeDee and Khi made their way outside and headed in my direction.

"What was that all about?" Khi's nosey ass asked. That nigga was always noticing some shit.

"Nothing. She brought me a bottle of water," I said, holding the water up so that they could see it. "How did everything go?"

I followed behind KaeDee and Khi and completely zoned out. I saved Taylana's number in my phone under the name "Troy" and went to shoot her fine ass a text.

Me: You the dinner and movie type? Or the Netflix and chill type . . . Dae.

Send.

Troy: It don't matter as long as I'm with you.

Me: Just tryna see if I'm eating at the table or what's on the table.

Send.

Troy: Lol lol . . . you corny as fuck. But eat me on the table please daddy.

Me: not shy at all . . . just the way I like em. lol

Send.

I chuckled as I hopped in the back seat, knowing shorty was bad for me and bad for the business we had going on with Tamar, but like they say . . . Dae was always fucking up.

Chapter 4

Deonna

I walked inside of She is Beauty with Skylarr's big, chunky self glued to my hip. I had promised my brother-in-law Khi that I would pick her up from his mother's house and bring her to Tangie's to get her hair braided. I felt bad for my little bro. This was the second time that Briana had put him through this drug shit, and I knew now that their daughter was around, it had to be much harder for him. He pretended like he was cool, but I knew, deep down, Briana's relapse had to be eating him up.

"Hey, Tangie," I said as I walked over to her talking to some brown-skinned chick that was working the front desk.

"What's up, Deonna? Hey, pretty girl," Tangie said, reaching for Skylarr. Surprisingly, Skylarr went right to her. I smiled and looked around Tangie's shop. Things were really coming along for her, and the place looked a lot better than the last time I was there.

"Khi said to call him when she's done getting her hair braided, and he's going to come pick her up."

"Girl, look at this baby's head. I can't believe Briana would let her hair get like this. She's too young for her hair to be all tangled up and in knots."

"Exactly. I tried, and so did Khi's mother. We gave up, and Khi said to just bring her to the professional, so here she is. Work your magic, boo."

"Only for Khi, because he knows I don't even deal with babies this young. Oh, and forgive me for being rude. Deonna, this is my cousin, Cuba. Cuba, this is Deonna. Her and her husband KaeDee own a law firm, one of the best in the city," Tangie said.

I could feel my phone vibrating in my clutch, and I pulled it out to see that I had several messages from my husband. I briefly looked down at them, and then brought my attention back to Tangie and her cousin.

"Cuba? That's a cute name. Nice to meet you, girl. I hate to be rude myself, but KaeDee just text me saying he's back from his business meeting, and I need to get back to the office quick."

"Okay, girl, we understand. I'll see you soon for your appointment anyway, and we can chat then."

"Cool," I said absentmindedly as I turned to leave the shop. Once I made it outside and into my car, I opened KaeDee's messages and read them all over again.

KaeDee: Where the fuck you at?

KaeDee: I'm back from my meeting and need to see you now! Get to the office.

KaeDee: And hurry the fuck up.

I locked my phone and placed it in my cup holder. Cranking my car, I pulled out of the parking lot and headed across town to the office, wondering what KaeDee was so hostile about. My husband and I had been married for the past four years. We met when I was a just a struggling freshman in college at Howard University, and he was in his last year of law school. He came to my rescue when he offered to pay for my tuition after he overheard me begging the school's cashier to give me more time when I'd fallen behind. I thought it was odd for a man that didn't even know me to want to help me out like that, but KaeDee was that type of man. He was genuine, had a good heart, and just wanted to see others succeed in life. That alone had me open and wanting to know more about him.

After a few dates and many long conversations, I was in lust and ready to give KaeDee my all. I wanted to explore a life with him. I could tell that he was the kind of man that I needed in my life and that would make me happy. I was so used to dating niggas in the streets that had records, that didn't mind robbing niggas, that was selling dope, and all that shit, that I wanted something different, and KaeDee was that different. At least that's what I believed.

After KaeDee graduated and came back to Dallas to start his law firm, he proposed to me after us dating for only eight months. I had gladly accepted, and within a few months of being engaged, we were married, but still living apart. Life was good, things were good, and I was happy. There was no drama, no crazy baby mamas, no looking over my shoulder, or no paranoia every time a cop was in the area. KaeDee was the man of my dreams—hell, the man of every woman's dreams, but then, it all changed drastically. The man that cared so much about my dreams and goals no longer did. Everything was everything that he dreamed of and what he wanted.

It wasn't until our home was done being built and I finally reunited with him in Dallas that KaeDee requested that I change my major to the criminal justice field and help him run his firm. He wanted us to be the Bonnie and Clyde of criminal defense attorneys, and shit, what woman didn't want to be her husband's ride or die? I did that shit with no questions asked. I enrolled in the degree program at the college and never looked back, and even though I would miss dancing, I figured there was always later.

In my second year of the degree program, I got pregnant with our daughter, Chanel, but I made sure that didn't stop me. KaeDee was counting on me, and I was going to make sure he never regretted the day he made me his wife. I was so stoked and proud that I couldn't wait until the day I graduated and was able to stand next to my husband every time he fought a case in that courtroom. I was definitely ready to be the Bonnie to his Clyde. The only problem was that I didn't realize how much that statement would hold true.

The life I thought I had escaped was the one I had walked right back into, only deeper than I had ever been. KaeDee was just another thug in a suit, using his law firm to cover up his drug activities, and I had no idea until he wanted me to know. I felt so deceived and so betrayed. I felt like I didn't know the man I had married, and I had been misled into something that I hadn't even asked for. Things were so different now for me. I had a daughter that I had to look after—a daughter that I felt safe keeping and giving birth to, because I felt safe with the man I had fallen in love with.

KaeDee had deceived me so badly that, for a moment, I had fallen out of love with him. Things were rocky, but when I came to my senses and realized what I had in my man, I got my shit together, and got it together quick. I knew better; what KaeDee did for a living didn't make him. He was a loving and caring man that would never let anything happen to his family. He suddenly was the man I fell in love with again, the man that I would do anything for. I was Bonnie; he was Clyde. Together, we were a force to be reckoned with, and I loved this shit.

I stepped out of my 7-series BMW and armed the alarm as I made my way toward the office. Once I stepped inside, I nodded to the receptionist and gave her a smile before I made my way to KaeDee's office. I could see through the glass window that surrounded his office that he was in a conversation with two men dressed down in suits. Their backs were to me, so I couldn't tell who they were.

KaeDee's eyes locked with mine as I came closer. I held my hand up to let him know that I would be in my office, but he signaled for me to come in. I could see that the worry lines were riddled in his forehead once I pulled the door and stepped inside.

"Hi, baby. Sorry. I got back as soon as I could. Do you need me to handle—"

"Mrs. Davis," one of the men turned to me and said.

I looked from him to KaeDee, who sat behind his huge oak desk. He absentmindedly toyed with the picture frame in front of him, something he did when he was frustrated and wanted to snap. It held a picture of him, Chanel, and me; a reminder of what he had to lose if he ever fucked up and made the wrong decision. Never once did KaeDee return my glare. He slammed the photo down, causing it to shatter. Pieces of glass scattered across his desk and onto the floor.

KaeDee got up from his seat, and his six-foot-four frame seemed like a huge statue as he stood there and adjusted his tie. I watched as he rubbed one hand over his smooth chocolate face and cleared his throat before he then rubbed one hand over the waves in his low-cut fade. KaeDee was a man of very few words, only speaking when he felt he had something of importance to offer. He was so calm in this moment as he walked around his desk, but based off his demeanor, I could tell that he was burning with fire on the inside. Briefly, KaeDee's dark hazel eyes wavered over me before he walked out of his office and left me alone with the two men.

"Mrs. Deonna Fortson," the man said again, but I was too busy looking after KaeDee.

"It's Prince now . . . KaeDee!" I yelled after him, but he kept walking down the long hall.

"We have a warrant for your arrest. I'm Agent Porter. This is Agent Cryer."

"What?" I said, finally looking them over in full. That was when I noticed the badges that hung from the pockets of their suits.

A warrant for my arrest? For what?

"Did you once used to date a Mr. Tyrin Walker?" Agent Porter asked.

"Yeah, I . . . that was five or six years ago. So what?" I rebutted, crossing my arms over my chest.

"Did you used to handle books for him? A little accounting work for his car wash?"

"I don't know what you're talking about. I would like to speak to my husband, please."

"He's going to meet us downtown. If you can turn around and place your hands behind your back, please, Ms. Fortson," Agent Cryer said to me.

"What am I being arrested for? I need to see the warrant," I said stubbornly. I refused to put my hands behind my back and be arrested for anything. Yeah, I used to date Tyrin Walker, and yeah, I used to do accounting work for him, but that was many years ago. I was young at the time, only nineteen when I first met him. I walked away from him when things took a turn down a path that I wasn't interested in traveling.

"Laundering money for Mr. Walker's drug business back into his car wash," Agent Porter said as he handed me the warrant.

I took a look at what I was being accused of, and my breath seemed to get caught in my throat. They had me down as doing business with Tyrin as recently as six months ago. I had to wonder if my husband saw this, and if he did, did he read into it in detail? How was I going to explain this shit to him? How was he going to react when he found out that, after all the hell I had given him for hiding his life from me, I had also been hiding mine from him?

Chapter 5

Khian

I parked in front of my homegirl Tangie's beauty shop and stepped out of the car. My mind was all over the place from dealing with baby mama drama, my shit being missing, and all the goonies I had lost the night before. I felt so muthafuckin' guilt-ridden. I was supposed to have been there, and I felt like if I had, maybe I could've saved a few of my li'l soldiers—especially the homie Cocoa. She was a mother before anything, and her and Tramell was just doing what they had to do to feed their youngin'. Shit wasn't fair, but we had to play this by ear.

I completely understood why my li'l bro Dae flipped out like he had, but I didn't get this far by being no dumb nigga. Every move we made had to be calculated, and it just wasn't smart to do anything based off emotions. Dae was one emotional-ass nigga. That's why he stayed tipping a bottle or gone off that lean. He let too much shit get to his ass, and the nigga was always acting like he was one bottle away from jumping off a bridge. I ain't know what was wrong with my youngin', but he needed to get his shit together. Every time I tried to sit him down to see what was up with him, he always said it was nothing and that I was always in his business. One thing I wasn't about to let happen was Dae fucking up everything we had worked so hard to build because he was always in his feelings. I was gonna let him make it on this one, though, because since we all grew up together, I knew Tramell and Cocoa were homies.

When I pulled the door open to She is Beauty, Skylarr immediately took off running in my direction. I knew that Tangie could get her right if no one else could. She had my shorty looking a hundred times better, and that brought a smile to my face. Just looking into Skylarr's eyes made me think about her trifling-ass mama, but I'd be damned if I called that bitch up to see how she was doing. I was sure she was somewhere getting laced, not giving a damn if her daughter was good or not. That was how it was when that monkey was on your back. Not a thing in the world could talk you out of getting your next fix.

"What's up, bro?" Tangie said as her short ass walked up to me. "You know you can't be coming all up here looking like that. You got all my clients sweating and shit. Bitches coming all out the shampoo bowl and getting water all over my floor just to get a look."

I chuckled and looked around, and that was when I saw her. Our eyes met, but she turned away from me like she wasn't just talking that hot shit the night before. I picked Skylarr up and left Tangie standing there as I made my way over to her. She looked at me, rolled her eyes, and went back to what she was doing on the computer.

"You gonna run everybody off with that stank-ass attitude. I guess you so used to talking to whack-ass niggas you don't recognize a boss when you see one," I told her as I reached over the counter and cut off the computer screen. She looked up at me with a frown on her face, and I shook my head, because her damn hair still wasn't combed.

"You don't see me working?"

"I don't give a fuck about you workin'. You oughta be happy a nigga trying to talk to your ugly ass."

She laughed. "But I'm not happy, and you should've took that as your cue last night to not try and talk to me again."

"So, you do remember a nigga from last night?"

"I do . . . and I see the both of you clean up well."

"And I see you don't," I shot back.

"I wasn't trying to, but I still impressed you enough for you to take time out your day to bother me again, so that says something."

"I can tell you ain't got no nigga—or at least he ain't hitting it right, because you wouldn't be talking like that if I was in your life."

"But you're not, nor do I want you—"

"Damn, what the hell is going on with you two over here? Khi, you didn't tell me you knew my cousin Cuba."

"Cuba, huh?" I said as I bit down on my bottom lip while eyeing her. I could tell she was low-key feeling a nigga no matter how hard she tried to play. They always felt the kid. Shit, I was the streets, and the streets was me. Everybody knew who Killa Khi was, and if they didn't know, it wasn't that hard to find out. "Cuba got a smart-ass mouth that I'ma have to fuckin' tame."

Tangie laughed. "She just—"

"I don't know this nigga, Tangie, and he don't need to know shit about me," Cuba said, and I had to look at her ass funny.

"Okay, what did I miss?" Tangie asked just as the door chimed and Rue's bitch ass walked in.

"Hold her right quick," I told Tangie as I handed Skylarr to her and made my way over to Rue.

"What up, Khi?" Rue said and held his hand out like I was gonna dap his thieving ass up or something.

"Don't muthafuckin' 'what's up' me, nigga. You sure is shining right now. What lick you done came up off of?"

"Man, don't even come at me like that, bruh. You'll know if I hit you—"

"I'll come at you how the fuck I wanna come at you!"

"Khi! Khi, please don't do that shit in here. And don't forget you got Sky with you."

"Yeah, nigga, don't forget you got your daughter with you," Rue slid in, and it was only seconds before I would have my hands wrapped around his throat, ready to break his fuckin' neck.

Cats like Rue wasn't respected in the streets, period. He was the worst kinda nigga, and it was a wonder he was even still alive. He made his living by ganking niggas for shit that they worked hard for, but I guess he knew who to fuck with, 'cause as far as I knew, he had never even breathed in my direction. I didn't know who had done us in the night before, but seeing Rue walk up in there decked with diamonds when I knew he ain't work for none of that shit made me snap. I was acting like Dae, and I needed to calm down.

I let Rue go and stepped a couple of feet away from him before I adjusted my suit. Tangie handed me Skylarr, and I reached into my pocket to pull out a few hundred dollars to pay her. I would catch Rue in the streets later. I looked over at Cuba, and she was staring at me while I headed to the exit. I didn't know why, but seeing her again just made me want her even more. I would tame that feisty-ass attitude and have her calling me daddy in no time. I winked my eye at her, and she hurried and threw her head down like I hadn't already caught her looking.

"I'll catch you on the block, Rue," I told him before I walked out of the shop and headed to my car.

***

It was going on seven when I pulled up to the crib and spotted Briana hanging on the outside of the gate. I shook my head as I pressed down on the remote to open it and drove down the long driveway. Rubbing my hands across my head, I sighed and looked through the rearview mirror at my daughter peacefully sleeping in the back seat. Skylarr hadn't asked about her mother since I picked her up, and I didn't even know if it was a good idea if Briana saw her. I didn't want or need Briana playing no pop-up games in her life with that in-and-out shit. I knew she wasn't clean and most likely didn't have any plans on getting that way anytime soon, so until then, she just needed to stay the fuck away.

By the time I pulled Skylarr out of her car seat and made it up to the house, Briana had made it down the driveway. She stood behind me, sniffling, as I stuck the key inside the lock and unlocked the door.

"Are you high?" I asked without even looking over my shoulder at her.

"No, you know I wouldn't come here if I was," she sniffed, and I opened the door and walked inside. Briana followed me in the house and closed and locked the door behind her. "Can I put her in her bed?"

"Don't fuckin' wake her, Briana."

"I won't."

I handed Skylarr over to her and watched as she took her up the stairs and to her bedroom. Making my way up the stairs as well, I headed to my room and straight to the bathroom. The meeting with Tamar earlier that day went good, and I was glad that I was able to catch up with him while he was in town. He was what I was striving to be. Every time we linked up, he always dropped some jewels on a nigga, letting me know what to do and what not to do in this game. I listened every time he spoke, because he wasn't that much older than me, and I knew that if he could get in the position he was in, then I could too. We both started from the bottom and had family to look after just the same. He told me how he started out with his brothers by his side, too, and how they were no longer there, but I wasn't trying to have that be my story. My brothers were my life, and I wished that Dae would take the time out to hear what Tamar was saying. But just like earlier, it always seemed to go in one ear and out the other.

Once I showered and took care of my hygiene, I sat on the bed and rolled me a blunt before I headed back downstairs. Briana was standing in front of the fridge for a few seconds before she pulled out a few things and set them on the counter. As I headed to the back yard to light up the hay, I wondered what kinda shit she was on, since she had brought her ass all the way from the hood to my crib. Briana was a sneaky-ass broad, and I didn't have no trust left in me to give her. She was up to something. Briana was always up to something.

"Where the hell is Selena, and why the hell does your house look like this? That bitch don't clean up, and shit, that stove don't look like it's ever been used," Briana said as she stepped outside. I couldn't help but notice the track marks on her arms as the dim light from the back yard was shining over us. Seeing her like that was sickening, and hell nah, it didn't make me feel bad for what I did to get money. Shit, dope was gonna get sold whether I was the one to sell it or not.

"Why the fuck are you here?" I asked and took a hit off the hay.

"Because I just want to apologize. I don't know what happened . . . how I let myself get back on this shit again. But I know that I have done it before, so I know I can quit again. I just need your help. You know I can't do it without you."

"You don't want or need my fuckin' help. If you wanted to stay clean, then you would have. I really think you do shit like this for my attention. We got a muthafuckin' daughter to take care of, and you need to focus on her and not some dick that you'll never have again!"

"It's not even about that, Khi. You know what I went through as a child! I told you! And it . . . it gets hard for me sometimes. You always have to be so damn hard on me," Briana cried.

"What you mean? We got a baby to look after, Bri," I said as I stepped in front of her. "You're her mother, but if you got a problem being that, then you know it's nothing for me to replace you."

"Replace me? Khi, I wish you would have Sky calling that bitch Selena Mama. Don't play with me like that. You know I can make your life miserable if I choose to."

I chuckled before I hit the weed and took a step away from her. When Briana made threats like that, I always had visions of myself strangling her or blowing her muthafuckin' head off. She knew a few secrets that I mistakenly let go before I knew what type of chick she really was. Every now and then when she wanted to flex, she would try and use that shit against me, but it never worked, and it never would. I would body Briana in a heartbeat before I ever let her bring me or my brothers down. She knew that shit, too. I just hoped she never forgot it.

"Go clean yourself up, Bri. Stay the fuck away from Sky until you do. Don't make me have to hurt you," I told her as I turned my back to her.

"So, you're not going to help me, Khi?" she asked as she began to cry again.

"Only somebody that can help you is you. You'll figure it out when you're ready."

"I don't have any money. How am I supposed to pay for treatment?"

"I don't fuckin' know! Like I said, you'll figure it out. Say good-bye to your daughter, and then get the fuck out."

"You never loved me, Khi. You never did!"

"Maybe I fuckin' didn't, but it's too late to figure it out now. Go, Bri, because you pissing me off, and I don't wanna fuck you up no more than you already are."

"If something happens to me out here, it's your fault. You just remember that."

"I ain't tripping. I've lived with worse. Lock the door on your way out."

Briana stood behind me for a while before she stormed off and went inside the house. I shrugged my shoulders and walked over to sit in the lounge chair next to the pool when I heard the back door open and close again. I thought that Briana had come back to say something else, but when I looked it up, I realized it was Selena's ass.

Shit, I need to change them locks. The fuck these bitches wanna bother me today for? Damn! I thought as I took a huge toke off my weed.

"Damn, soon as I leave, you have that bitch up in here cooking and cleaning for you and shit," Selena said, and I sighed.

"You know how Bri is. Anything to make a nigga happy," I told her as I went to sit down, but she grabbed me.

"I leave to go visit my mom and clear my head, and you got her up in here. Where's the fuckin' respect, Khi?"

"Oh my God, what the hell is wrong with y'all today? All these emotional-ass rants and shit. You didn't get my text?"

"Yes, and that's why I went to my mom's house to give you a chance to cool down. We need to talk."

"Nah, I'm good. I don't need to calm down. I've told you too many muthafuckin' times about putting your hands on me, and you seem to don't understand. Only reason I didn't knock you the fuck out was because you're carrying my seed. The next time, I won't give a fuck, so it's best for you to leave. I don't want to end up feeling like no ho-ass nigga because you couldn't keep your hands to yourself."

"We can't talk about it, Khi?" Selena asked as she rubbed her hand over her stomach.

"There's nothing to talk about, Selena. I'm good on all that. If I wouldn't have been arguing with you last night, I might could've made it to Tramell 'n them on time. You not good for business, ma, and I told you when I first started fucking with you that I can't have nothing fucking with my money or with my fam. You thought you was special or something?"

"You're just gonna throw me out on the street . . . while I'm pregnant with your child?"

I laughed. "You read my text, man. Don't play with me. Do I need to leave while you pack your shit, or are you gonna be able to do that with me in the house?"

"You're fucking her. Just admit it! Tell me the fuckin' truth, Khi!" Selena yelled, and I sighed. I didn't have time for this shit.

I tried to walk around her, but she grabbed my arm once again and shoved me in the chest. Sucking my teeth, I pulled in a deep breath and went to move Selena's hand. She hauled off and slapped me in the face. I shook my head and tried to let that shit go, but Selena wanted to keep testing my patience. She knew what type of nigga I was, but it was like she wanted me to beat her ass or something. Shit, if I had to beat a bitch to get her to act right, then I didn't need to be with her.

Selena brought her fist up as if she was going to punch me, but I caught her ass and lightly shoved her back. She stumbled a little bit but caught her footing before she could fall. You would think that would stop her and get her to leave me the fuck alone, but not Selena. Her ass never backed down and never left well enough alone.

"You don't even put in the effort with me anymore. You used to go so hard on making sure that we worked out, but you don't even try anymore. You don't love me, Khi!" she yelled, and I had heard that shit enough for one night.

"Fuck I need to try anymore for? The first time you put your muthafuckin' hands on me, I knew then I fucked up and made the wrong choice, so there was no need for me to put effort into shit!"

"Then why ask me to marry you? Why keep me around if you knew you no longer wanted to be with me?"

"'Cause I didn't wanna have another bitch out here carrying my seed without doing shit the right way. I don't want my fuckin' kids growing up in a broken-ass home, but you silly-ass bitches don't know how to appreciate shit."

"Silly-ass bitch? No, nigga, your junkie-ass baby mama is the silly-ass bitch. I swear you put that bitch and your pissy-ass daughter—"

Before she could even finish that fucked-up-ass statement, I had my hand around her throat and lifted her off the ground a couple of feet. I stared into Selena's green eyes, wanting to make sure that she knew how fucking serious I was with her. She had the game all the way twisted if she thought I was gonna keep being some sucka-ass nigga when it came to whether I would hit her back.

"Don't you ever in your muthafuckin' life say some slick-ass, disrespectful shit about my daughter. You want a nigga to get out of pocket with you, then you got it, bitch. I will fuckin' murk your ass, Selena, if you pop off foul about Sky ever again. Spoiled-ass broad. Take your ass back to your fuckin' mama's house, and I'll have your shit sent to you. Let this be the last time you contact me unless it's something concerning my child,"

I told her as I released her and caused her to hit the ground.

She sat there for a minute and gasped for air while I walked inside to check on Skylarr. Briana's hard-headed ass stood by the window, and I already knew that she had seen everything that had taken place, even though I had told her to leave a long time ago.

"Y'all getting on my nerves. I feel like I need to move and don't tell either one of you bitches where I live," I said to Briana as I walked toward the staircase.

"Your house needs cleaning and shit. You look—"

"I just thought about that. How the fuck you gonna come clean up my shit when you had my daughter over there living in a fuckin' pigsty? Man, get the fuck out, and take Selena's ass with you."

I took the stairs two at a time and pulled my cell phone out of my pocket once I had made it to the top. Thinking about how bad shit with Selena and Briana was had me thinking that it was definitely time for a change. I had completely lost all respect for both of their asses. I had dated both of them for the wrong reasons in the beginning. Briana was a beauty with exotic features and a bad-ass body, and Selena was a half-breed with one of the fattest asses I had ever seen. All that super-ficial shit had landed me in this shit I was in, but there were some other things and somebody else I wanted to explore. Cuba. Seeing her again that day confirmed everything I had been thinking and feeling. She was the one, and like they said, third time's a muthafuckin' charm. Shit, at least it better be. I needed a change in my life for real—someone to hold me down and someone I could do the same for. Neither Briana nor Selena had what I was looking for, and although I didn't know Cuba, I just knew that she was it.

Me: Aye, you gonna help me get your cousin or nah?
Send.

Tangie: You need help? Say it ain't so . . . lol. Cuba ass is a tough one, but I got a feeling you'll be just what she needs after what she's gone through.

Me: What has she gone through?
Send

Tangie: If I tell you, she'll kill me. But I will definitely help you get her. You have something for her to do? Like more work? In the evening time? She can use the money, but nothing illegal. Maybe she can babysit for you since you having that little issue with Briana . . . ???

I looked down at Tangie's last message and thought about it for a second. I wasn't the kinda nigga to have mad bitches around my kid, especially with how young she was, but damn, I was desperate. Something about Cuba had a nigga stuck in his thoughts, and I usually didn't stay there too long if it wasn't about no money. I thought about the fact that I had mad-ass laundry to handle and the other little shit around the house that could be tidied up, and I figured maybe having Cuba around wouldn't be too bad.

Me: Set it up, but give me about a week tho. I need to handle some shit with these crazy-ass bitches, and then I'll be ready.
Send.

Tangie: Alright bro, you know I got you.

Chapter 6

Amber

One Week Later . . .

It was 7:30 in the morning, and I had gotten up about an hour ago to fix my man breakfast in bed. Yesterday, Tramell's baby mother, Cocoa, was laid to rest along with two others, and I knew Dae was taking it very hard. He seemed to be so defeated when he came home a few hours earlier after staying out all night, having only enough energy to shower before he was knocked out and snoring right next to me.

I knew little things like this breakfast had always made him feel better. He would say all the time that he appreciated the effort I gave to put a smile on his face even though he was such an asshole all the time. It was nothing to me, because I loved my man. We had been together since I was a freshman in high school and he was a sophomore. All the girls were so in love with the Prince brothers, and I felt like the luckiest girl in the world when I started dating Daelan Prince. He was so charming and caring at such a young age. He was always looking after me and making sure I had everything I needed. Dae would give me the clothes off his back just to see me smile, and for that reason, I fell deeply in love with him, and I knew the feelings were mutual.

Back then, my mama's boyfriend that lived with us apparently had a thing for young girls. He had been hitting on me nonstop until one day, he could no longer resist me. My mama caught him touching all over me and forcefully trying to remove my clothes. He was able to convince my mama that I was the one that had come on to him. He said that I was always tempting him by wearing my jeans too tight or my shorts too short. He convinced her that I was a fast-ass little girl that was too eager to get some dick and that she should keep a better eye on me.

That was the day I found out that some bitches ain't shit. My mama didn't even ask me or care to know my side of the story; not that she needed it anyway. She took her boo's word and threw me out on the street with the clothes I had on my back and no shoes on my feet. I went straight to Dae with everything that happened, and that was the first time I really saw how tight Dae's bond with his brothers was. They went to my crib and fucked my mama's boyfriend up, and then grabbed up everything they could that belonged to me.

Dae convinced his mother and grandmother to let me stay with them. They were apprehensive at first. Dae told them that if I was going to have to live on the streets, then he was going with me, and his mama was not for nothing. They allowed me to stay, and I slept on the floor in the room with the boys every night, with Dae's arms wrapped around me. I guess Dae's mother and grandmother knew what would happen if they allowed me to stay, because not even six months later, I was pregnant, and then later gave birth to our son, Daelan Jr. two days after my fifteenth birthday. D.J. was now five years old.

Dae was love. He was everything that love represented, but that was all back when we were younger. Over the past few years of Dae ripping and running these dirty streets, he had completely done a 360 from the tall, lanky boy that I met in high school. He was no longer soft and serene when it came to how he treated me. Most times that I looked in the eyes of the man that I loved so much, I didn't even know who he was, and I didn't even know if he knew himself.

"Babe . . . babe," I said as I flipped on the bedroom light and made my way toward the bed. Dae's sexy body was on display, showing damn near every inch of his caramel skin besides what was covered by the briefs. His stomach was ripped with a firm eight pack, and his huge biceps showed how much he took care of his body. I knew the ladies loved my man; they always had. He was a dreadhead, unlike the rest of his brothers, and I made sure that they were always neatly tamed. Dae had these sexy hazel eyes that seemed to turn dark whenever he was angry and lighten up whenever he was in a good mood or happy. As of late, they always stayed dark—at least whenever he was in my presence.

"Babe," I called out again just as D.J. came bolting into the room and jumped on the bed all over his father. He should've been at school, but Dae's paranoia wouldn't allow me to drop him off this morning. He was afraid that whoever hit them last week was probably not finished, and God forbid that anything happened to D.J. in the process. I was cool with my little man being home, though. I would rather he be right there with me where I could watch him at all times anyway. Maybe since all this had happened, I could talk Dae into allowing me to homeschool D.J. like I had wanted to do in the beginning.

"Daddy! Daddy! I waited for you last night," D.J. said to his father, and finally Dae came to. He opened one eye, yawned, and stretched before completely opening the other one. I smiled as I watched the two of them interacting with each other. No matter how much of an asshole Dae could be sometimes, he never let it show with D.J.

"This food is gonna get cold if you don't eat it soon. And D.J., did you finish your breakfast?" I said as I moved closer to the side of the bed.

"Just sit the shit down," Dae said as he stared at D.J. strangely before he continued to tickle him. I went to place the tray of food down onto the nightstand when I noticed the reddish marks that were on Dae's chest, with a few around his neck area. My breath caught in my throat, and my hands became shaky, causing the food and drinks to spill from the tray.

"Ahhhhh!" D.J. screamed as he reached for his leg that had been hanging over the bed. "That was hot!"

I quickly set the tray down and tried to go to D.J.'s aid, but Dae grabbed me by my hair and pushed me back. I tumbled backward and threw my hands back to catch my fall.

"What the fuck is wrong with you, Amber?" Dae yelled as he quickly sat up in the bed to examine D.J.'s leg.

D.J. had tears running down his face as he dramatically ran his hand up and down his leg. I could see that he was a little red, and I assumed that some of the coffee had fallen onto his skin. I immediately felt bad, but I damn sure didn't do the shit on purpose like Dae was acting. That was my baby, and I would never do anything to hurt him. The blatant disrespect that Dae was continuing to show was really starting to get to me. It's not like I didn't know that he was cheating on me, because he always had, almost from the beginning of time. I was always having to fight some chick over Dae.

There was a time when he used to do his best to hide his infidelities, but now, he just didn't give a damn anymore. I don't know how many times I'd gone through his clothes to do laundry only to find the scent of perfume or makeup stains. Condom wrappers and sometimes even used condoms would pop up all over the damn place. I didn't know what I had done to deserve the things that Dae had started doing to me over the years. It was like he no longer loved me, and I had threatened to leave several times when I thought I reached my breaking point, but Dae would always guilt trip me into staying. He would even use D.J. against me and tell me that I couldn't take him if I ever left, and of course, I wasn't leaving my son behind.

"I didn't do the shit on purpose, Dae, damn," I finally said as I jumped up from the floor and ran into the bathroom.

I grabbed a rag from the cabinet and wet it with some cold water, and then grabbed a tube of Neosporin from the medicine cabinet. When I turned around, Dae was standing directly behind me. His eyes were so fuckin' dark that they scared me. I couldn't help but glance at the marks on his chest again. I wondered how, if he was so fuckin' hurt about his people being killed, was he able to gather up the strength to get some pussy? And why not get it from his girlfriend? I couldn't even remember the last time we had sex, but I really didn't even know if I cared. He always made it like it was something that he was forced to do whenever we were intimate. In order to save myself the embarrassment, I hardly ever asked, and he never attempted.

"You did do that shit on purpose," Dae barked, causing me to jump back a couple of inches.

"No, I didn't! Why would I purposely try to burn my son?" I asked, and when I attempted to go around him, he pushed me back.

"The fuck you mean? Bitch, you know why! Every time me and that nigga bonding, you always gotta step in like that shit kills you or something."

"Your ass is craz—"

Whap!

"My ass is what?" Dae asked after slapping me across the face. I brought my hand up to my lip, and I felt it beginning to swell. Holding back my tears, I looked up at Dae. His six-foot-one, muscularly-built frame seemed to tower over me as it always did whenever he was angry with me. He hated when I talked back to him, but hell, he wasn't my father, and shit, he *was* crazy. To think that I tried to burn my son was the dumbest shit in the world, and only a *crazy* person would even think some shit like that about me.

"Look, I ain't trying to fight with you!" I yelled to Dae as I held my hands up in surrender. I could see that he was burning with anger, and usually when he got like that, it was nothing that I could do to get him off of me. I wasn't trying to go there with him. Not that day. Hell, not any day, but especially not that day. Not while D.J. was just feet away in the other room.

Dae made one move toward me, and I tried my best to dodge him, but he grabbed me by the back of my hair and pulled me into his chest. His big, bulky hand wrapped around my throat, and he squeezed tightly as he ran his nose down the side of my neck as if he was smelling me or something. He then brought his lips up to my ear and began to whisper.

"She was a pretty, dark-skinned bitch with a fat ass, in case you was wondering," he said, and the tears began to slide down my face. "You better learn how to keep your emotions in check when my son is around. You understand me?"

I nodded my head and tightly shut my eyes. Just as Dae went to let me go, there was a light knock at the door. I rushed over to the sink to wet the towel again. I turned on the cold water, placed the towel underneath, and then wrung out the excess. I placed the towel to my lip, hoping I could keep some of the swelling down. D.J. was a smart boy, and I didn't want him to think that it was *ever* okay to hit a woman. He looked up to Dae and wanted to be just like him, and normally, that would be okay, but not this time and not in our situation.

"Amber, are you okay?" I heard Deonna say from the other side of the door. I had completely forgotten that she was here. I picked my head up and looked through the mirror at Dae. He looked back at me with a smirk on his face before he turned around to pull the door open.

"What the fuck do you mean is she okay? Bitch, are you okay? My brother still hadn't gone upside your head yet? Let you had played me like that, I would've had your muthafuckin' face in the dirt, scandalous-ass bitch."

"Dae!" I yelled at him to stop. Deonna had been staying with us since a couple of days after her arrest. She needed a place to lay her head and didn't have access to any money to get a hotel.

Apparently, she had gotten into some legal drama that she didn't really go into details about. KaeDee bailed her out, but by the time she made it home, he'd had the locks changed and wasn't answering any of her calls. All of her belongings, including her wallet that held her ID and credit cards, were inside of her office, which KaeDee had made sure to deny her entry to as well. It had been damn near a week since she was released, and KaeDee had yet to contact her.

She could stay with us as long as she liked, and I told her so without even thinking to check with Dae, because I didn't think I had to. We were family, and I knew that if I had been in a similar situation, Deonna would do the same for me.

"Nigga, don't flex, okay? Just because you go around here putting your hands on Amber like that makes you some big, bad-ass man, don't think that you can do the same to me. I fight men too." Deonna rolled her neck and smiled almost like she was testing Dae.

Deonna was a pretty girl. She had some radiant brown skin, sleek brown eyes, and a figure to die for. All her curves were home grown and fit her five-foot seven frame perfectly. She loved to work out and took great care of her body. She rocked a short cut that fell chin length that she always kept laid. I admired her so much. She was a businesswoman, her husband's partner and confidant, and I hoped that whatever she and KaeDee were going through could be fixed. They were the type of couple that I wanted Dae and me to be.

Deonna stood there with her arms folded across her chest and just stared Dae down. I could feel things about to take a turn for the worse when Dae bucked at her like he was going to hit her, and Deonna brought her hand back to slap the shit out of him. He punched her in the face, causing her to stumble back and trip over the thick carpeting in our bedroom. I ran to them and pulled at Dae's arms when I felt like he was about to hit Deonna again. He pushed me off of him and stood over Deonna as she tried to pick herself up off the floor. I could see that she was dazed, and I felt so fuckin' bad.

Yes, everyone knew that Dae was a hothead and that he had an anger problem, but I didn't believe that they knew just how bad it was. I didn't want people to see this side of him, because I knew that it was just a phase he was going through. Whatever demons Dae was facing out there in them streets was really fucking with him, and he hadn't yet figured out how to cope with it. That was part of the reason why it was so easy for him to convince me to stay when at times I so badly wanted to leave. I didn't want to neglect my man in his time of need and then be accused of not riding for him when things got bad.

"What the hell is wrong with you, Dae?" I screamed as tears poured from my eyes. I slowly moved over to help Deonna in fear that he would attack me again. "Just leave. Just fuckin' leave!"

"You're what's wrong with me! Every time I try to be happy with your ass, you come along and fuck it up and make me act like this!" Dae threw out, and I shook my head repeatedly. I refused to let him do this to me that day. This was how it was every time when he realized he'd gone too far. He would toss it all back on me and really have me wondering if I truly was the reason for everything he did. Usually, I would fall for it, but not this time. I woke up in a great mood, ready to cater to his every need, but his blatant disregard for my feelings had brought us to this point.

"I don't care, Dae. Just whatever . . . just go!" I said, and finally, he walked away. He got dressed in a T-shirt and jogging pants, threw some Jordans on his feet, and bolted out the door.

As soon as he was gone, I ran to grab my cell phone to call Khi. He picked up on the third ring.

"What up, sis?" Khi answered.

"It's Dae. I can't hide this shit anymore. He's been hitting on me, been doing it for years, but this time he's hit Deonna too. I don't know what to do anymore, Khi," I told him, and all I could hear was his light, then heavy breathing before the line went dead.

Chapter 7

Cuba

I pulled up to the address that Tangie had written down for me and made a stop in front of the heavy iron gate. Looking at the numbers laid out across the gate, I double-checked that I had the right address. I went to press the button on the keypad, but before I could, the gate started to open. I drove through once it was fully open and went down the long driveway until I came to a stop behind a cocaine white Maserati.

Looking in the rearview mirror, I brushed my hair down as best I could with my hand, and then stepped out of the car. Even though it was just a mini-mansion, I could tell that the home would look just as good on the inside as it did on the outside. I made my way up the steps and raised my hand to knock, but the door swung open, and this stalking-ass nigga stood on the other side of it. I turned around to leave, but he stepped out and grabbed my arm. I couldn't believe that Tangie had set me up like this, and I couldn't wait to get back to her and let her know how fucked up it was.

"Damn, where you going?" he asked me.

I rolled my eyes at his cocky ass and jerked my arm away from him. I couldn't help but give him the once over. He was rocking a wife beater, and a pair of pajama pants that hung low around his waist and exposed his print that I wish I would never have seen.

"You and Tangie got me fucked up. What's this, some kinda joke or something?"

"Chmmp . . . man, bring your ass in this house. She said you needed to make some extra paper, and I was looking for somebody to help me out around here."

"I feel like this was a setup."

"So, what if it was? You wanna make some bread or nah?" he asked, and I thought about my home situation. Over the past few days, I had noticed how Camp would always stare at me whenever Tangie wasn't in the room, and I had even heard him late night creeping by my door too many times for me to be comfortable with. I would lock the door at night and even put a chair up under the doorknob, but I really wanted to get the fuck up out of there as soon as possible. I didn't even have the heart or courage to tell Tangie what was going on for fear that she would take Camp's side and throw me out on my feet.

I needed that roof over my head since I didn't have anyone else right now. My mother and father had pretty much tarnished my name with the rest of my family, having them believe that I had Alaska killed, so no one really wanted anything to do with me. It hurt like hell, but it was motivation for me to get on my grind and do what I had to do so that I never had to go to any of them for anything. Tangie paid me $7.50 an hour for thirty hours a week. It was all she could afford for the moment, so as mad as I was that they had set me up, I wasn't going to turn down no extra bread.

I took Khi's lead and followed him inside his home. His foyer was decorated with huge pictures of Martin Luther King Jr., Malcolm X, Tupac, Scarface, and Biggie Smalls. I smirked and continued to follow him as he took me to the spacious living room. I watched as he sat his daughter down on the floor, directly in front of the TV. I looked around at the toys scattered here and there and saw little things that could be cleaned, but not much. Most of this shit looked like he threw on the floor on purpose just to look like he had some shit for me to do, but I wasn't tripping. If he wanted to pay me to be in his presence, then I would gladly accept. As long as he knew I wasn't fucking for the cash, then we were good.

No lie, Khi was fine as fuck. He had a dark caramel skin tone, a baby face with little to no facial hair besides the goatee that was lined to perfection. He had some eyes that seemed to be a hazel color in the light, but dark brown in the night. Khi kinda reminded of Derek Luke's sexy ass, especially since I had just sat up crying the night before while watching *Antwone Fisher*. His swag was better, though. He had this gangsta-ass edge about him, not to mention he was cocky as fuck. But as fine as Khi was, I had sworn off his type after Rue. There was no way I would ever go down that road again only to be fucked over and left hanging like I had been three years ago. I shook my head at the thought.

"Come on, let me show you around," Khi said as he pulled me out of my thoughts. He waved for me to follow behind him, and I did. He showed me to the kitchen first. It was a huge open area with stainless steel appliances and granite marble countertops. Interior design magazines had become a fascination when I was locked up, so I had a good eye for detail. I would study those magazines for the better part of my day and daydream of how one day I would be designing homes for celebrities and the rich.

"You don't know how to wash dishes," I said as I pointed to the sink that held a few glasses and plates, along with silverware and a few bowls.

He chuckled and looked me up and down. "You don't know how to comb your hair?" he asked, and I couldn't help but laugh.

"I keep it like this to keep niggas like you away, but I see it didn't work," I told him as I followed him around the house, going room to room. So far, on the bottom floor, I had counted three bedrooms and two bathrooms. All of them were clean, and it was just another confirmation that he really didn't need me there. It made me smile on the inside to think of the lengths that one would go through to have little ol' me in their presence, but I had to stay in game mode at all times. I couldn't let shit like that having me remove the block that I had around my heart.

Once we made it upstairs, he showed me where his daughter slept, which was a princess-themed bedroom, and then showed me to the master bedroom. I couldn't take my eyes away as I stood in the doorway of the room. Out of every room in the house, Khi made sure that his room was fit for a king. The bed had to be custom-made, because it looked to be the size of two king-sized beds put together. The four bed posts were built into the ceiling, and there were huge gold shams that hung down that you could pull open and closed like curtains. Whoever had done this room for him had done such a good job that there was nothing about it that I would do over.

When I had finally taken a breath from my excitement and went to turn around, I bumped directly into Khi's firm chest. He looked down at me with that cocky-ass smirk, and I quickly diverted my attention to something else, which just so happened to be his dick again. I threw my gaze to the floor, but when the soap that he bathed in tickled my nose, I had to take a step back from him. He grabbed at my arm, but I took another step back.

Why the hell does he have to smell so good? I thought as I became frustrated.

"I'm just to here to work for you, okay. Whatever ideas you have about me, I'm not that type of girl."

"And what kinda girl is that?"

"I know you don't need me here. Your house isn't really even dirty, and shit . . . you could do the little bit of mess you do have all by yourself."

"But then that would defeat the purpose of why I told Tangie to get you to come here."

"I'm not fuckin' you for money, Khi," I finally told him as I threw my hands across my chest. I was nervous but hoping he would understand that I was only there to do the real job of cleaning and caring for his daughter even if it wasn't much.

He looked down at me, and his tall ass had the nerve to laugh at me. "Trust me, when you do give me that pussy, I'm not gonna have to pay for it," he said as he turned around to walk away.

I took a deep breath, and then let it out as I followed him down the stairs and into the living room where his daughter had fallen asleep on the floor. He picked her up and was headed to lay her in her bed when the doorbell rang.

"I can take her for you," I said to him, and he handed baby girl to me and made his way toward the door.

I had only made it about halfway up the stairs before I heard Khi's loud voice along with another going back and forth. I peeked over my shoulder briefly before I continued up the stairs to lay little mama down in her bed. I pulled back the covers to her Princess Tiana bed set and laid her down before I pulled the covers up over her. There were a few toys scattered about over the floor, so I picked those up and tossed them inside a toy box that sat at the end of her bed. Once I was done, I left the room and headed downstairs to really get started on my *job* by washing the dishes and cleaning up Khi's kitchen.

Khi stood in the foyer of his home with another guy who damn near looked exactly like him. They stood at the same height, had the same caramel skin tone, with those same dark and mysterious hazel eyes. The other guy wore his hair in dreads and was just a little more on the rugged side than Khi, but I could tell that they were brothers. The dreadhead looked at me with a mischievous glare, and I smiled at him briefly as I made my way toward the kitchen.

"Aye . . . aye, come here," he called after me, and I stopped midstride. I tucked my hands over my chest as

I waited for him to approach me. The whites of his eyes were red, and his pupils looked glazed over. I could smell the alcohol on his breath the closer he got to me, and I knew that he was wasted. "Don't I know you?"

"No, you don't," I said as I shook my head and frowned up my face. I went to walk away, but he grabbed my arm and pulled me back to him.

He looked down at me and stared idly in my face like he was waiting for me to recognize him, but I didn't. I had never seen dude a day in my life, but I guess that liquor had him gone and thinking we'd met before.

"Can you let me go?"

"You sure I don't know you, shorty?"

"I'm positive. Now let my fuckin' arm go!" I yelled, and that's when Khi finally stepped in.

"Aye, Dae . . . go to my office, nigga, and I'll be there in a minute," Khi told him as he peeled him away from me. Dae placed his hands into his pockets and bit down on his bottom lip. He looked me up and down real good before doing what his brother told him to do.

Khi licked his lips before he stepped into my space and looked down at me. I attempted to walk away from him, but his cocky ass grabbed my arm and made me stand right there under his glare.

"You niggas sure love grabbing on a bitch. Can you let me go?" I asked him, and he smirked.

"I'll be back," he told me as he let me go.

I shrugged my shoulders and walked away from him. I didn't know if this job was going to work for me. Khi's ass made me feel things that I did not want or need to feel. I was going to hold out for as long as I could, but I knew that it would be only a matter of time before I caved in. I could feel it.

Chapter 8

KaeDee

I banged on the door and waited for someone to open it. I had left the office as soon as Khi called me and told me what happened with Amber and Deonna. I couldn't believe that Dae had been doing some ho-ass shit like beating on his damn lady as much he walked around confessing his love for her every second he got, but I guess I shouldn't have been that surprised. That nigga grew up in the same house as the rest of us, but one would think that he had been raised by a beast or some shit instead. He was always in some shit. That nigga didn't know how to act, which was why I didn't understand why Khi hadn't done what the fuck I had told him to when it came to the business. Khi always went on and on about how he refused to let anyone ruin what we all had built, but it was like he couldn't see that Dae was going to be the cause of our downfall. Khi had a real live soft spot for Dae, but I didn't, and wanted that nigga out. He was too fuckin' hotheaded and always making some dumb decisions, because it sounded good in that fucked up head of his.

Going after them Arabs like he had wasn't a smart move at all. Now, instead of us being focused on getting our paper together and properly planning to go after who had hit us when we had the valid evidence, we were constantly looking over our shoulders and waiting on them to hit back. Dae had broken Amin's jaw and nose, and he had to get a few stitches above his eye, but other than that, he was going to be just fine. But just like always, Dae was unable to leave well enough alone. Amin was found dead days after leaving the hospital. Although Dae claimed to know nothing, I knew better; Amin's blood was all over Dae's hands. When them Arabs came at us, they were gonna come hard, and it wasn't going to be anything that we could do to stop them. We just had to be ready.

Amber had finally come to open the door, and immediately, I noticed that her bottom lip had been busted. She didn't even look at me and had diverted attention to the floor before she spoke and wrapped her arms around me. I hugged her back and stepped inside of her and Dae's home.

"Why have you been holding that in so long, Amber? You're family, and you know we would've been pulled you and D.J. out of this situation with no problems," I told her as she continued to look at the floor.

"It just started over the past few years, and it's progressively gotten worse. I just didn't know how to tell anyone, and every time I got the courage to do so, he would always convince me that he wasn't going to do it again. Dae is sick, KaeDee. I don't know what's going on out there or what he's seen, but it's fucking with his mind. One minute he can be so calm, cool, and loving, and the next, he will snap and turn into this monster," Amber said as tears fell from her eyes.

I knew that she wasn't lying, because I did notice that whatever was going on with Dae hadn't started affecting him until the past few years. We all thought that the nigga was just having a hard time after our uncle was murdered some years back, but shit, it had been a while since, and he was still cutting up. I didn't understand it, but I honestly no longer had it in me to care. He was Khi's problem now. Khi wanted to be a softy about the way he handled him, like Dae was still a little-ass boy, then that shit was on him. After the shit with Amin and him hitting Deonna, I was officially washing my hands of the little nigga.

"It's gonna be okay, Amber. Maybe you and D.J. should go and stay with Moms until Dae calms down," I told her, referring to my mother, who was pretty much her mother as well. "Or either come to the house or to Khi's. It doesn't matter. Just somewhere other than here."

"No, it's gonna be okay. I know deep down that he hates to disappoint you and Khi, and hopefully, now that you guys know, he won't do it again," she said, and I didn't push. I just didn't want anything further to happen to her, and I damn sure didn't want that nigga hurting my nephew.

"Where's Deonna?" I asked Amber, and she pointed down the hall toward their guest bedroom. I kissed Amber on her forehead before I made my way down the hall.

The room was dark, but I didn't see Deonna anywhere. I noticed the light that peeked from underneath the door of the bathroom. Before stepping in that direction, I dropped Deonna's Louis bag with all her personal belongings on the bed. I knew that had I not been so stubborn and given her these things a week ago, she would've stayed somewhere else, and the altercation with Dae would've never happened. I made my way over to the bathroom, twisted on the knob, and pushed the door open. Deonna damn near jumped out of her skin when she saw me, causing something that she held in her hand to fall on the floor.

I walked over and picked it up, noticing that it was a pregnancy test. The word *pregnant* appeared in the screen, and I looked down at Deonna as she sat on the toilet, refusing to return my stare. I could see the bruising over her jaw from where Dae had hit her, and I bit down on the inside of my cheek as the anger I felt brewed inside me. I guess Khi knew what he was doing when he told me to check on the ladies and that he would talk to Dae. I could kill that nigga right now for this ho shit that he was doing. Hitting on females was a punk-ass move, and Dae knew better.

Although I was mad at my wife, I didn't like to see her in this state, especially now that I knew she was carrying my child. I gritted my teeth and placed my hands in my pockets as I tried to hold my composure. So much was going on lately that it had been hard for me to stay the calm guy that everyone knew me as. I felt like at any moment I would snap. I hoped that Deonna wasn't about to tell me no shit that would make me do the same thing to her that Dae had done. I had never put my hands on a woman before, and I didn't intend to, but shit, I didn't know how I would react if Deonna told me something I didn't like.

Her and this ex of hers, Tyrin Walker, had done some business together since me and her had been married, and Deonna ain't never said shit about it. Hell, I had never even heard this dude's name before the FBI came parading through my firm and slapping a twenty-page warrant on my desk that had my wife's name written all over it. I thought it was real funny how she flipped out on me and was ready to leave a nigga when she found out what my *true* profession was when all along she knew that she had dated a well-known drug kingpin out of Miami before I even came around.

Shorty was a real-life actor. She had pretended to be this good girl in college that came from a good family with morals and shit, but hell, now I didn't even know what part of that shit was even true. I had never met Deonna's parents before, or any of her family, for that matter. She claimed that she was the black sheep of the family and that everyone was mad at her for pursuing a dream in dance when her family contained a line of doctors and nurses. Shit, who the fuck knows?

"So, you pregnant?" I asked, finally breaking from my thoughts as I held the test in my hand. I looked at it once more before I tossed it in the trash and took a seat on the edge of the tub.

"Looks that way," Deonna said with a sniffle.

My wife was so fuckin' beautiful to me. She had those eyes that my mama always preached to her boys about to look for in our women. I knew when I met her in college that she was the one for me, which was why we didn't date long before I proposed to her and gave her my last name.

I pulled Deonna's hands into mine, and they trembled underneath my touch. "Look at me," I told her, and she brought her eyes to mine. Tears leaked down her face, and she tried to wipe them away, but I held onto her tighter. The love I had for this woman was undeniable. She gave me my first and only child, and I made sure that I gave Deonna and Chanel the world. Deonna was my life, my partner, and my Bonnie in this fucked up world that we lived in, but she was a liar that I no longer trusted. What I did back then was to protect her, to protect myself, and to protect my brothers. She kept her life from me in an attempt to deceive me, but the truth always came to the light.

I took one hand and pulled the hair from Deonna's face before I rubbed my palm down her skin that seemed to be coated with caramel as it glowed from the light that shone down on her. I hadn't noticed the glow until now, but it was evident, and it made her look even more beautiful.

"Tyrin Walker," I said, and just speaking that nigga's name out loud caused my body to heat up. I stood up, loosened my tie, and then placed my hands in my pockets, afraid of what I might do with them. "You know that nigga stepped into my office today, right?"

"What?" Deonna said.

I tried to read her expression to see if she had known that the nigga was in town or not. I wanted to know if she had been in contact with him, and if not, I wanted to know when was the last time they'd spoken. "What did he want?"

"He wants me to defend him in court. He says that if I defend him and get him off, then he won't have to testify against you," I said with a shake of my head.

"Wow . . . that muthafucka. Testify against me? How is he going to testify against me?"

"He's claiming that he didn't know anything about his books and any extra money that came through the doors of his carwash. He's saying that he's never touched the books or seen the books, and that you were the only person that had access to them."

"He's lying. He checked over them with a fine-tooth comb each time to ensure that I never missed a fuckin' dime."

"What the fuck does it matter, Deonna? Your name is on that shit! And not to mention you were there with that muthafucka six months ago. That was when you was supposed to be in Miami with Selena, fucking vacationing, but instead you doing work for that nigga. Did you fuck him, Deonna?"

"No . . . no!" she yelled, and I just didn't know if I could believe her.

None of that shit sounded right to me. I couldn't believe that she would go out of her way to work on his books one fucking time. She had to have fucked that nigga while she was there. Had to.

"I don't believe you, Deonna. You've lied to me about every part of your life before we met, so how do I know if what you're telling me now is the truth?"

"I only lied about Tyrin because I was ashamed of that part of my life. I didn't want anyone to know that I was involved in that type of life. That's why when I got with you and found out that you were no different, I was so upset."

"Was that the last time you saw him?" I asked her and noticed how her eyes danced around before she laid them on me.

"That was the last time. I haven't had any communication with that man. I swear to you, KaeDee. I wouldn't do that to us."

"What the fuck you mean you wouldn't do that to us? You did this shit to us when you never told me about it in the first place! You should've said something. How many women have we defended for the same shit, Deonna? You can go to jail, and if you do, what the hell do you think it's gonna do to us, to Chanel?"

"I thought that I was leaving all that in the past. I never knew that it would ever catch up to me, babe. I am so sorry. I swear I hate that I didn't tell you the truth. You have to forgive me so that we can move on from this."

"I left your purse on the bed. I gotta go," I told her as I exited the bathroom.

"Wait, baby, wait. Please let me come home. I miss Chanel . . . and I miss you too."

"I'm going to defend your punk-ass boyfriend on the strength of Chanel and our baby that you're carrying in your stomach. . . . That is my baby, right?" I asked without even turning to look at her. I didn't even want to see if there was doubt. The thought of Deonna carrying another man's baby infuriated me. I took in a deep breath and willed myself to stay cool.

"What kind of question is that, KaeDee? Of course it's your child," she answered.

"I'll be in touch. For now, get you a hotel, and I'll think about if I want to continue on with this marriage or not," I told her before I walked away and left the house.

I made my way to my 2015 pearl-colored Bentley Continental and disarmed the alarm. Once I pulled the door open, I sat down inside, cranked the ignition, and pulled out of the driveway. I had a feeling about Deonna that I just couldn't trust, and my instincts had hardly ever led me wrong.

When I pulled out of the gated community, I drove a bit down the road and pulled into a nearby gas station. Pulling up to the pump, I got out and slid my card through the machine before I started to pump the gas. After a couple of minutes, I was pulling away from the pump just in time to see Deonna's BMW pass me by. She was so focused on where she was going that she didn't even notice me. I waited for a few moments before deciding to pull into traffic a few cars behind her. I wanted to see where she was headed as I followed her onto the freeway, keeping my distance once we both picked up speed in conjunction with the other cars.

Twenty minutes later, she exited into downtown Dallas and drove a few miles down the road before pulling into the parking lot of the W Hotel. She parked her car next to a brand-new Aston Martin, and I didn't even think twice about it until the door swung open and Tyrin's bitch ass stepped out. My jaws clenched as I pulled into a parking spot that had them in my direct line of vision.

Tyrin pulled Deonna's door open, and she stepped out and directly into his embrace. I shook my head as I watched the interaction between the two of them. They didn't seem to be two people that hadn't seen each other in six months. The way that Tyrin touched the side of Deonna's face and stared down at her, I knew that everything she had told me was a lie.

He leaned over and tried to kiss her, but Deonna turned her head and stepped away from him. He said something that I couldn't quite pick up from reading his lips, and Deonna slowly nodded her head in response to him. Taking her hand into his, he led her toward the hotel, and I reached over into the center console, pulled my pistol, and stepped out of my ride.

Chapter 9

Deonna

Hearing that Tyrin was in town and had been up to the law firm had me heated. I didn't know what the hell he was trying to do by coming to see my husband, and I wasn't about to have him messing up my relationship. What he and I had ended years ago when I picked up and left Miami to start my life over in D.C. I admit that I did make the mistake of allowing him to entice me into seeing him when Selena and I took that vacation to Miami months back. Shit, Tyrin had always been tempting to me. He claimed that he only wanted to have dinner, but I should've known that being in Tyrin's presence would only lead to my panties ending up on the floor and us making love into the wee hours of the morning. It never failed. That was the first and last time that I had ever cheated on my husband, and I hoped that by Tyrin being there, he wasn't looking to stir up any drama.

I had only done his books for him while I was there because he claimed that he had to fire the last girl and had gotten super behind. After that one time, I warned Tyrin to never contact me again, but of course, he hadn't listened. It hadn't mattered, though, because I made sure that I never replied to any of his efforts to reach out to me.

He'd always hated it back then whenever I said that I was leaving him, and he couldn't understand why I wanted to mess up a good thing. What we had was good, too good, but Tyrin was bad for me. He didn't fit the lifestyle that I wanted for myself, and for that reason, I had to move on. I could never have kids with him or even settle into one place, because shit was always popping off when it came to Tyrin. He lived life on the edge, and the thrill of the game excited him. Muthafuckas was always shooting at him, he had been robbed more times than I could count, and I was sure that he was responsible for part of the high body count in Miami.

Tyrin wasn't anything like KaeDee, who was careful and more calculating. He lived his life one day at a time, and I couldn't roll with that. I had to go, had to get away from him before I ended up dead, on a cold-ass table, forcing my parents to have to come out and identify me.

"Bae, stop walking so slow," Tyrin said as he pulled me from my thoughts and to the reservations desk.

I nervously looked around and hoped that no one there would recognize me. I didn't even know what the fuck I was doing there with Tyrin. The minute KaeDee left, I had contacted Tyrin and told him that it was fucked up that he was trying to railroad me in the way that he was. He claimed that he could explain. He asked me to meet him so that we could talk in person, because his line was most likely being tapped by the FBI. I knew that meeting up with Tyrin was the last thing I needed to do, but somehow, I convinced myself that I needed to hear what he had to say.

"Why are you getting a room, Tyrin? Let's just find a private area in their lobby for us to speak," I said, knowing damn well the reason he wanted to get a room. I wasn't slow, and I knew how this shit was going to go. I could feel my pussy throbbing with anticipation as I suddenly thought of how I knew Tyrin was going to fuck me. He always got down in the bedroom, and if I were handing out trophies, he would definitely be crowned king.

Shit, I thought as I started to feel guilty as hell. I had just found out I was pregnant not even an hour ago, and there I was ready to be fucked by a man that wasn't my husband. *What the fuck am I doing here?*

"Come on, let's go," Tyrin said as he grabbed my hand and pulled me toward the elevators.

I had ample time to say no and just turn around and walk away, but I didn't. I got on the elevator with Tyrin, rode up to the thirty-ninth floor, got off, and followed him to the room. My heart beat heavily against my chest as we walked inside, and Tyrin immediately put his arms around me.

"Shit, I fuckin' miss you, girl."

"Hmmm," I moaned as he slid his ferocious tongue across the back of my neck. He slid his hand underneath the pencil skirt that I wore and rummaged his fingers in between my thick thighs. I shuddered at his touch. I closed my eyes and allowed my head to relax against his chest as his fingers made love to and danced against my clit.

"That nigga hitting on you, Deonna?" he asked, I guess noticing the swelling on my jaw.

"No," I said as I shook my head, and he slid a finger inside my pussy. "Wait, wait . . . wait!"

"Don't play with me, Deonna. Take this shit off and let me taste that pussy," Tyrin said as he backed me up toward the bed.

I put my hand up to stop him and stared into his decadent, light brown eyes. Tyrin's pretty-boy looks always fooled people into believing that he was one of the good guys that could be trusted, but they were always sadly mistaken. Tyrin was a light-skinned nigga with baby features. He was every bit of thirty but looked to be more like twenty-five years old. The fade that he rocked was always spinning with waves, and he kept it cut low and

neatly tapered. His facial hair was to a minimum. with
only a slight peach fuzz on his chin. He stood at five feet
ten inches, chiseled and firmly built, with some sexy-ass
bowlegs.

"You're a snitch now, Tyrin?" I asked him as he removed
his shirt and got down on his knees in front of me. I
looked down at him as he licked his lips and tried to pull
my skirt up. "Stop it, Tyrin, and answer me."

"Take this shit off," he said and reached behind me
to unzip my skirt. He tugged at it until it came from
around my thick hips and pooled around my ankles. Tyrin
removed my Louboutins from my feet one by one and
tossed them to the side. He pulled the skirt away, and then
came for my panties.

"No, I'm serious. Answer me. You really gonna snitch
on me if my husband doesn't defend you?"

"Man, what the fuck you gotta bring that nigga up for?
Fuck your husband," Tyrin snapped, reminding me again
of another reason of why I had left him. His attitude
wasn't shit to play around with, and I always feared back
then that one day he would stop taking shit out on them
streets and bring it home to me. He was big on verbal
abuse and had never put his hands on me, but I didn't
know if and when that shit would change, so I didn't stick
around to find out.

"See, this why I can never stay in the room with you for
too long. I'm gone," I said as I kneeled down to pick up
my skirt.

There was a knock at the door. I looked at Tyrin to see if
he was expecting anyone, and he shrugged his shoulders
and made his way over to the door. He didn't even check
to see who it was before he pulled the door open.

"It's for you," Tyrin said and stepped to the side while
I was in the middle of pulling my skirt up over my butt. I
instantly began to sweat, and my heart beat achingly in

my chest as I looked up to see that it was my husband standing on the other side of the door. The look of hurt was evident in his eyes, and I could only imagine what it looked like to him. Although I hadn't fucked Tyrin, I was pretty sure that it looked like I did.

I held my hand over my chest, feeling as if I was going to have a fuckin' heart attack when KaeDee punched Tyrin in the side of his face so hard that it sent him flying across the room. I jumped back and covered my mouth, watching as KaeDee pounced on Tyrin and pounded his humongous fist into every part of his body. I had never seen my husband this angry before. It was like he snapped and transformed into the Incredible Hulk. His big, burly body was frightening, and I feared that he was going to kill Tyrin.

"KaeDee!" I yelled, trying to stop him, but he just kept going. I couldn't believe that I had fucked up this bad. I don't know why I had even gone there knowing that I was a happily married woman. I knew the things that Tyrin did to me. I knew what being in a room alone with him would do to me. I could almost never say no to him, which was why I had opted to stay away from him before now. I loved my husband, but truthfully, I don't think I had ever really fallen out of love with Tyrin. Leaving him was the hardest thing that I'd ever had to do, but I loved my life, and I didn't want my parents to ever have to bury me, so it was something that I'd had to do.

KaeDee was something every woman needed in her life. He was caring, loving, strong, and charismatic. He was as fucking smart as he was strong and giving. He had the greatest head in the world on his shoulders and would do anything for those that he loved. He was the greatest provider ever, a fantastic life partner, and he was my heartbeat. Without my heartbeat, I couldn't live. KaeDee was what I needed to keep breathing, but then whenever

I thought about Tyrin, which I tried my hardest not to do often, he was what I needed to stay alive inside. He excited me whether I wanted to admit that or not. Tyrin was like a fuckin' drug, and being that I was a strong woman, I was able to stay away from him, but whenever he was in my face—or like that day, in the area—I had to have him.

KaeDee my oxygen, Tyrin my satisfaction, and both completed me and made me whole. Seeing my husband about to take Tyrin away from me started to slowly kill me on the inside. When KaeDee pressed his pistol to Tyrin's head, I began to choke. I huddled over and coughed uncontrollably, suddenly and finally admitting to myself that I had been missing Tyrin something serious. I realized that now, and I knew that if we could all walk out of there that day, I would not deny my feelings for him any longer.

"KaeDee, please," I begged him for his sake and mine. I stepped forward, hoping that maybe I could talk KaeDee out of the mistake he was about to make. "Baby, remember Chanel back home. What will she do without her daddy? And this baby that I'm carrying, this could be the son that you've always wanted."

"You preg . . . pregnant again by this nigga? Where the fuck is my child, Deonna?" Tyrin asked, and I watched KaeDee's eyes go blank as he looked at me and then down at Tyrin. He was ready to squeeze the trigger, but thank God the police came in right in time. I don't think I had ever been so happy to see the police a day in my life.

"Freeze!" one of the officers yelled as he pulled his weapon and pointed it at KaeDee's back. KaeDee quickly dropped the pistol and didn't hesitate to lie down on the floor and place his hands over the top of his head.

Chapter 10

Khian

I sat in the car and waited for Daelan to bring his ass on so that we could go and bail KaeDee out of jail. He ended up having to spend the weekend in Lew Sterrett and wasn't able to see a judge until this morning. They granted him a $500,000 bond, and I had stopped by a bail bondsman's office a few hours ago so that they could post it. He was supposed to be released no later than two in the afternoon. It was already going on 1:30, and Daelan still hadn't brought his ass out yet.

I honked on the horn a few times and was ready to pull out my cell to call when he finally emerged from the house. He had a Styrofoam cup in his hand, and a blunt hung from the corner of his mouth. It fucked me up to see my li'l bro so fuckin' careless like he was. It seemed like he and Emon didn't appreciate shit. They had it the fuckin' easiest out of all of us, and maybe that was the fuckin' problem. KaeDee, Cass, and I had made this dope game shit easy for them, so they really didn't know what it meant to work for shit.

Emon's dumb ass got locked up on his eighteenth birthday after he was gifted a Porsche Panamera by me and KaeDee. He took it out joyriding with two of his homies, and they never made it home that night. They had almost a pound of weed in the car, pills, and Emon's ass was strapped with a nine millimeter. KaeDee took on Emon's case when he was fresh out of school, and he did the best he could, but unfortunately, it wasn't enough. Emon got four years, and KaeDee beat himself damn near to death about it, but shit, it wasn't his fault. We taught Emon and Dae better, but them niggas didn't listen to shit. They thought they knew everything, but they both were dumb as fuck. They never thought shit out and always acted on impulse.

KaeDee wanted me to put Dae out and have him doing something else besides this dope shit, in fear that he was either gonna fuck up our connect, or have us going to war over some bullshit. I heard what he was saying, but at the end of the day, Dae was my youngin', and I couldn't just snatch this shit away from him. He put in work, too, and even if it wasn't as much as the rest of us, he still did his part.

"Man, what this nigga done did to get himself locked up? I bet it's behind Deonna's bitch ass," Dae said the moment he sat down in the car and closed the door behind him. He took a sip from the Styrofoam cup, and then took a pull from the blunt before passing it over to me.

"You ain't hear me blowing for your ass twenty minutes ago?" I said as I pulled out of the driveway and sped down the street, causing Dae to waste a little of his *drank* on his shirt. He looked over at me, and I blew a cloud of smoke into his face, smirking at the few drops that had made small stains.

"Bitch," he said, and I laughed.

"I don't know what that nigga did, though. He told me he didn't wanna talk about it when I talked to him yesterday. All he wanted to know was where was Deonna's ass at."

"Pussy-whipped-ass nigga. I betcha all this shit has something to do with why that bitch caught them charges.

I knew I couldn't trust a ho with no hair. Baldheaded ass."
Dae shook his head and moved his dreads out of his face.

"Fuck is you talking about, nigga?" I laughed and pulled
onto the highway. "Anyway, bruh, since you want to duck
and dodge a nigga's conversation and shit, we about to
talk about this shit now since you ain't got nowhere to go."

Dae sighed. "Damn, told you it ain't shit wrong with
me, bro. Why the fuck something gotta be wrong?" Dae
asked and sat back in his seat, looking defeated.

"What you mean why something gotta be wrong? When
the fuck has it been normal to snap out on everybody the
way you've been doing? Then you over there beating on
my sis like some ho-ass nigga. . . ."

"Man, don't act like you ain't never hit on no bitch
before. I done seen you choke Briana's ass out a few
times."

"Man, don't try and twist this shit around, Dae. But
yeah, I have put my hands on Briana and Selena, and it's
fucked up no matter if I felt like they deserved the shit or
not. We not them type of niggas, though. Come on, fam,
we don't beat on women."

"What I do with my girl is my business. I don't dictate
how you run your bitches, so don't try and dictate how I
run mine."

"I ain't trying to dictate shit, Dae. I'm just telling you,
you looking like a real ho-ass nigga for that shit. You
beating on Amber, bruh. Beating on her like she another
nigga."

"Fuck that ho. I don't even know why I'm still with that
bitch."

"Really? That's how you feel? Shorty that done held
you down through all the fucked-up shit you be out here
doing, you feeling like that? Man, what the hell is wrong
with you? Please talk to me. I'm begging you, bruh."

"Look, I don't wanna fuckin' talk about this shit, a'ight? Man, leave me the fuck alone. I'm good!"

"Straight up, youngin'. You got that. Long as you know it won't be no more talking and straight action coming from me."

"Yeah, and like you scare me, ho-ass nigga."

"We gon' see, you bitch. You pussy-ass bitch."

"Man, what's up with that broad, though, that was at your house the other day?" Dae asked, changing the subject.

I was dead-ass for real with his ass, though. It wasn't going to be no more talking from me, and every time Dae fucked up, I was coming straight for his head. KaeDee was already fed up with him, and I was the one that kept giving him all the chances. I couldn't have him out there making me look bad just because I wanted to spare that nigga's feelings.

"You tell me. You fucked?" I asked him, referring to Cuba. I had peeped how he was checking shorty out like he knew her the other day when he came by, but I never got a chance to ask him what it was all about since he ran out on me the minute I asked him what was going on with him.

"Nah, she just look familiar; that's all. Maybe she went to school with a nigga or just used to be around the way in the hood. She just look like somebody I know, but I know I ain't fuck."

"Like you would remember," I joked.

"Nigga, you might be right about that, but shit, I don't think I fucked."

"Shit, I hope not, 'cause I'm definitely tryna see what that box like."

Dae laughed and snatched the blunt out of my hand. He took in a long pull and blew the smoke out before he looked over at me. "She might be what you need, though.

I knew from jump that Briana and Selena wasn't 'bout shit, but I couldn't tell you that."

"I was wrong about Briana, but Selena was some shit that really went too far, and I tried to make it work for the sake of me not letting her go before she fell in love, and then my dumb ass went and got her pregnant."

"Yeah, you is dumb for that shit. I could tell that li'l ho low-key crazy, bruh, so I know you got your hands full with that one."

"I really do care about Selena a lot. I just never been in love with her. I should've never dragged her along like that."

"So, you think little mama is what it is? She look like she ain't shit but sixteen years old. You check her ID?"

I laughed. "Cuba don't even know what I'm about to do in her life. It's been so long before I went hard behind a woman, but I could feel like this won't be a mistake. I'm all in on this one."

"What? And you haven't even had the box yet? Nigga, is you for real?"

"It's them eyes, bruh," I said, and Dae laughed before pulling his dreads from his face.

"You and KaeDee with that eye shit Mama used to talk about. Fuck that. I don't believe in that shit. That's why I never listened to her when she started talking about it. If that shit was so accurate, then why the fuck you got it wrong?"

"Nigga, I was only nineteen when I met Briana, and if you did listen, you'd know Mama always told us that we may get it wrong a few times before we get it right. I believe in that shit, because Mama said that Daddy taught it to her. She said that he knew that she was the one for him when he first laid eyes on her. She gave him five boys, and when he got locked up and left her to raise us alone, she still held that nigga down, and still fucking do so after him being gone for eleven years."

"That's because she just that thorough. She a rider, but that ain't got shit to do with her fuckin' eyes. I wish you stop telling people that shit too. You and KaeDee sound real fuckin' stupid."

I shook my head and sighed. "You just a lost cause, my nigga. A lost fuckin' cause."

I pulled into downtown Dallas and drove down Industrial Boulevard until I made it to the Lew Sterrett Justice Center parking lot that sat right across the street. I parked as close as I could to the front, and Dae and I hopped out and made our way to the jail. KaeDee stuck out like sore thumb as he paced back and forth, puffing on a cancer stick. I knew my brother had to be stressing if he had resorted to the nicotine.

"Aye," I called out, and KaeDee looked over at us and tossed the cigarette to the ground. He walked toward us, and with every step he took, I swear to God I could see the ground shaking. This nigga was heated, and I knew that if KaeDee was pissed about anything, it had to be something serious.

"I need a fuckin' drink," he said as he walked past Dae and me and headed across the street to the parking lot.

We all got in the Mazi, and I peeled off, waiting on KaeDee to grace us with the details that had led to him being locked up over the weekend. I thought it was kinda funny that we hadn't heard from Deonna, but I guess that was enough for me to know that all this shit had to do with her.

"Bruh, I don't know why you ain't just kill that ho and that nigga. I already know this shit is about her. I'm just glad that it's not me in trouble this time, though. I'm happy as fuck it's not me that y'all picking up from county," Dae said before sipping on the lean from his cup.

"Shut the fuck up, Daelan," KaeDee snapped, and I couldn't help but laugh.

"A'ight. I'm just saying that y'all niggas always got something to say about me getting in trouble and shit. I'm just glad I ain't do—"

"I oughta snap your muthafuckin' neck right now," KaeDee said as he wrapped his big-ass arm around Dae's neck and squeezed as hard as he could. Dae's drink fell out of his hand and into his lap, and he brought his hand up to try to pull KaeDee off of him. I shook my head and kept driving like I ain't even see the shit. I knew it had to be a reason KaeDee opted for the back seat rather than sitting up front where there was more leg room.

"Keep talking that shit. Your ass is always running your muthafuckin' mouth, and I'm getting sick of it. Shut the fuck up some got-damn times and listen, nigga! Listen! You gonna fuck around and get your ass into some trouble that Khi can't get your bitch ass out of. Notice I fucking said *Khi* and not *we*. I refuse to come to your rescue any fuckin' more. You put your hands on my wife, and because of that, I want to fuckin' kill you, but I know it would cause my mama some pain, so because of that, I'm going to spare you. But if you ever . . . in your mutha-fuckin' life . . . touch my wife, I will hang your ass by your muthafuckin' balls, nigga, and I mean that literally. You know how I give it up, so don't fuck with me, *Daelan Prince*. You giving us a bad name out here, nigga. Get your shit together or go the fuck away!"

KaeDee released Dae, causing him to take a sharp and deep breath as he fought to fill his lungs with oxygen. He began to cough, and I glanced over at him to see tears falling down his face. Nobody said anything after that. We all rode in silence all the way to KaeDee's side of town. Once I pulled into the gated community where KaeDee lived, I drove four blocks down the street to his home. It was only four houses on his block, his being the biggest one. He lived in an eight-bedroom mansion that he had built at the same time he opened his law firm.

As soon as I pulled up to the gate and placed the car in park, Dae angrily hopped out and slammed the door behind him. I watched as he paced back and forth with his dreads hanging as he looked toward the ground.

"Let me tell you something. Dae is gonna fuck this shit up for us. I'm telling you right now, Khi, to take care of him. You always talking about you'll never let anyone fuck up the business, but I guess Dae is the exception. Give him something else to do and stop fuckin' playing before we don't have shit left," KaeDee said, and I sighed.

"A'ight, I hear you. I heard you the last time."

"Come on, bruh. You know I know what the fuck I'm talking about. Cass will be home in a few months. How the fuck you think he gonna feel if he comes home to us having no connect, or in the middle of a war? You saw the look on Tamar's face when that nigga yawned in the middle of the damn meeting. He's too disrespectful, too hot, and too damn dumb to be in this shit."

"We not gonna lose the connect, and Cass ain't got shit to worry about. I'll never let that happen. I worked too damn hard to get it going in the first place, and I'm not about to let Dae fuck up nothing for us."

"I can't tell, bruh. Look at this nigga, bruh. Look at him," KaeDee said, pointing out the window at Dae.

I looked at him, and all I could see was that at some point, I had lost my brother, and I didn't know where and to what. This wasn't the Dae that any of us was familiar with. Something had happened, and I just wanted to know what so that I could do what I needed to help him out of this state.

"What happened with Deonna?" I asked, changing the subject, and KaeDee began telling me everything that took place, from the time the FBI came rolling into his office to him being seconds away from killing that bitch-ass nigga Tyrin Walker from out of Miami, and to him almost being killed by the cops. I shook my head the whole damn time, not believing that my sis even got down like that. She didn't seem like the type, but nowadays, you couldn't really tell the hoes from the good girls anyway.

I felt bad for my brother, because he really loved his wife. I remembered when he first called me and Cass from D.C. while attending school, telling us how he felt that he had met the one. I had never heard that nigga sound so happy in my life. As soon as he had graduated college, he came home and got this house built, bought Deonna an engagement ring, and had her move here as soon as the house was done. Deonna and KaeDee were what I wanted, but now I wasn't so sure about that.

KaeDee said that he was going to check into this Tyrin cat, because he didn't trust him, and he was going to do some digging into Deonna, too, because he felt like he no longer knew her. Shit, I felt the same way. That bitch had fooled us all. He wanted me to take him to get his car out the pound in the morning, but that night, he said, he just needed to think and get his head straight, and I understood.

Once we were done talking, KaeDee stepped out of the car, and then entered the code that he needed to get inside the gate. Dae's ass wouldn't even get back in the car until KaeDee was out of sight. He went to say something, but I hushed his ass by turning up the music on him. I needed to fuckin' think as well.

When I made it back to the house, the first thing I did was head up to Skylarr's room. It was going on two weeks since I took her from her mama, and I knew there was no way I was ever going to give her back. I loved having my daughter right up under me, and little girls needed their daddies more than anything. I hadn't seen or heard from Briana since the night she had come asking for my help. I was a little worried about her, and I felt a little bad about turning her away, but this was what she had done to herself. She only got clean the last time because I forced her to for the sake of our daughter, and this time I wanted it to be something she wanted to do on her own. I didn't feel like her getting clean was something she wanted to do right now, otherwise she would've never gone back on that shit. Knowing her, she only came to me asking for help so that she could please me. That was why I was so hard on her and told her what it was straight up. I wanted to make sure she knew that it was never going to be me and her again, so if she was going to clean herself up, she needed to take me out of the equation.

As soon as I made it to the top step, I could hear Cuba and Skylarr singing nursery rhymes and shit. That brought a smile to my face, especially when I peeked into the bathroom and saw them dancing on the ABC carpet that I had laid out in the middle of the room. She usually didn't get there until after six most evenings, but I had Tangie let her have the day off since I had to pick up KaeDee from the jail.

"Where is Skylarr, where is Skylarr?" Cuba sang as she held on to Skylarr's little hands.

"Here I amm, here I amm!" Skylarr responded to her.

"How are you today, little girl?"

"Vewy well, thank you."

"Run away, run away," Cuba told her, and Skylarr ran around the room. She started spinning around in circles, and that was when she noticed me. She took off running toward me and hugged my leg like she always did when she saw me.

"Hey, you're back. I didn't think you would get back so early or I would've had dinner ready," Cuba said, seeming

embarrassed. If she had only known how much I fuckin'
admired that shit. . . .

"It's cool. I can order some pizza or something. I'm in
for tonight, so you can chill out," I told her as I looked her
over. I noticed that she had finally taken the time out to
do something to her hair, and that let me know that I was
making progress with her ass. She wore her natural hair
and had straightened it out to have it fall down both sides
of her full, round face.

Cuba's job was to take care of the house and take care
of Skylarr, but she made sure to take care of me too. Every
day that she cooked, Cuba was sure to make something
for me too. I hadn't had a homecooked meal by a woman
other than my mama since me and Briana were together,
since Selena's ass didn't know how to cook besides
making hot dogs, tacos, and spaghetti, which I refused to
eat. She didn't even try to learn, either. My moms would
even call her up to come get some lessons on the shit that
she knew I loved to eat, but Selena figured her pussy and
her good looks was enough to get her down the aisle.

"Okay, I'm gonna go use the phone to call me a cab and
wait outside then. I will see you all tomorrow after I leave
the shop," Cuba said.

I put both of my hands up to block her exit. I stood in
the doorway and stared at her as I wondered what her
last nigga had done to her to make her shy away so much
from affection. I could tell her ducking and dodging me
like I had the plague wasn't nothing but a defense mech-
anism. She wanted the kid, but some bitch-ass nigga had
her scared to enjoy her muthafuckin' life.

"Nah, stay," I told her.

"That's okay," she said as she quickly shook her head
and shot her stare down to Skylarr. She tried to kneel
down and play with my daughter to keep from having
to deal with me, but I gently grabbed her by her throat

and forced her to look up at me. I leaned over and pressed my lips against hers before pulling her bottom lip into my mouth.

"I said stay, a'ight." I let her go, picked up Skylarr, and turned around and walked out of the room.

Chapter 11

Cuba

My eyes shot open, and I looked around the room until my eyes landed on the digital clock on the nightstand. It was going on one in the morning, and I wondered how long I had been asleep. I was still holding on to an old iPad that I had found tucked away in one of Khi's guestroom's downstairs. Not only had I developed a love of interior design while locked up, but I had also fallen in love with urban fiction books when my cellmate, Tiffany, had given me a book called *The Coldest Winter Ever* to read. I could relate so much to Winter Santiaga by the end of the story that it had me wanting to read more and more.

When Khi told me to stay, I ended up making him dinner, and then hid in one of his guestrooms. That fuckin' kiss he gave me had me so fuckin' wet that I didn't want to be anywhere near him for fear that I would end up with his dick inside of me. I grabbed the iPad from the closet, lay in bed, and started reading *Chi-Town Hood Affairs* by Nicole Black until I guess I fell asleep. A smiled cracked my face when I thought about Jay's crazy ass, but it was quickly wiped away when I heard yelling coming from another part of the house.

I sat up in bed and made my way over to the door. I pulled it open slowly, careful not to make a sound. When I stepped out of the room, the yelling was louder, and I could make out Khi's voice, along with some female. I stood in the hallway, where I was able to have a clear view to the kitchen in which they both stood face-to-face. The chick had her back to me while she rolled her neck and pointed her finger into Khi's face. She was about five foot eight, with long, pretty brown hair, and she had light brown skin. I had never seen her since I had been working for Khi, but I figured she was probably Skylarr's mom.

"I swea' to God it's something wrong with your ass! You mad 'cause I don't wanna give your crazy ass no dick! You sneak into my house in the middle of the night, Selena, trying to get some dick from me while I'm fuckin' 'sleep. You don't think that shit is crazy?" Khi yelled, seeming to be frustrated as hell.

"Not when you're my man, no, I don't," she shot back.

Hearing her call him her man made me tense up a little.

"I'm not your fuckin' man, Selena, got damn! What the fuck you don't understand about us being over? I'm done, my nigga, got damn!"

"Khi, no. Please no. I've been so miserable without you. I can't eat; I can't sleep. Please. What about the health of our unborn baby?" she cried and began to say some shit in Spanish that I couldn't understand.

I watched as she brought her hand up and touched him on the chest. She then wrapped her hands around Khi's neck and laid her head on his chest. He seemed to be so defeated by this chick as he stood there and allowed her to hug him for as long as she needed.

She cried for a good while before she turned her head toward him and tried to kiss him. He pushed her away, but that didn't stop her. I knew that I should've walked away then and minded my own business, but when the chick dropped to her knees and went for Khi's pajama pants, I was stuck. He didn't seem too pressed to push her away this time when she pulled at the string, untied it, and pulled his dick from his pants. His thick muscle sprang to life and caused my mouth to water.

"Shit," I said under my breath—or at least I thought I said it under my breath. Khi's head shot up, and he looked directly at me. I tried to back up, but shorty saw me too, and her entire face turned red. She cocked her head to the side, and her eyes grew wide. This bitch seemed like she had come straight out of an exorcism as she grabbed a knife from the counter and charged in my direction.

I backed away and took off running down the hall and back into the guestroom. I slammed the door shut behind me and locked it. I didn't have anything to protect me from this broad, and I wasn't about to be involved in any kind of shit that was going to have me back in jail. Fuck this shit and fuck this job. Khi wasn't even my damn man, and I'd be damned if I was going to be fighting his damn baby mama over his ass.

"Aghhh, shit! You cut me, you stupid bitch!" I heard Khi scream, and my eyes grew big, but I refused to be another victim. In that instance, instincts that I didn't even know existed inside of me kicked in, and I ran into the bathroom that was connected to a bedroom located on the other side of it. I ran into the bedroom and slowly pulled the door open to see Khian still wrestling her crazy ass over that knife. I shot out the room and made a quick dash for the stairs and ran up them two at a time.

I ran inside of Skylarr's room and closed and locked the door behind me. She was still asleep, but I didn't know how crazy that bitch was, and I didn't want Skylarr to wake up and walk into anything. For some reason, I felt the need to protect her from her own mother. Khi had custody of his daughter for a reason, and I shook my head at the thought of his ass having another child with her. I paced back and forth across the bedroom floor, silently praying that everything was okay with Khi. I hoped she hadn't cut him too bad and that he was going to be okay.

What seemed like hours passed by before I heard Khi calling out for me. I was a little hesitant about opening the door, but since I didn't hear that dumb-ass girl screaming at the top of her lungs anymore, I felt like maybe it was safe. I pulled the door open and went to stand at the top of the stairs. Looking down, I saw Khi at the bottom with his back to me. He had a towel wrapped around his arm that was practically covered in blood.

"She gone?" I asked, and he quickly turned around and looked at me with a surprised look on his face.

"How the fuck you get up there?' he asked.

"I came out the other bedroom. I was scared and didn't know if she would try and hurt her own daughter," I told him as I hesitantly made my way down the stairs.

"She's not Sky's mother."

"You got two baby mamas?" I asked with a frown on my face.

"Fuck does it matter? But look, I appreciate you for looking out for my little one."

"Yeah, okay," I said, sort of taken aback by this nigga's tone. I wasn't the one that told him to lay down with that crazy bitch, but I was sure he thought shit was everything just based off the fact that the broad had a fat ass. It didn't matter, though. I was about to leave him up in this bitch to deal with that attitude of his alone. I walked over to the bar area and grabbed the cordless phone from its base. I had memorized the cab company's number, so I started dialing and placed the phone up to my ear when it began to ring.

"Yes I would like to—"

"What the fuck you doing?' Khi asked as he snatched the phone out of my hand.

I turned around and mugged him like he was crazy. He stood there, dripping blood all over his carpet. He should've been focused on whether that bitch had hit an artery instead of worrying about what I was doing.

"I'm calling a cab. Can you give me back the phone, please?" I held my hand out, and he turned to walk away like he hadn't heard me.

"I told you to stay."

"No, I'm not fuckin' staying here to deal with your dumb-ass baby mama drama. I'm not your girlfriend, nor will I ever be! You got that bitch trying to kill me like we fucked or something. I'm not beat for this shit, and I be damned if I sit around here and end up gettin' in trouble because you can't control that crazy-ass ho. Fuck this shit and fuck this job! I quit, and I'm leaving, so give me back the damn phone."

"Cool," was all that Khi said before he handed me the phone and headed up the stairs to Skylarr's room. I redialed the number to the cab company and looked up just as Khi looked at me. I turned my back to him, and quickly after, I heard the door slam.

"Hey, what happened? Are you okay?" Tangie asked after opening the door for me. "I thought you said you were going to stay the night at Khi's."

"I don't even wanna talk about it," I told her and made my way toward the guestroom. I just wanted to curl up in the bed and go to sleep, but I guess Tangie didn't take the hint when I told her that I didn't want to talk about it, because she followed me into the room.

"Are you okay?"

"Yes, Khi just had some drama going down at his house, and you know I'm not trying to be mixed up in no shit like that. I'm still on probation, you know," I said, and she looked at me and shook her head.

"Damn, okay. You just scared me for a moment, that's all. It's late, and you knocking on the door like that had me worried. Get you some rest, and I'll see you in the morning."

"I want to go see my parents in the morning if you don't mind. I'll stay over a couple of hours to make up for the time I miss. I know that they probably don't want to see me, but I won't know that at least until I try. And spending that time with Skylarr has me really thinking about my nephew. I can't stop wondering if he looks like Alaska . . . and, well, to see if he looks like Rue or Bry. Have you seen him?"

Tangie shook her head, and something about the way she looked told me she was lying. She had been keeping shit away from me that she thought was going to hurt me, and that was cool while I was locked up, but now was not the time to be hiding shit from me. I was a big girl, and I could handle it. Hell, after doing three years in prison, I honestly didn't think anything could hurt me worse than that.

"I think going to see your parents is a good idea, Cuba, but at the same time, I just want you to be prepared for the worst of what could possibly come out of seeing them. You know that they blame you for Alaska even though the muthafucka responsible is still out there. I don't want you to get your feelings hurt. If you want, I can go with you."

"No, it's okay. I want to do it by myself," I told Tangie, and she nodded in understanding.

She made her way over to the dresser and grabbed a gift bag that I hadn't even noticed was there. She walked back over and handed it to me. "I had been thinking about what kind of gift to give you as a welcome home present, and I realized today when Khi called me a hundred damn times trying to get in contact with you that you can really use your own cell phone." She smiled, and I stood up to hug her.

"You're too good to me, and you didn't have to do this."

"Umm, everybody needs a cell phone, honey. Don't worry, the bill is paid for up to a few months, so it's not going to interfere with your savings."

"Thank you so much, Tangie. I swear, one day I'm going to pay you back for everything."

Tangie waved me off and walked out of the room, closing the door behind her. I got up and locked the door, and then placed a chair under the knob. Stripping down to my underclothes, I pulled the box out of the gift bag and smiled, seeing the brand-new iPhone. I had just gotten one as a gift from Rue right before being locked up, and I had never gotten a chance to enjoy it. I rushed to open the box and set up my new phone. I was like a kid in a toy store as I downloaded all kinds of apps and logged back into my Facebook page after being gone for three long years. I even took a bunch of selfies that I uploaded to Facebook and this app called Instagram that I had never heard of until now.

I must've played around on my phone until I was dead-ass tired, because the next thing I knew, I had woken up to the sun shining in my face and the iPhone laying on my chest. I picked it up and looked at the screen to see that it was a little after eight in the morning. I also noticed that I had a text from a number that I didn't immediately recognize. Once I opened it up and went to the app, I saw that it was from Tangie.

Tangie: Good Morning, boo. Be sure to lock my number in, and I'll see you when you come in. Good luck with your parents. Tangie.

Me: Thanks so much, Tangie, once again! I fell asleep
playing on this thing, and now I'm tired as hell, but I will
see you soon.
Send

I got up and went to the closet to find something to
wear. I was so nervous thinking about my parents and
wondering if they would allow me to see my nephew. It
had been so long since I had seen and talked to them that
it had me sweating even thinking about it. I loved my
parents so much, and Lord knows that if I could go back
and change things, I would. I didn't understand why they
had it out for me so bad. I knew that I had gone against
them a lot when it came to Rue, but I was a young, dumb
teenager. They acted like they had never been young
once and had never made mistakes before, but hell, I
had to remember my parents was some damn Goody
Two-Shoes.

My mother had worked as an English teacher for the
Dallas Public School system for thirty-two years before
she retired, and my father had worked at Parkland
Hospital as a registered nurse for more than fifty-one
years. He had just gone into retirement a year before
I graduated high school. They weren't rich or anything
like that, but their salaries combined had afforded us the
opportunity to live in a good neighborhood and attend
good schools, so it killed them that we always ventured
off to the hood and dated niggas like Rue and Bry.

I shrugged my shoulders and was pulled out of my
thoughts when I heard twisting and turning of the doorknob. I froze and stopped everything that I was doing,
but I knew the muthafucka knew that I was in there. I
shook my head, hoping and praying that he wouldn't try
to get up in there. The door began to twist again, and

somehow, he was able to get the door unlocked, but the chair under the door stopped him.

I backed away, but remembered I now had a phone. I swiped it up from the bed and started to record everything that Camp was doing. If anything ever happened to me, I wanted to have proof that Camp was responsible for it.

"I'm calling the police!" I yelled, and he tried to push the door open again, but thank God for the chair. "You keep on pushing, you gonna break the door, and Tangie's gonna wanna know how her door got broken."

Finally, he stopped trying and walked away from the door, but now my ass was scared as fuck to leave out of there. What the fuck was he doing there anyway? That nigga was usually up and gone to work before Tangie, so why in the hell was he still there?

"Man, I gotta get the hell up out of here," I said to myself as I realized I might've fucked up by quitting the little hustle I had going on with Khi. I pulled up my text message icon and went to send Tangie a message.

Me: Please send me Khi's number.

Send.

I set my phone down on the bed and began to get dressed while constantly looking toward the door. After I was dressed, I checked my phone to see if Tangie had responded. She had. Quickly, I clicked down on the number, and then clicked down on SEND MESSAGE when it popped up.

Me: Khi, please forgive me for last night. I just freaked out after that shit popped off, but I really need my job. Trying to get on my feet and get my own crib. Please tell me the job is still mine. Cuba.

Send.

After I sent the message, I sat down on the edge of the bed and put my head into my hands. I didn't know what the fuck Camp's ass wanted with me when he had a chick like Tangie by his side. What the fuck was wrong with niggas? Tangie had her shit together. She wasn't one of them bitches that sat around collecting government assistance and waiting on a nigga to take care of her. She was educated and had her own business that made her her own damn money. She was so fuckin' kindhearted, and I knew for a fact that she loved Camp's dog ass. Why the hell couldn't that nigga appreciate that shit?

Niggas would fuck over a good woman all behind some new pussy that wasn't even worth it, and hell yeah, I was saying I wasn't worth it. What the hell was I going to do for that nigga? I only made $7.50 an hour, and the extra cash that Khi gave me didn't even begin to add up to what I knew Tangie was doing. I was living in her guestroom, didn't have a damn car, and just until last night, I didn't even a phone. How dumb was this nigga?

"Ughhhh!" I screamed, debating whether I wanted to tell Tangie what was going on. I felt like she deserved to know that her man wasn't shit, but what if she already knew and decided to get rid of me instead of him? I shook my head and began to pace the floor. Khi hadn't texted back, and I had yet to hear Camp leave the house. I was going crazy in this bitch and felt like I could really use some good hay to calm my nerves. Damn, I hated the fact that I was on probation and couldn't smoke like I wanted to.

After going crazy in my bedroom for an hour, I finally heard the door open and close. I made my way over to the window, peeked out the blinds, and spotted Camp once he stepped off the stairs. He walked through the parking lot to his car. I quickly ran to the door, removed the chair, and ran out of the room. I opened the door, took my key from my pocket, and locked the door.

I hurried down the stairs and took off running until I made it to the bus stop. By the time I sat down on the bench to catch my breath, my phone buzzed. It was Khi finally getting back to me.

Khi: Yeah, but your ass owe me a fuckin' big-ass meal for the way you walked out on me while I was damn near dying. That was some ho-ass shit, big-headed-ass girl!

Me: Sorry. But I got you. Definitely . . . thank you so much ☺

It took a couple of bus rides for me to make it to my parents' house, and it was already going on noon. I knew I had told Tangie that I was going to make up the hours I was late, but I was thinking of just not going at all. I wanted to spend as much time at my parents' house as I could if they allowed, plus Khi texted back saying he needed me at his crib no later than five.

Taking in a deep breath, I walked up the sidewalk that led up to the front door and rang the doorbell. I heard little feet running toward me on the other side of the door, and it caused me to smile with nervousness. I was so excited to see my nephew. I bet that he looked just like Alaska, and just thinking about it caused tears to form in my eyes.

"Who is it?" I heard my mother say from the other side of the door.

"Cuba!" I yelled with a smile.

"What do you want, Cuba?" she asked, and my heart began to beat wildly in my chest.

"Mama, open the door, please. I want to see my nephew," I said as the tears I held onto spilled down my face.

"Who is it, Nana?"

My nephew's voice sounded so angelic, and I really, really wanted to see his little face. I held my hands together and took a couple deep breaths. I silently prayed to myself that she would just open the damn door. I could feel myself shaking on the inside as what seemed like minute after minute passed by. After realizing that she just wasn't ready to forgive me, I turned around and walked away.

The moment I made it to the end of the sidewalk, I heard the locks clicking and the door unlatching from the hinges as it came open. I turned around, and my mother stood there with a scowl on her face. I hurried back down the sidewalk and laughed with joy as I caught a glimpse of my nephew poking his head between my mother's legs.

"Hi, Mama," I said to her, but I couldn't keep my eyes off him. I kneeled down and just stared at him. He had the most beautiful eyes I had ever seen, with smooth milk chocolate skin. He looked so familiar to me, but I knew it had to be because I had imagined what his face would look like thousands of times when I was behind those walls. He was everything that I thought he would be, and I wanted to hug and hold him so bad. He was the only piece of Alaska that I had left.

I held my hands out for him to come to me, and he smiled at me and tried to make his way to me, but my mother grabbed him and pulled him back.

"You saw him; now you can leave. Don't you ever come by here again, Cuba. I'm warning you that I will call the police if you do."

"What?" I asked and grew angry.

"You heard what I said." She pulled my nephew into the house and slammed the door shut. A few seconds later, I heard the locks latch and their footsteps as they moved away from the door.

I broke down by the time I made it back to the bus stop. I felt like I was going to explode. I just couldn't understand how my mama could be that way to me. She knew I wasn't a bad person, and I knew deep down she knew that I wasn't responsible for Alaska's death.

She just wanted someone to blame, and I had been the perfect scapegoat for her.

I sat at the bus stop, sulking in my thoughts and feeling like I wanted to die. I hadn't felt this bad and low since I stepped foot into that raggedy and little-ass cellblock and they had closed those bars behind me. I had tried plenty of times to kill myself in the first few months that I was there. One time, I had almost made it when the lights went out and I tied a sheet to the bars and slid my head inside the noose I had created. Had it not been for my cellmate hearing me gag, I would've fucking succeeded, and right about now, I wished I would have. I spent a month in solitary confinement after that on suicide watch, and I just knew that shit was going to make me go crazy, but it had made me stronger and gave me the strength I needed to get through that bid. I longed for that same strength now, because I felt like stepping into the street and letting a car hit me. That shit there felt so fuckin' bad.

I looked down at my phone as it vibrated in my hand and noticed a number that I didn't recognize. I slid the bar across the bottom of my phone and placed the phone to my ear. I used the bottom of my shirt to dry up the tears that had leaked down my face.

"Hello," I answered after clearing my throat.

"What's up? I really need to see you."

"Who is this?" I said disgustedly. I already knew who it was on the other line and wanted to know how he'd gotten my number. I shook my head, knowing that it had to be Tangie's ass, because she and Khi were the only two people that had my shit.

"It's Rue. Damn, you don't know my voice, girl?"

"How the hell did you get my number, muthafucka'?" I asked, pissed as hell that this nigga wasn't trying to leave me alone. I hadn't even had this number for more than twenty-four hours yet, and already he was on my line.

"Aye, calm down, girl. I got your shit off of Facebook. I got on a few minutes ago and saw you had logged back on and updated your profile. Did you forget we was friends?" Rue asked, and I cursed myself under my breath. I couldn't believe that I didn't even think of that and was pissed as hell that I was so careless with my info like that. Facebook was on some bullshit about helping me keep my account secure from hackers and in case I got locked out, so I added my number, but damn, I didn't think everybody was gonna be able to see the shit. I made a mental note to block this nigga as soon as I got the opportunity.

"So, that don't mean take my number and call me."

"I really just wanna talk to you, Cuba. Look, this shit has been eating me up for three fucking years, and it was nothing that I could write in a letter or say over no phone without incriminating myself, and it's not like you had a nigga on the visitors list."

"So just incriminate me instead, huh? You a fuckin' coward, Rue, and I don't wanna talk to you. I don't wanna hear your explanation. I told you that already."

"Cuba, please come put one in the air with me and hear me out. I promise you, if after that you don't wanna hear from me, then I'll never contact you again."

Against my better judgment, I told Rue that I would come to where he was at, and he agreed that he would meet me downtown so that we could go back to his place from there to talk. Maybe I did need to hear him out to see what he had to say. It could be possible that things had happened differently than how I perceived them. For Rue and I to be together as long as we were, I really couldn't see how he could do me like that, but they always said that niggas would damn near sing like a lullaby to keep themselves out of jail when facing them football numbers. Who knew what kinda time Rue was facing after that night? I held onto the possibility that just maybe Rue wasn't the coward that I thought he was, with the hope that twelve had railroaded me for whatever reason. I could take that better than I could the nigga that I had been holding down allowing me to take the fall for nothing.

"Umm, I think I'm fine sitting out here," I told Rue as he tried to pull me into his bedroom.

"Man, come on. I don't be smoking all over the house like that. I ain't gonna touch your little ass—not unless you want me to," he said, and hesitantly, I followed him to the back of his apartment and into a bedroom that was located on the right.

He walked over to the dresser and grabbed a sack of weed and a couple of cigarillos. I'd had my first meeting with my probation officer the second day after I got home, and I wasn't due to see her again for another couple of weeks, since I already had a job and had passed my last drug test. I didn't know how often they planned to test me, but I anticipated that it was going to be often considering I was locked up for a drug-related offense. Right about now, I didn't give a fuck and would figure out how I was going to pass that muthafucka at a later time, because all I wanted to do was get high. I needed something to ease my mind and bad.

"Nice bedroom or whatever . . . but is this where you and that bitch Anastasia sleep?"

Rue laughed. "Hell, nah. I don't live with her. She has her own place out in Pleasant Grove. You know I don't bring people to my house. Shit, you're the last chick that I've had up in my spot, and that was when I had the last spot down Marsalis."

"Oh . . . okay, I guess." I walked over to the bed and sat down on the edge of it. I pushed out a deep breath, sucked it in, and then exhaled all over again. Rue came to sit next to me as he put the fire to the hay. He took in a few puffs, and then handed it over to me.

"When I saw your pic on Facebook . . . man, that shit brought back so many memories."

"Don't, Rue. You said you wanted to explain your side of the story, and that's all I'm here for—that and the weed," I said as I held my hand up to stop him. I wasn't trying to hear none of that sentimental shit. I took a puff of the weed and looked over at Rue, waiting for him to talk.

"A'ight, so check it. All I know is that them niggas came to me while I was sedated in the hospital, in pain, with bullets in my muthafuckin' back, asking me where the dope came from and talking about, if I survived, I was going down for twenty to life for that shit. I kept trying to tell them that I ain't know shit about no dope and that whoever had shot us must've planted the shit there. I said that shit over and over again. They finally left me alone, and I thought they believed that shit until they came back.

"They woke me up talking about they had a statement from you saying that I had just bought the dope from some cats out the South, and that they came back to get it back when they shot up the car. I ain't believe that, but then they showed me the written statement from you, and I just flipped out. I started saying all kinds of crazy shit. All I kept thinking about was how you and Alaska was in the back seat, whispering and shit, and I kept wondering if you had set me up since you was so quick to tell on a nigga. To me, it was making sense, since you was the only one that walked away that night without being hit and how them niggas knew exactly where we were at. My mind was all over the place after reading that shit, so I said whatever I could to hurt you, knowing that they were recording me and was gonna let you hear it."

"But I didn't write shit," I said as I angrily stood up from the bed. "I didn't say shit about nothing! It wasn't until I saw that you was really about to let me go down that I tried to tell them everything that happened, but they said it was too late. They said that you had signed a statement and that you would testify against me if you needed to."

"I did, but hell, I didn't know they was gonna believe me. Shit, I didn't know they was gonna believe my ass, man. I swear to God I ain't know. I thought they knew that I was saying shit just to hurt you—like the text messages and me claiming to be fucking Alaska and possibly being her baby daddy. I just knew they was gonna call me out on that, but they never did. All they kept saying was that they needed somebody to go down for that dope, and they said that whoever went down was going down for murdering Bry and shooting me and Alaska too."

"So, you never slept with Alaska?" I asked as I threw my hands on top of my head.

"Hell no! I never slept with her—ever. I would never do no shit like that to you."

"Then how did you know she was pregnant to even claim her baby? I didn't even know until that night from when she told me while we was in the car. That's what the fuck we was whispering about."

"They told me. That fat, white cop kept asking me why would you want to have your pregnant sister murdered, so that's when I threw that shit out there about me sleeping with her. I was mad, a'ight? It was fucked up that I lied like that, but it was too late when I realized that they set me up for that shit. They used that fake-ass statement against me, hoping I was going to give them the name of some connect or something. They thought they had some

big-time drug case on their hands. All they cared about
was that dope, Cuba. Muthafuckin' drugs rule the world,
so if they got some nigga that was pushing a lot of weight
and confiscated a lot of bread, that meant bonuses and all
that bullshit for them.

"They wasn't trying to find out who killed Bryson or
who had me and Alaska laid up in the hospital like that.
When I wouldn't give them what they was looking for,
they said that you was definitely going to go down and
that they was gonna give you life if I didn't give somebody
up. I finally told them that me and Bry had robbed some
niggas for them keys and that they must've figured out
it was us and came to get their shit back, but they didn't
want to believe me. They felt like I was trying to protect
my *supplier* and that I was just saying anything to keep
the heat off of him.

"I promise you that I tried to retract all that shit I had
told them when I realized they was just using us against
each other, but it was too late. Why you think you only
got that little bit of time that you did get? They knew that
you didn't have anything to do with that dope or us getting knocked like that. They just wanted to punish you
for not snitching. That's what they do. That's why you got
so many muthafuckas out here being labeled as snitches
and shit, because they start throwing all kinds of false-
ass charges on the table for stuff they know you ain't have
nothing to do with just to get you to start tellin' on other
people.

"The only thing is, in your situation, they used you to
get to me, and then turned the tables and tried to use me
against you because I didn't have info that they wanted.
They didn't wanna believe the fuckin' truth when I tried
to tell their asses, though, so it wasn't shit I could do
about it. It was what it was, and I know it's fucked up, but
it wasn't like I didn't try, Cuba."

I heard everything that Rue was saying, and it all sounded believable, but still, I just didn't know. None of it changed the fact that I had spent the last three years of my life behind bars, though, and that he was the cause of it all. Shit, whether it started off with twelve playing mind games with him and lying on me just to get him to talk, he should've never fallen for the shit to begin with. Rue knew damn well that I wouldn't have set him up. What reason did I have to even do that? Bry and my sister died that night all because of the decision they made to go out and take some niggas for their dope.

"Say something, Cuba," Rue said, pulling me out of my thoughts.

I looked down at my phone, realizing that it was almost three o'clock. I stood up from the bed and looked over at Rue as he waited for my reaction on everything he'd just told me. I shrugged my shoulders, not really feeling like I had a change of heart about the nigga. At the end of the day, everything he said could be the truth, and then it could be a lie, too. It was not like he didn't have three years to think up the perfect story to tell me. All I knew was that on my plea deal paperwork, his name was in big, bold letters as a witness to my crime, and I would never forget that.

"I appreciate you for trying," I said, giving him the benefit of the doubt. "But it doesn't change that I lost three years of my life. You niggas fucked around and robbed the wrong niggas. They came back at y'all when me and Alaska just so happened to be with y'all. I lost my sister and went down for it all. From the jump, no matter what the faggot-ass police told your ass, you should've been a man and told the truth from the jump. A real nigga wouldn't have played no tit for tat bullshit with twelve like that and would've easily called them on that bluff. A real nigga would've really just swallowed their pride and stayed quiet . . . but again, I thank you for trying. I have to get to work," I said as I walked out of the room, with Rue following behind me.

"I heard that you working for Khi. Is that true?" Rue asked, and I briefly turned around to face him.

"Who told you that? Anastasia?"

"She might've said something about it. But you need to be careful around that nigga. Do you really think it's smart to be around him being you on probation?"

"You and that bitch shouldn't be discussing me," I said as I ignored his question and turned to leave.

On my way out, I noticed a picture on the wall near the door that I hadn't noticed when I first came in. It was my nephew. He had that same chocolate face and hazel eyes. "Oh my God, that's him."

"Yeah, B.J."

"That's his name? B.J."

"Yeah, that's what I call him, but it's Bryson Jr.," Rue said, causing my heart to melt.

"Oh my God, I love him so much, and I don't even know him."

"You haven't seen him yet?" Rue asked, sounding surprised.

"No . . . well, yeah. I just came from by there when you called, but my mother only let me see him for a brief second before she told me to never come by again and closed the door in my face. You know she blames me for Alaska's death."

"Nah, I didn't know that, but maybe I can help you with that."

Chapter 12

Daelan

Two Months Later . . .

"Shit . . . hmmm, fuck, Dae," Taylana moaned as I moved in and out of her. She wrapped her legs tighter around my waist, and I sucked her right nipple into my mouth, suddenly feeling a gush of her juiciness spill out of her. She arched her back and tried to pull her nipple from my mouth, but I grabbed her arms and pinned them down on the bed.

"Aghh, fuck," I groaned as I gave her a few long and deep strokes.

Taylana's eyes rolled into the back of her head as her pussy became tighter and wetter. She wrestled her way out of the hold I had on her and reached up and wrapped her arms around me. She started throwing her hips back at me and moaning loudly.

"You 'bout to come?" I asked as I flicked my tongue over her nipple before sucking it back into my mouth.

"Yes, wooo, yes, I'm about to come, baby," she crooned and began to scratch my back and moan even louder.

I felt her walls gripping me even tighter before they started contracting all around my dick. She began to scream, and I grabbed hold of her legs and threw them up over my shoulders. I pounded slow and deep inside her until I felt myself about to come. I sped up, and then quickly pulled out, allowing my nut to spill out all over her stomach. I rolled over onto my back and fought to catch my breath, while Taylana got up to grab us some towels.

"Shit," I said, feeling my fucking toes tingle. I moved my leg up and down, and then shut my eyes.

I felt myself dozing off, but the minute Taylana came back and dropped a towel on my face, my eyes shot open. I took the towel to clean the sweat from my forehead, while she took another one to wipe my dick off. She tossed the towels on the floor, and then climbed in bed to lay beside me.

Things had been cool as fuck with Taylana. We had been talking ever since I met her at her brother's vacation spot. I never intended to still be dealing with her after all this time, but after I took her out a few nights after we met, I got a taste of what that box was like, and I was having a hard time letting her go. Not to mention she was just a muthafuckin' pleasure to be around. I hadn't met anyone as real and laid back as her in a long-ass time. She had me getting rid of all my shorties—except for Amber, of course—and making shit all about her.

I even had her pick up and move from Miami to be with me, and we got an apartment together. I was living foul as fuck, knowing damn well I was practically married with a kid at home, but I felt like Taylana was love. She was what I once had with Amber, and what I lost with someone else. I couldn't, at least not right now, let that go. Nobody understood me and all the shit that I was struggling with, but ever since I had been with Taylana, I felt less stressed and even less angry. I hadn't even put my hands on Amber in a long-ass time, and even though I knew that I couldn't be with Taylana forever, I was just enjoying the time that I could be.

"I'm thinking I want to tell Tamar about us," Taylana said, pulling me out of my thoughts and causing me to groan.

Damn, I thought as I shook my head. Just when I was thinking I could figure this shit out to make it a forever situation, she had to bring that nigga up. How the fuck was she gonna tell her brother about us? One thing I wasn't was a ho-ass nigga, and not too much scared me these days other than KaeDee, but hell, I wasn't trying to fuck up my bread. Not my muthafuckin' cheddar. That nigga Tamar find out I'd been sliding up in his little's sister pussy raw-dog style, I could guarantee that he was cutting that check off, and shit, no amount of pussy was good enough for that. I'd rather have plenty of hell on earth than to be broke. Fuck that. And then let all that shit happen and that muthafuckin' sumo-wrestling-ass nigga KaeDee was gonna definitely murder my ass. I was still having nightmares 'til this day about that nigga choking me in my sleep after he caught my ass slipping in the car. I hadn't talked to his bitch ass since the day he had me standing on the outside of Khi's car, crying like a bitch and talking to myself. I swear that was the only nigga in life that I feared. He was having problems with his bitch, too, so I knew for sure he wouldn't hesitate to murk me and call it a day. Taylana had lost her muthafuckin' mind, but I was going to make sure she got it right.

"Bae, don't nobody need to know about us but us. You know my people would kill me if they found out that I was mixing business with pleasure . . . and so would your brother. Ain't no need in fucking up a good thing by involving people in our business."

"I don't think it's going to be as bad as you think it is. My brother knows that I am a grown woman and that I'm fucking. Shit, he can't stop me from talking to who I wanna talk to. I'm falling in love with you, Dae, and want my brother to know the real reason why I came all the way to Dallas to live. I can't keep having him think that I'm attending college when I'm not."

"I didn't tell you to tell him that. Maybe you should go enroll in college or something, bae, 'cause I ain't tryna meet dude that way. I do business with this man, shorty. You think he gonna be cool with me, knowing I been fucking his sister behind his back? If anybody did me like that, I would feel like I couldn't trust them. We just gonna have to keep things on the low for now, and hell, maybe one day . . . but not right now. Just wait and see how everything goes with us. It's only been a couple of months."

Taylana sighed and threw her head back on the bed. She crossed her arms across her naked chest, and I rolled over on top of her and began to suck on her nipples. She ran her hands through my dreads, but she refused to look down at me. I could tell that she was pissed, but hell, I wasn't about to let this shit fuck up my money just because she no longer wanted to lie. I told her off top that we could never tell anyone what was going on between us, and she agreed, so she couldn't change her damn mind now. Fuck that.

"You know what? You kinda remind me of this chick I used to talk to. Y'all don't look alike or no shit like that, but y'all kinda got the same personality and qualities that it's kinda scary."

"Don't be comparing me to no other bitch, Dae."

"Man, it's not even like that. She died not too long ago, and she had really meant something to a nigga, so I kinda feel like the love that I had got to experience with her, I'm now able to experience with you. It's like a nigga getting a second chance or something."

"Okay, I don't know if I should feel honored or like I have been reincarnated or some shit," Taylana said, and I groaned and hopped out of the bed.

"There you go with that attitude. I'm about to shower and bounce. Hopefully by tomorrow you'll be over this shit," I told her and walked into the bathroom.

Taylana had picked the perfect time to catch an attitude any muthafuckin' way. Amber had been blowing me up nonstop about when I was coming home, because she claimed Li'l Dae wanted to see a nigga, but I knew it was really her. I loved my girl, no lie. I just didn't know how to get back to what we used to have. I didn't know how to get over what was fucking with me and, until I did, I knew I could never be happy with Amber. Every time I saw her, I tried my hardest to remember what we shared, the type of chick she was, and how she was really down for a nigga, but it never worked. I would always snap and just straight lash out on her. Even then, she still stayed around, she still stayed down waiting for a nigga to get right, but I just didn't know how.

Taylana was a great ass distraction from it all, and I often thought about just taking her ass and getting the fuck away from there, but I couldn't leave my youngin', and Amber really did need a nigga. I wasn't the type to leave them out there on stuck all just because I couldn't figure out how to get my shit together.

I hopped in the shower and tried to shake everything off. When I was done, I opened the door, and Taylana was standing right in my face with a scowl on hers and tears running from her eyes. She had my phone in her hand, and I knew that the little bit of happiness that we did have was about to come to an end.

Bitches always wanna go through a nigga shit, I thought as I snatched my phone out of her hand.

"Who the fuck is Amber?" she asked me.

"Why the hell are you going through my phone?" I asked and shot around to the side of the bed that I slept on and grabbed my shoes.

"I said who the fuck is Amber, and why the fuck is she texting you asking if you would be home tonight and if you want her to warm up dinner? You cheating on me, Dae?"

"No! That's a chick that I used to mess with, but I quit fucking with her a little bit after we started fuckin' around. I didn't know that me and you were gonna go this far . . . and shit, she just a little slow to let it go," I tried explaining, hoping that Taylana would buy it and leave me the fuck alone. Nobody told her nosey ass to go through my phone any damn way, so I ain't give a shit about her tears. Like they say, you gonna always find something when you go looking for it.

"You expect me to believe that, Dae? I knew something was up. It seems like every time I start pouting or complaining about something, you always wanna jump up and leave," she said as she got in my space.

"'Cause I ain't about to sit here and deal with your fuckin' attitude."

"Because I said don't compare me to some bitch you was fuckin'," Taylana shouted, and I shook my head and walked around her ass.

I argued too much with Amber to be dealing with that shit from another bitch. So, hell yeah, I didn't give a fuck how I felt about Taylana; I wasn't about to deal with it from her. Every time I sensed she was on some bullshit, I was out the door and taking my ass home.

"Nah, because you sitting here making all them fucking sounds and poking your stank-ass lip out. Then you wanna go through my shit. Fuck outta here, man." I sat on the edge of the bed and slid my feet into my tennis shoes. Standing up, I pulled my dreads from my face and headed toward the door. "Look, I'll holla at you tomorrow."

"Nah, you holla at Amber tomorrow."

"A'ight, shorty, cool. Trust me when I say you'll be calling me before I come calling your ass."

"I seriously doubt it. You must got me confused with that dead bitch you was comparing me to."

I froze and could feel my jaw clenching. I tightened and loosened my fists before sliding my hands into my pockets. That shit pissed me off, and I did my best to calm down. I had to remember who this chick was and what I stood to lose if I fucked her up. I shook it off, sucked my teeth, and walked out the door. Fuck her.

Chapter 13

Amber

I heard the sound of Dae pulling into our garage, and I rushed into the bathroom to clean up my face. I didn't want him to know that I sat there crying for him every night. I guess he was really mad at me for telling KaeDee and Khi what he had been doing to me, because he hadn't really been home since. I felt it was time that someone knew. It was getting worse, and too many times I had seen Dae zone out when he was around D.J. and stare at him all funny. I didn't know what that was about, and I didn't want him ever getting to the point where he would hurt our son.

I cleaned my face and straightened out my hair a little bit. I rushed to the bed to climb inside, but the vibrating of my cell against the nightstand stopped me. It was four o'clock in the morning almost, and didn't nobody contact me this late unless something was up. I grabbed up my phone and looked at the screen. It was from a number I didn't recognize. Once I completely opened the message and read it in its entirety, I realized that somehow, one of Dae's hoes must've gotten his phone. She had the nerve to be questioning and going off on me about *her* man. The bitch even had the nerve to tell me that I needed to leave Dae alone so that *they* could be happy. With the way I was feeling at this moment, that might not be such a bad idea. Shit, somebody needed to be happy, because clearly, I wasn't, and it didn't seem like I would ever be.

I took my hand to dry the tears that had fallen again
and turned around to see Dae standing right behind me.
His eyes were as dark as night, and he was breathing like
he had just run a mile. He pulled his dreads from his face,
and then reached out and snatched my cell phone out of
my hand. I guess he'd seen the message and recognized
the person it had come from. I knew that I shouldn't say
shit to this fool about it, but I was so sick of being treated
like I was some ordinary bitch on the streets. I was the
mother of his child and the woman that had been holding
him down through every single fucking thing.

There were times when Dae was out making so many
mistakes and fucking up the family business that his
own brothers didn't even want to bother with him. They
turned their backs on him and only dealt with his ass
from miles away. Niggas would be out in the streets
laughing at this man. His so-called friends were exactly
that—so-called. But of course, dumb-ass Amber was right
there to pick him up and help to build his ego back up. I
was the one that went to Khi, begging for them to give
him another chance. He straightened up for every bit
of six months and was right back to doing the same ol'
bullshit.

There had been so many times where Dae was supposed to be handling business, but instead he'd be laid
up with some bitch, getting high and throwed off some
lean. He would end up passing out, and whatever little
trick he was with that night would take him for product
and money that he wasn't even supposed to have on
him. We'd had to come up off our savings to replace shit
so many times that it made me sad and angry to even
think about. We would be struggling with no money for
food, or could barely even pay our light bill, because Dae
couldn't dare tell his brothers we were broke because he
refused to keep his dick in his pants. I had held this man

down through all of that shit and then some, but do you think any of that mattered? Every chance he got, he took it as an opportunity to spit in my face and walk all over me.

Most would call me stupid and even weak, and maybe I was all that, but I was the type of woman that just didn't walk away from shit I put my time, love, and hard work into. I had put a lot of work into this relationship. Sacrificed a lot. Invested a lot. Stayed up late nights crying a lot. Got beat the fuck up and down a lot. I had given and taken too much for me to just walk away and give somebody else a chance to appreciate what I knew I had. I knew what kind of man I had in Dae. I knew what kind of potential he had, because I'd witnessed it with my own eyes. But at the end of the day, it was time for me to stop waiting around for him to live up to that potential. I just hoped that for the next woman, he could be as great as I knew he could be. I no longer had it in me to stick around and find out.

"I'm not even going to say anything. Like she said, I need to leave y'all alone and let you two be happy. Me and Daelan will be at Khi's."

"You ain't finna go no muthafuckin' where! Damn, soon as a nigga mess up, you wanna fuckin' leave me! You act like you perfect or something!"

"Soon as you mess up? What the hell do you mean soon as you mess up? Dae, your ass been messing up! I'm just getting to the point where I realize that you ain't gonna ever stop messing up. You want all them bitches you keep chasing after, trying to find whatever it is that you're not getting here, then go ahead. I will move out your way and let you do you."

"Because all we fuckin' do is argue! All you do is nag and complain. It's like you always judging every little thing I do. I'm a messed-up-ass nigga. I know that shit, but if you wanna keep fuckin' arguing and pointing that shit out every time I'm in your face, then fuck it. I'll be in these streets."

"You're not even making sense, Dae. You don't even make sense right now! How the fuck can I judge you? How many times do you go out there and fuck another bitch that it no longer counts as a mistake? I nag because you tell me you're happy with me and that you love me, when you obviously are not happy and it's impossible that you even love me. Talking about being perfect? No, I'm not perfect, but ask me how many niggas have I fucked?"

Suddenly, Dae snapped and wrapped his hands around my throat. He threw me down on the bed and climbed on top of me. I held back my tears, no longer wanting him to see that every time he couldn't control his anger or couldn't express his feelings in another way, it hurt me. I had to be strong and show him that what he was doing no longer affected me, even though it would never hold true.

I closed my eyes, refusing to look at him. I would sit there and wish that he killed me, wish that this would be the time that he went too far, but I had a little boy that loved his mother, and I had to be there for him.

"Like you ain't never fucked another nigga before. Admit that shit! Tell the fuckin' truth! You know you fucked that nigga," Dae yelled, forcing me to open my eyes and look at him.

I didn't know what the fuck he was talking about. I had never cheated on Dae . . . ever. What the fuck was he talking about?

Chapter 14

Khian

I was downstairs on the bottom level of my house, where I had transformed the entire floor into one area full of shit that made me happy. I had weights, a bar, pool table, a couple of big-ass TVs that I kept on the sports channel, and other manly shit. I guess you could call it my man cave, but I only went down there when I was stressed the fuck out. I practically lived down there when I was with Selena.

I still hadn't figured out who took my shit and killed my fam, but with me practically running shit on my own, I really didn't have time to investigate anything. Dae had given us more problems to worry about. After him beating up old man Amin at the local food mart and most likely being the one that killed him, the Arabs had sent a few threats our way. Dae was acting like it wasn't shit to him. He was so in his feelings that I hadn't seen or really heard from that nigga since the day KaeDee choked his ass out in the car. I told him that he needed to watch his back and keep in constant contact with me, but that nigga basically said fuck me.

Not only was he ducking and dodging me, but he wasn't handling any of his responsibilities on the business end of things, and I was really thinking about putting Tramell into place to take his position. Tramell was out of the hospital and healing from the gunshot wounds that he suffered that night we got hit, and all he talked about was wanting to stay busy so he wouldn't have to think about Cooca. If Dae didn't want this shit, then I wasn't going to force it on him.

I think I was really starting to realize that I wanted this for him more than he wanted it for himself. Everybody was telling me to let Dae go. Even Cass's ass was screaming the shit from behind them walls. I was the one that gave him another chance the last time KaeDee had had enough of Dae. I just didn't want to give up on my little brother. I had envisioned that we would all be bossing up and taking over the streets together, but everything wasn't meant for everyone, so it was time for me to move on. I was tired of putting myself out there for Dae to turn around and make me look like a fool. With everything that was being thrown my way, or that I was already dealing with, I didn't have time to worry about that nigga anymore.

Briana had disappeared, and I tried to force myself not to care, but I did share a child with that woman, and at one point, I loved her. I didn't know if she was dead, or skipped town, or somewhere needing my help. I had checked out all the drug rehabilitation centers in the area, and none of them had her as a patient. I even had some goonies from my crew keeping a lookout for her, but so far, nothing. I regretted allowing her to walk out of my house without giving her the help that she had asked for, thinking I was teaching her a lesson. That shit didn't do nothing but turn around on me. Most days, I couldn't think without wondering if she was going to be found dead in an abandoned building or in the bottom of a fucking river. I knew how this dope shit went, and I didn't want any of that for Briana.

Selena wouldn't stop bothering me. Her ass was using every little thing about the baby that she could to get to me. I had attended the sonogram appointment with her to find out that we were having a little girl, and she thought that me being happy about it meant that I wanted her ass back. I allowed her to keep the car I bought her, put her up in a nice little three-bedroom house, and even told her she was welcome to move the fuck on, and she still didn't get the hint. For some reason, she thought I was just going through a phase, but I was going to show her better than I could tell her. I was just waiting on Cuba's little pretty ass to let me behind them walls so I could knock them bitches down.

Lately, she had been spending more time with me than at Tangie's crib, and I wasn't even tripping about it. After she would cook dinner and put Skylarr to bed, we would sit up some nights, smoking and talking about a bunch of bullshit that kept us laughing and entertained. She was a pleasure to be around, damn near like one of the homies, but I could see that she was still scared to let go of whatever was keeping her from giving a nigga a chance. Every time I thought I was making progress with her, she would pull back and take her ass home, but I wasn't giving up. I hadn't had any pussy since I stopped fucking with Selena, and I wasn't looking for any but Cuba's. I had plenty of options, but I was going to hold out until I got hers. Something was telling me that she was worth it.

I downed the last of my Cognac and set the glass down on the bar. I had gone back over to my weight bench to do a few more reps when I heard the doorbell ringing. I shot up and grabbed the remote from the couch and turned the TV to the surveillance system. Seeing the cab on the outside of the gate had me wondering what was up. The only person that took cabs to my crib was Cuba.

I walked over to the intercom system that was installed into the wall and pressed the button that opened the gate. Before going up the stairs, I grabbed my phone from the bar to see that I had a bunch of missed calls and text messages from Cuba.

Cuba: Can I come over?

Cuba: ????

Cuba: Please Khi. I am so scared. Please can I come over?

Cuba: Can you answer the phone? I don't know what to do. I can't stay here anymore. Please answer.

Cuba: This nigga gonna make me kill him. I cannot live here anymore. Please pick up.

I frowned at her last message as I rushed up the stairs to open the door for her. What the fuck did she mean, and what nigga was she talking about? I ran my hand over the waves in my head, getting pissed. Shit, I didn't know what was pissing me off more: the fact that she was dealing with some nigga, or that I was all in my feelings about the shit when I hadn't even fucked yet.

What nigga? The fuck? I thought as I pulled the door open for her.

She stood there with her hair all over her head, and her shirt had been ripped down the middle. I pulled her into the house and shut the door behind her.

"This was sitting at the gate," she said. She was in tears, and her hands shook as she handed me a yellow envelope. I took the envelope from her and pulled her into the kitchen after noticing her swollen lip. Setting the envelope down on the kitchen cabinet, I grabbed a sandwich bag and filled it up with ice.

"What the fuck happened?" I asked, placing the bag on her lip.

"I don't think I can stay there anymore. He won't leave me alone, and tonight, we got into a fuckin' fight with me trying to keep him off of me. I only had enough money on me to pay the cab, because I ran soon as I was able to get free, so I didn't have time to grab any money so that

I could go and stay at a room . . . and I don't want to go back, Khi," Cuba rambled on, and I didn't understand what the fuck she was talking about. I wrapped my arms around her and looked down at her.

"Look, look . . . aye, chill the fuck out, man. Just calm down. I can't even understand what you saying right now," I told her. "Go upstairs and find something to change into, and then meet me out back so you can tell me what's going on."

Cuba nodded her head and did what I told her to. I ran downstairs to my man cave to grab the blunt and a sack of weed that I had been enjoying for myself. By time I got back upstairs and made it into my back yard, Cuba was walking out wearing one of my long T-shirts. She had the homemade ice pack in her hand as she made her way over to one of the lounge chairs to sit down. I sat down beside her and waited for her to tell me everything that was going on.

"So, what's up, man?" I asked as I lit the blunt. "What's going on? What nigga you dealing with, and why you ain't tell me you had a nigga? That's why you don't wanna give me a chance, but yet you got some nigga over there beating on you."

"Come on, you know I live with Tangie."

"I don't know what the hell you got going on. You don't talk to me about what's going on, ma."

Cuba sighed. "It's Tangie's boyfriend, Camp. That nigga has been trying to fuck me since I moved in, and tonight, he came too close. Tangie went out with her homegirls to the club, and she didn't even say shit to me, so I had no idea she was gone. I went to take a shower as usual, and when I came back and went into my room, he tried to come in. I ran to put the chair on the door like I always do to keep him out, but he pushed it open, and the door popped me in my mouth."

"Did he touch you?"

"When he got inside the room, he tried to pin me down to the bed and take my clothes off, but I was able to fight him off. I grabbed my purse and left," Cuba explained, causing my jaw to twitch.

"A'ight, I'll handle that nigga."

"No . . . no. I don't want to cause any problems with me and Tangie. She's been too good to me, and I don't want nothing like that between us. I just wanna get out of there. Just take me to get my money that I saved up, and I will find an apartment with what I have. I don't want Tangie to know. Please don't say anything to her."

"A'ight." I nodded and passed her the blunt. I let that shit go in one ear and out the other. Tangie didn't have to know a muthafuckin' thing, but like I said, I was going to handle it.

"I've just been through enough these past three years of my life, and I don't want any problems with anyone. I don't need the drama, you know. I just wanna live, man."

"You the one that's refusing to live," I told her, and she looked at me briefly before taking her eyes to the ground.

"I'm sorry for bringing you all this drama. Just being here brings me peace, you know, especially Skylarr. I love that little girl upstairs, and I just appreciate everything that you're doing for me. I know that you had me here for other reasons in the beginning, and it's not like I don't like you or anything like that, I just . . . man, I just been through so much and . . . damn," Cuba said. I could tell that she was trying to keep herself from crying.

"You love my daughter?" I asked her.

"How can I not love her? She tells me she misses me every time I come here and tells me not to leave her again." Cuba laughed as she wiped the tears from her face. "She always wants to comb my hair."

"Somebody needs to comb it."

"Shut up!" Cuba laughed and hit me on my shoulder.

I grabbed her arm and pulled her toward me. She looked at me, no longer smiling.

"Why you shaking for? I scare you?" I asked her, and she turned her eyes away from me. I grabbed her chin and forced her to look at me. "I scare you?"

"No . . . yes," she said, just above a whisper as she nodded her head.

I pulled Cuba on top of me and ran my hands through her hair. Gently gripping a hold of her hair, I pulled her to me and kissed her lips. She kissed me back and slid her tongue into my mouth. I took my hands and roamed them all over her body.

Just as I was about to pull her shirt over her head, I heard the door open. I looked over and saw Daelan's ass. He wouldn't answer any of my calls or return my text messages, so I knew for him to be there, something had to be wrong.

"Bruh, I need to talk to you," he said as he tossed his dreads from his face.

"Go inside. I'll be in there in a minute," I told him, and he did as I said.

"Cuba," I said and kissed her lips again. "Do I scare you?"

This time Cuba shook her head as she looked into my eyes. I pulled her in for another kiss, and then I took her hand and placed it on my hard-ass dick.

"Do this scare you?" I asked, and she shook her head and shyly laughed. "You sure about that,? 'Cause he's a beast. You see how bitches be sneaking in a nigga's house when he 'sleep and pulling out knives and shit."

"Umm, and I see that you still haven't changed your locks or your gate code. You must like it."

"Nah, I'ma change it, and I'ma give it to you," I told her as I smacked her on the ass and pulled her up.

"Oh, really?"

"Yeah, 'cause you ain't going back to Tangie's. And I want you to be able to come and go without me having to be here to let you in. But, aye, let me talk to this nigga for a minute. Go and check on Skylarr, and I'll be up there in a few," I said to her as I pushed down on my dick, forcing it to go down.

We walked inside, and Dae's ass was pacing back and forth until he laid eyes on Cuba. They stared at each other for a moment before she took the stairs, and I told Dae to follow me to the basement. As soon as we got down there, he went to the bar and poured himself a drink. His whole demeanor told me he was off his square. His appearance was wild, and I could tell that it had been the last thing he'd been worried about. I shook my head as I watched him down a glass of Henny and then pour himself another one.

"Man, bruh . . . man, look, don't be mad at me, a'ight? But I don't know what the fuck to do. I fucked up. Okay, I know I fucked up. I just need you to tell me how to fix it, and we can't tell KaeDee. I just wanna fix this shit before it becomes a real fuckin' problem."

I leaned against my pool table and crossed my arms over my chest. Dae downed his second glass before he started pacing again. He mumbled a few words before he stopped and looked up at me.

"Bruh, you know me and you be fighting and shit all the time, but you know I look up to you more than anybody. Man, you just be expecting too much from a nigga and damn, you always been like that. Like, damn, fam. You harder on me than Cass and KaeDee. Like, them niggas say what they gotta say and then leave me alone, but you always on my fuckin' case, Khi. Damn, man, you act like you hate me."

"How the fuck do I act like I hate you? The nigga that's always defending your pussy ass. I'm always defending you to Cass and KaeDee when you don't even deserve to be fuckin' defended. That's why I'm always on your case, because them niggas gave up on you a long time ago. They don't give a fuck no more. Everybody is tired of you fucking up, Dae. Everybody, man."

"I know, man, and Amber trying to leave me, bruh. She said she was gonna call you so she can come stay with you. Can you please tell her to stay and give me another chance? Bruh, please. You and Amber all I got left. And if y'all give up on me, then what the fuck I'm gonna do?" Dae's ass cried, dropping real fucking tears.

I shook my head and sighed. "What the fuck you do to Amber now?"

"Man, you gonna be so mad at me, bruh," Dae said and went to pour himself another drink.

"Man, what the fuck did you do?"

"Shorty . . . Tamar's sister."

I took in a deep breath and let it out. I could feel my jaws twitching and my body heating with anger. He didn't even have to say anything further. I should've known that fucking day we met up with Tamar at his spot and seen them talking outside that Dae was up to something. This nigga was always doing some shit, not even thinking of what the consequences could be. I turned my back to him and grabbed one of the pool sticks from the table.

"That bitch going crazy. She keep texting Amber and shit. She texting me, talking about if I don't come home, she gonna tell her brother that we been fucking and that the reason she moved down here is so she can be with me. I don't know what the fuck—"

I turned around and smashed the pool stick in the side of Dae's face, causing the stick to break in half. I then grabbed the pistol that I kept stashed on the underside of the table and removed the safety. I walked over to where Dae was laid out on the floor, rolling back and forth, trying to stop the blood that leaked from his face. He looked up at me, his eyes bucked, and he threw his hands up to stop me, but I pounced on his ass. I kicked him in the stomach, his face, just snapping the fuck out on him before I knelt down to get closer to him. I took the butt of the pistol and smashed it against Dae's head. At this point, I didn't give a fuck if I killed this nigga. That's how mad he'd made me. I went to bat for him every single time he did something crazy, and this was how this nigga wanted to repay me. Fuck him! Turning the gun back around, I pointed it at Dae's head and wrapped my free hand around his throat.

"Muthafucka, give me one reason why I shouldn't pull this trigger, Dae! One muthafuckin' reason, nigga!" I yelled.

"I'm sorry. Just tell me what I need to do to fix it. I fucked up, Khi. Man, damn," Dae cried as blood seeped from the side of his mouth.

"Look at me!"

Dae looked up at me as tears fell down each side of his face.

"End it! Change your muthafuckin' number, and I swea' to God if I hear anything else about you contacting this girl . . . Just fuckin' end it, Dae."

"A'ight, a'ight. I'ma end it."

Chapter 15

Cuba

After walking past Khi's brother Dae a few moments ago, I was starting to feel like I knew him also. It was something about him that I couldn't quite place. I knew he wasn't somebody that I had spent time with, because I had only been with one person in my life, and that had been Rue. Rue had been my first of everything and the last man that I had spent time with, so I didn't understand why the sudden familiarity was hitting me like this. I shrugged it off, though, figuring that one day it would come to us, and we would find out where we had known each other from. Shit, it really wasn't that damn important to beat my brain up about it.

I peeked my head into Skylarr's room to see that she was still asleep. I noticed that her blanket had fallen off, so I walked inside and covered her up. I smiled down at her, suddenly thinking about the kiss that I shared with her father moments earlier. I could still taste him on my lips as I ran my tongue across them and then bit down on my bottom lip.

I had fought so hard to deny the attraction that I felt for Khi, but it was just something that I no longer wanted to do. Seeing how patient he had been with me, although I had given him so much attitude, made me like him that much more. He showed me that he was really interested in me and that he was willing to wait for me to come around. Taking down the walls completely that Rue had forced me to put up wasn't an option, but I'm not gonna lie and say that I didn't want to explore something with Khi. I was beginning to realize that I couldn't allow my past experience to change the way I lived today. I was too young to be sitting around scared to love again just because one fucked-up-ass situation had scarred me. I just hoped that Khi wouldn't make me come to regret it.

I headed into the bathroom to shower as I thought about how much money I had saved up and whether it would be enough to get me a place. I knew that Khi was talking about me staying there with him, but I didn't wanna get too dependent on him like that. Besides, we still really didn't know much about each other like that. I hadn't told him about where I had spent the last three years of my life, and I wasn't even sure I wanted him to know.

After turning on the shower and waiting for it to heat up, I stepped inside and closed the glass door behind me. I ran my head under the water, wanting to wash away any of Camp's scent that may have been on me. I shook my head just thinking of how close that muthafucka had gotten to me this time. He was one sick-ass nigga, and I had decided that I was going to tell Tangie what had been going on. As soon as I got my shit out of her house and got away from there, then I would let her know what kind of creep she was laying down with every night. I owed her that much, and hell, if she wanted to be a way about it and take her nigga's side, then that was on her; but as a woman and me being fam, I felt like I had an obligation.

Once I pulled my head from under the water, I felt a brush of cold air hit my skin. When I looked up, Khi stood on the outside. He stared at me for a second, and my eyes wandered from his eyes and down to his dick. His shit was so thick and long that it caused a lump to fill my throat. It had been so long since I had a man inside of me that I didn't know if I could even handle him. I hoped that Khi couldn't sense how scared that I was, but it seemed like this nigga was always in tune with me.

Khi stepped into the shower, and I turned around to face him, refusing to look up at him. He towered over me, his body like a statue, his abs sitting rock hard on his perfectly sculpted body. He stood before me looking like a chocolate god.

I placed my hand on his firm chest, and Khi took that as an opportunity to pull me into him. Finally, I brought my eyes to his, and we just stared at each other for a moment before Khi suddenly knelt down before me and swooped me over his shoulders in one quick motion. He stood back to his feet and placed me against the wall.

Quickly, I grabbed for his head as he locked his juicy lips around my hard and erect clit. I had never experienced oral before, and the feeling was tantalizing. My eyes rolled, and I tossed my head back as my mouth dropped open.

"Oh, shit," I cried out as Khi sucked and circled my clit with his tongue. I went to push his head away, feeling as though I could no longer take the tongue lashing that he was giving me. It felt so good, yet I felt like I had to get away. My breathing quickened as Khi gripped me tighter and forced my legs around his neck. "Oh my God, Khi! Khiiiii!" I screamed as I did my best to push him away from me. Tears began to fall from my eyes as I reached my peak and began to explode. This was also something that I had never experienced before, and I swear I was able to get a dose of what Heaven must've felt like. The way my body shook as Khi continued to pull everything out of me, it felt like my soul was slowly leaving from me. "Oh, fuck! I can't take no more! Aaghhhhh!"

Khi finally pulled me down, and I wrapped my legs around his body. He looked at me, and I was glad that the water hid my tears. I was so embarrassed and felt so inexperienced. Rue had never taken me to such heights, and I wondered what the hell we had been doing for damn near four years.

Khi grabbed the washcloth and got it nice and soapy before using it to wash my body. Every part of me that he washed, he ran his tongue over, sucking and kissing damn near every part of my body. Once he was done, he stepped out of the shower, grabbed a towel, and dried himself off. He then grabbed another towel, handed it to me, and pulled me out of the shower. The moment I wrapped the towel around my body, Khi picked me up and carried me to the bedroom.

He lay me out on the bed and pulled the towel away from me. Dropping down to his knees in front of me, Khi pulled me to the edge of the bed and dove head first into my pussy. I tried my hardest to take this shit, but Khi had me squirming and screaming at the top of my lungs. I had come so many times that I thought I was going to die, especially the last time when I squirted. I was ready to climb under the covers, put my thumb in my mouth, and go to sleep, but Khi wasn't done with me.

"What the fuck you think you doing?" Khi asked and shook his head. "You done? Shit, I'm just getting started."

"Wh-what," I stuttered as Khi pushed me to the head of the bed.

"Look, let me tell you something before we go any further. Don't go falling all in love with a nigga and acting crazy and shit."

"Whatever. Ain't nobody about to fall in love with your ass. Don't you go falling in love," I told him, not feeling as confident as I tried to sound. If he was able to satisfy me with his head game the way he did, I could only imagine what his dick game was like. I sighed, knowing it was too late to turn back now.

"Shit . . . why the fuck you so tight? When the last time you had sex?" Khi asked as he tried to slide his thick-ass, mushroom-looking head inside of me. "Relax."

"I'm trying to," I said to him.

"Relax, Cuba. Relax, baby. I ain't gonna hurt you."

I nodded my head and relaxed my legs to the side. It took a little force, but Khi was finally able to enter me. I instantly moaned as I threw my hands around his neck and looked up at him. I stared into his hazel eyes, unable to stop the tears that slid down my face. It was just feeling so good to me that I couldn't stop the emotions that ripped through me.

"Damn, your shit is so fuckin' wet. Hmm," Khi groaned. He dropped his body onto mine as he slowly slid in and out of me.

I was still so sensitive from all the oral he had given me that I felt myself about to come again. I shut my eyes and dug my fingernails into Khi's back.

"Damn . . . oh, fuck. I'm about to come again," I said, and that seemed to make Khi go harder.

He dug into me deeper, and each time he stroked me, his dick seemed to grow harder. My mouth dropped open, and I gritted down on my teeth as an orgasm ripped through my body, causing me to scream out.

"Aghhhh, fuck!"

I wanted more. I wanted to feel that feeling again. I was loving it. It was a high that I could get used to, and I wanted that shit over and over again. I could already feel myself getting addicted.

Damn, what is this man doing to me?

I threw my hips into Khi and squeezed my muscles around his dick. I just wanted to come again . . . and again . . . and again.

"Damn, baby. Shit. Give me that pussy," Khi said as he stroked me into another orgasm.

He and I had sex for what seemed like hours before each of us no longer had the strength to move. When I looked over at the digital clock on the nightstand, it was going on five in the morning.

"I didn't mean to be crying like that while we was having sex," I told him as I laid my head on his chest.

"That shit don't bother me, bae. Why you saying that like you did something wrong?" Khi chuckled.

"I've never had oral before, and tonight was the first time I had experienced an orgasm."

"What kinda niggas you been dealing with, man? You serious?"

"Yes, I'm serious. And I've only been with one person before you today."

"Shit, I knew I liked you for a reason."

"I got something that I want to tell you."

"You wanna hit this?" he asked and passed me the blunt that he'd rolled up a few minutes ago.

"When I ran into you at Wal-Mart that day, I had just gotten out of jail, where I had spent the last three years."

Khi sighed, and I could feel his body tense up. "Why you just now telling me this, though? The fuck you go to jail for?"

"That's why I don't say anything. I don't want nobody judging me."

"I'm not judging you. Shit, I ain't perfect, but don't you think that's something you should've said before I brought you around my damn daughter?" Khi sighed and got up from the bed.

"Khi . . . I didn't do anything wrong."

"Yeah, whatever," he called over his shoulder before leaving the room and slamming the door behind him.

I had tossed and turned so much after I confessed to Khi that I'd been to jail that I couldn't even go to sleep. By time my eyes did start to get a little heavy, it was going on ten o'clock, and Skylarr had come inside saying that she was hungry. I got up, took a quick shower, and took her downstairs to make some breakfast. Dae was sitting at the island and going through his cell phone. I looked at him, noticing that his face was bloody and swollen, and one of his eyes was damn near shut. I wondered what the hell had happened, because he didn't look anything like that when I had seen him last night.

"Where's Khi?" he asked.

I shrugged my shoulders and walked over to the fridge to pull out some eggs and bacon. I grabbed a bowl from the cabinet and a skillet to fry the bacon. As soon as I began to crack the eggs open, I could feel Dae standing behind me. I turned around and looked at him before putting my attention back on my food.

"I just get a feeling about you every time I see you that I know you from somewhere," Dae said, and once again, I just shrugged.

"Well, when you figure it out, let me know."

"Did we fuck?"

"Sure didn't," I said confidently.

"Did we go to school together?"

"I went to DeSoto High. What school did you go to?"

"Nah, I went to Lincoln, but I was never in that bitch. Maybe I used to fuck one of your friends or something."

"I don't have any friends."

"You got a sister?"

"Why the fuck does it matter? We didn't fuck, so . . ."

"Because you seem like a real sneaky-ass broad to me and, I wanna know where the fuck I know you from."

"Daddy!" Skylarr yelled, and Dae took a couple of steps back as Khi entered the kitchen.

He was dressed down in a black-and-gray suit with a pair of red bottoms on his feet. I wasn't sure how to take him after last night, so I didn't say anything and went back to seasoning and scrambling my eggs. I heard the soles of his shoes clicking against the kitchen floor and knew that he was coming in my direction. Moving my shoulders around, I threw my neck from side to side and tried to relieve some of the tension that I suddenly felt. Khi wrapped his arms around me and kneeled over and snuggled his face into my neck.

"I'm sorry, a'ight," Khi said into my ear before he kissed the side of my face. "We'll talk about it later, though."

"Bruh, I don't think you should trust her," Dae blurted out, and we both looked over at him.

"How the fuck would you know who to trust, nigga? Grab one of my suits out the closet and get dressed. We got a meeting to get to," Khi told him.

"A meeting with who? The fuck I gotta wear a suit for?" Dae asked with hesitation.

"A meeting with Tamar. Some shit done popped off, and he called a few of us to meet him at his spot at one."

"Why I gotta go, though?"

"You scared or something?"

"Nah . . . I'm . . . I'm just saying. What if shorty told him and that nigga calling us over there as a setup? I broke it off with her like you told me to."

"Then you ain't got shit to worry about, nigga. You either gonna be in this shit or not, Dae. You gonna prove to me that you want this or what?"

"A'ight, a'ight. Just take me by the house, though, 'cause you know I'm not with wearing no suit, nigga," Dae told Khi.

Khi kissed me one more time. "See you later, ma," he said to me, and I looked up into this hazel eyes and smiled at him.

"See you later," I told him and watched as he and his brother walked out the door.

Chapter 16

Deonna

I pulled up to my home just as KaeDee was driving out of the driveway. I knew that since it was Sunday, I could catch him there rather than at the office. I placed the car in park and hurried and climbed out before he made it out of the gate. I stood there as the gate opened, forcing KaeDee to have to stop his car. I could see through the window that he wasn't trying to deal with me.

We had gone through so much since he'd caught me in that hotel room with Tyrin, and I understood his frustration completely. KaeDee had worked his magic as usual and had gotten Tyrin and me out of the charges we were facing for money laundering, but ever since then, he'd made it clear that he and I were over. I'd made every attempt to contact him so that we could talk about things, but nothing was getting through to him.

I had been living out of hotels and off the money that I had in my savings since KaeDee put me out of the house and fired me from the firm that was supposed to be ours. I was only allowed to see Chanel every other weekend, and that was eating me up more than anything. I wanted my family back together so bad and for things to go back to normal. I really hoped that I hadn't lost KaeDee completely.

"What's up?" KaeDee asked as he stepped out of the car wearing a navy Brooks Brothers blazer with a white collared shirt underneath, gray slacks, and a pair of Giuseppe loafers on his feet. He adjusted the tartan on his head before sliding his hands into his pockets and leaning against the hood of his car.

"How is Chanel?"

"She's fine."

"KaeDee, I really want to come home and to fix our marriage."

KaeDee chuckled. "Why? Are you tired of that nigga Tyrin again?"

"I just wanna come home. I want us to fix this. Why are so you ready to give up on me?"

"I guess 'cause I found out how quick it was for you to jump in another nigga's bed. I mean, after you sit up and lied to me when I asked you was you or have you fucked that nigga . . . you told me no, and then I followed your ass to that hotel and found you getting ready to lay down with this man. Then we get up in this courtroom and I find out you was fucking the nigga while I was locked up for beating his bitch ass. What? You felt obligated to go and lick that nigga's wounds or something?"

I closed my eyes tightly, and then opened them again. I stared at the ground for a few moments before looking back at KaeDee. I could see that I had really hurt him, and none of it had been intentional. I was just struggling with the feelings that I had for two men in my life that meant something great to me, but I had come to realize that my family meant more to me than the excitement and fun that I had with Tyrin. After spending a few weeks with him, I woke up and realized that it would never work with us, which was why I had left him behind the first time.

"I made a mistake. Tyrin was a part of my past that I left behind, because it wasn't the life I wanted to live. When he came here and I went to talk to him about why he was bribing you into defending him, I had a weak moment. I started feeling things for him that I thought I didn't feel anymore. When I left Tyrin before I met you, I was still in love with him. I won't lie to you about that. Seeing him again, I just realized that things were left unresolved, and I made the mistake of wanting to see where things would go between us."

KaeDee sucked his teeth and pulled his hands from his pockets. He walked around the car and went to the driver's side to get in his car. I rushed over to him and grabbed the door before he could close it.

"I'm trying to be honest with you, KaeDee," I told him with pleading eyes.

"So, you've been fucking this nigga the whole fucking time you've been gone, Deonna?" KaeDee yelled as he slammed his fist into his steering wheel.

"It was a mistake, and I know that's not where I wanna be."

"But that's where the fuck you gonna be. Get the fuck away from me," KaeDee said and tried to close the door.

"KaeDee, he won't stop bothering me. I told him over a week ago that I was done with him, and he refuses to leave me alone. He said that I can't leave him again or he will kill me," I told him as I desperately held onto his door and tried to keep him from closing it on me.

"I don't give a fuck what that nigga told you! That's your problem. You deal with it. Now, get the fuck back!" KaeDee roared.

I stepped back and tried my hardest to fight the tears that threatened to fall from my eyes. KaeDee smashed down on the gas and bolted out of the driveway. I walked over to my car, got inside, and decided that I was going to hit Amber up to see if she had time to chat. She had been going through the fire with Dae's ass, and I knew if anybody knew what it was like dating a Prince, then she did. These niggas was the most stubborn niggas to ever grace this planet, and I couldn't believe I'd made the mistake of ever fucking over KaeDee.

Amber texted me back immediately, telling me to please come over and she would make us some Pink Panties, but I told her I would opt for a light wine instead, because I was pregnant. I turned my car around and headed for the expressway so that I could go to her house.

I had known Amber ever since I moved from D.C. to be with KaeDee, and she was one of the most kindhearted women I had ever met. I knew that I could be truthful with her about everything, and she would never judge me.

It took me about thirty minutes to get to Amber and Dae's place, and I quickly parked my car out front and went to ring the bell. Amber answered the door within seconds, and we hugged and walked inside to her entertainment room to sit down. As soon as I got comfortable on the sofa, I let it all out, telling her about my relationship with Tyrin, from when I lived in Miami, the things I did for him that led to my legal problems, and then, up until now, while I had been sleeping with him. I told her about how bad I felt and how stupid I was for fucking up a good thing with KaeDee over a man that I knew I could never be with.

"I'm not gonna lie to you, Amber. I know how KaeDee is, and he barely speaks to Dae now because of the things he's done. Girl, you got yourself—"

Amber and I both looked up at the sound of someone barging through the front door. She stood up just as Dae made his way into the entertainment room. He looked at me, and then pulled his dreads from his face before looking at Amber. His face was ridiculously swollen, and his right eye was damn near closed shut. I tried not to stare, but Dae was always in some shit. Amber was right. That nigga had pissed KaeDee off so much that he was on the verge of disowning him.

"So, that's your stuff by the door?"

"Don't act surprised, Dae. I told you last night that I was leaving. Khi told me that he would come and pick Daelan and me up later this evening after he got done with his meeting."

"Oh, that's what the fuck he told you?" Dae asked, seeming to get more upset. "What the fuck is this bitch doing in my house?"

I sighed and rolled my eyes, but I wasn't worried about his ass. I knew that he wouldn't dare put his hands on me again.

"Don't get mad at me because she's leaving your woman-beating ass," I told him and stood to my feet to leave.

"Bitch, fuck you, you dick-sucking, tranny-looking ho. Dyke-looking ass. Like you ain't out here sucking two dicks at time. I swear, hoes love to judge a nigga," he spat and looked at Amber angrily.

I was about to leave, but the look in Dae's eyes told me he was about to do something real stupid, and I wasn't about to let sis get her ass beat by this fool again.

"Got this ho and everybody thinking I'm just over here beating on your ass for no reason. Tell that ho why!"

"I don't know! You tell her why so I can hear this shit and find out too!"

"Oh, so you don't know why the fuck I be beating your ass? You gonna stand here and act like you don't know that Little Dae isn't mine?"

"What?" Amber and I said at the same damn time.

look it

Chapter 17

Daelan

I stood in my entertainment room, mad as fuck that Amber had this other ho there judging me like she was innocent. Neither of those bitches had the nerve to say anything about me and what the fuck I did. I knew I made hella mistakes, but I was sick of Amber faking shit and trying to act like she ain't never did nothing wrong. Every muthafuckin' time I looked into Little Dae's eyes, I knew he wasn't mine. My skin was dark caramel and I had hazel eyes, and Amber had a cocoa brown complexion with dark brown eyes, but somehow, we had created a little boy that was light as a muthafucka with light brown eyes. I waited year after year for this little nigga to darken up and start looking like me, but each year, he looked more and more like somebody else. He was not my son, and this ho was gonna admit that shit.

"Dae, you outta your fuckin' mind. You know damn well D.J. is your son. How could you say something like that?"

"What the fuck you mean? Have you not looked at your son lately? You gonna sit here and act like he don't look like that other nigga you fucked?"

"I'm not acting like anything, and he doesn't look like any nigga, because I haven't fucked anyone! He looks just like you! You're fucking delusional!"

"No, bitch, you fuckin' delusional. You wonder why I be out here running through these hoes. You the reason I'm like this. I was fuckin' fine until three years ago when I started realizing that he wasn't mine. That was supposed to be my first fucking son, and you fucked that up. You named him after me, knowing he belonged to someone else. Admit that shit, Amber! Admit it!"

"There's nothing for me to admit, because nothing ever happened. We're leaving this evening, so it doesn't even matter. We don't have to be in your life, Daelan. And if me and Little Dae being around is causing you so many problems, then we both will happily leave."

"You know what, bitch? You leave. You leave, and you leave the kid here. Whether he's mine or not, I'm the only man he knows, and I'm not about to let you come between us. Conniving ass," I said and walked off to my bedroom to get some clothes. I had Khi's ass outside waiting for me to shower and get dressed for this meeting we had with Tamar's bitch ass. His thirsty-ass sister acted like she couldn't take no for an answer and had been blowing my phone up ever since I told her the night before that we couldn't see each other anymore. I'd even told her that I would pay for her to move back to Miami and hit her off with a few extra coins if she needed, but shorty wasn't trying to hear that shit.

I could feel my phone vibrating in my pocket now as I made my way to the bathroom to quickly clean up as best as I could. Khi really flipped out on a nigga, but I knew that shit was going to happen. Even though I had fucked up again, Khi was giving me another chance to prove myself to him. He was right about everything. He was the only one of my brothers that constantly stayed on my ass and tried to help me. I fought with his ass like I hated him, but I loved that nigga 'til the death of me. I was gonna make sure I straightened the fuck up and did right. I didn't wanna disappoint him, plus I loved what I did. This dope shit made me feel superior, nigga.

Taylana: I really need to talk to you. Please answer me.
I know you're gonna be at my brother's today.
Taylana: Dae, I love you.
Taylana: Please talk to me. I can't take this. I'm hurting
so bad, Dae. I can't stop crying.
Me: It's over, Lana. Just stop contacting me, man.

I clicked on the word *details* at the top of the message
box, and then went under her name, scrolled down, and
clicked on *block this caller*. I had fun with shorty, but
she fucked up when she decided to send Amber that text
message. I couldn't have her out there going crazy and
shit like that, so I had to do what was best. And the best
thing was for us to end it before we really even got started.

Khi and I pulled up at Tamar's house a few minutes
before one, and KaeDee's punk ass was already on the
inside. I noticed Taylana's pink Maserati parked at
the front of the long driveway, and I started to get a
little nervous. I hoped she was gonna be cool, because I
would hate for me and my brothers to be in a real sticky
situation that I knew we wouldn't make it out of. Tamar
didn't allow anyone to bring guns inside of his house
outside of security, so we didn't even bother to try to
bring our shit in. I ain't gonna lie; being naked like this
had a nigga nervous as hell, mainly 'cause I didn't know
what to expect. It was just real suspect that he was calling
a meeting that day right after I told his sister to leave me
the fuck alone.

Shrugging it off, Khi and I got checked by security
and were pointed to the back of the house where the
everyone else was. As we headed to the back, it seemed
like Taylana's ass was watching and waiting for me to
come through the door. Khi spotted her before I did, and
he stepped on the outside of me and allowed me to walk

ahead of him. I made brief eye contact with her before diverting my attention elsewhere.

"Focus, nigga," Khi said once we walked past her.

"I'm good. Don't worry. I'm straight," I told him right before we entered a huge room that held two big-ass dining tables. Khi and I found KaeDee and took seats beside him. KaeDee nodded, but fuck that nigga. I was still mad at him over choking me behind his bitch. He should've been happy that I had the balls to do something he couldn't do. That bitch had been sucking another nigga's dick, so me punching her was hardly what she deserved. KaeDee whispered something to Khi, and Khi nodded his head before looking back at me.

"You good?"

"Damn, nigga, I said I was good," I said and sat back in my chair and folded my arms across my chest.

Tamar and two of his goonies walked in the room and commanded everyone's attention. I looked around and saw a few cats that I knew from around the way that got money in this dope shit. N.O., or some called him Qua, hustled a little further in the South, and this nigga Jaheim did his thang in the West. We used to beef with these niggas all the time over territory, but Tamar stepped up, hit us with that straight drop, then split everything up so that we all could see money.

I sat forward in my seat so that I could pay close attention to what was being said. When my phone vibrated in my pocket, I pulled it out and saw that I had a message from a number I didn't recognize. When I unlocked my phone and went to the message app, I saw that a screenshot had been sent to me.

"Shit," I said under my breath. Taylana's ass had sent me a message from another phone. Her stupid ass had screenshot a message that she was threatening to send to her brother if I didn't meet her in the bathroom. I looked around nervously, and then sat up so that I was close enough for Khi to hear me. "I gotta take a shit. That damn Red Bull kicking my ass."

Khi looked back at me suspiciously as I held onto my stomach and faked like it was hurting. I shrugged my shoulders and got up to leave the room. I spotted Taylana on the other side of this big-ass house, and she nodded her head for me to follow her. I looked around and didn't see anyone, so I quickly made my way in her direction, and then took her lead as she went into a bathroom that was about three times the size of my bathroom. She shut and locked the bathroom door as soon as I stepped inside.

"What the fuck you want? Is you crazy?" I said just above a whisper.

"I needed to see you. After you sent that text to me, I started feeling sick. I don't want to be without you. You know that I was really starting to fall in love with you, Dae. I was just in my feelings and feeling like you was cheating on me, so I reacted off emotions."

"Okay, and your emotions is what led you here. I told your ass what it was, and you didn't wanna believe me, so this is what the fuck we gotta deal with. My brother knows now since you wanted to keep threatening me, and I told him I was done fucking with you, so it is what it is," I told her, still refusing to admit that Amber was more than an ex. Shit, she was already in her feelings and hurting, and the way she kept trying to threaten me with going to her brother, I knew with the truth that she would more than likely do it. Fuck that. "I gotta go before they start looking for a nigga."

"Dae, wait," she said and grabbed my arm. She pulled me to a big, round couch that sat in the middle of her bathroom and pushed me down.

"What's up, man? I gotta go," I said as I looked up at her.

"What happened to your face? You have blood here," she said, touching the side of my lip.

I sighed. *Here she go, doing the shit that got a nigga hooked on her in the first place.*

She walked over to the sink, grabbed a towel, and wet it. Then she grabbed some ointment from a drawer. She walked over to me and pushed me back on the sofa. Straddling me, Taylana took the rag and cleaned my face up before applying the ointment.

"What happened?"

"Nothin'. I'll be like new in a few days. Ain't shit."

She pulled my dreads from my face, and then leaned over to kiss me. I turned my head from her, trying to make this shit easy on shorty, but damn, she wasn't making it easy on me.

"Come on, Lana. Nah, ma," I said as she reached behind her and rubbed her hand over my dick.

"Baby, why you so hard? I know you love me, Dae, and I know you want to be with me," Lana said as she ran her tongue across the side of my neck, causing me to shudder. I didn't even try to stop her when she unzipped my jeans and pulled my dick from my boxers. She stood up over me and stepped out of the pants she was wearing. Slowly, she slid down on my dick and had me biting down on my lip from her being so fucking wet.

"Shit, baby," I grunted and gripped her ass. "Ride this dick and hurry the fuck up."

Taylana pulled her shirt over her head and bounced up and down while pinching her nipples. I gripped her ass and guided her up and down. She tossed her head back as I threw my hips into her, forcing my dick deep inside of her.

"Hmm, mmm, shit. Yes, Dae, yes, baby," she moaned. "Just like that. I'm about to come."

"I'm about to come, too . . . shit, don't stop. Ahhh, fuck," I groaned as I bounced Taylana up and down on me roughly.

"I'm coming, I'm coming," she screamed, and at the same time, I pulled her off me as my nut shot out of me and I used my hand to catch it. I threw my head back on the sofa and panted until I caught my breath.

"Get me a towel. Hurry up 'fore my brothers come looking for me."

I lay there getting myself together while Taylana went to grab another towel. I heard the water from the sink come on and then cut off before she walked back over to me and cleaned me up. I stood up, stuffed my dick back into my boxers, and zipped my pants.

Taylana slid something into my hand.

"What the fuck is this?" I said, looking down and noticing that it was a pregnancy test. There was a big-ass plus sign with the word *pregnant* right next to it. I dropped that shit on the floor and rushed out of the bathroom, not giving a fuck who saw me. I couldn't believe this shit. Taylana promised me that she was on the pill before her ass moved down here, so I didn't see how the hell she even let this happen.

Damn! I thought and headed back to where the meeting was taking place.

"You straight?" Khi asked once he looked back at me as I took my seat.

I nodded my head but didn't say anything. All I could think about was that I had fucked up again. *Fuck!*

Chapter 18

Cuba

"Good morning," I said as I walked into She is Beauty.

"Umm . . . shit, good morning to you too. Is you okay?" Tangie asked with a sly grin on her face. She followed me over to my work station and eyed me up and down. She then grabbed my hand and spun me around. "Oh, you finally gave Khi the kitty, huh?"

"Oh my God!" I yelled as I playfully slapped her on her arm. "Not so damn loud."

"Oh, I already heard that," Anastasia's ugly ass said.

"Me too," another stylist, Tameka, said.

I looked at Tangie and rolled my eyes.

"Girl, we ain't crazy. We already knew that it would be sooner or later. Khi been claiming you since the first day he walked into this shop and saw you sitting there."

I couldn't help the smile that suddenly plastered my face. After Khi had come back from his meeting the day before, he apologized to me again for the way he walked out on me when I told him that I'd spent time in jail. I told him the truth about me catching a drug charge, but I didn't go into any other details. I wasn't quite ready to divulge that kinda information to him just yet. The fact that my sister died and my family thought I was to blame was one thing, but hell, I would never forget how he and Rue got into it on my first day of work, and I didn't want to cause more shit.

I could already tell that Khi was like those Alpha males that I used to read about in some of those books when I was locked up. His ass was already screaming out all kind of orders when he dropped me off there this morning and shit. I had to get used to that. I used to boss Rue's ass around all the damn time, and I didn't know how I was gonna deal with this new situation. And let's not forget my bad-ass attitude. Khi thought it was a front, but no, it was mad real. Jail just had a bitch scared to cut up, but bitches like Anastasia would be the first to get it when my probation was over. And Khi's baby mama, Selena. I really owed that special ho an ass-whooping.

"Well, I just try to keep bitches like Anastasia out my business, you know," I said after I kept noticing Anastasia's ass giving me a dry-ass, stank look.

What the fuck is she mad about? I hope she don't think I'm worried about Rue. I definitely don't give a damn about him. She must don't know that I know that she's not getting any head, and after what I've been experiencing these last couple of days . . . My gawd! I kinda feel bad for her, I thought and ended up giggling out loud.

"Girl, what the hell is going on with you?" Tangie laughed, and so did Tameka.

All I could think was, *If they only knew.*

"Look, Tangie, girl, I need to talk to you," I told her as I stuffed my purse into the drawer at my work station. "It's personal."

"Is everything okay?"

"Umm, let's just go to your office. I don't want anyone to hear what I got to say."

Tangie nodded, and we headed to the back of her shop to a little office where she had a desk, a laptop, and a small refrigerator. This morning before coming to work, Khi took me by Tangie's place to get all of my things. Tangie was already gone, so she had no idea that I was

leaving, and I didn't want her to go home to find out like
that. Plus, I was about to let her know what Camp's nasty
ass had been up to. It took everything in me to keep Khi
from fucking that nigga up, even though it would've been
a beautiful sight to see. Apparently, that nigga had gotten
laid off and was just laying his lazy ass around the house.
Part of me felt like he got laid off just so he could try to
get some pussy from me, but he was a fool.

"So, I am going to look for an apartment on my next
day off. I just wanted to let you know that I really appreciate everything that you've done for me. You have no
idea how much you mean to me, and I will never forget
the visits to come and see me, the letters, books, magazines, money . . . oh my God, just everything," I said to
Tangie, feeling myself get teary-eyed. I really hoped that
this news wasn't going to ruin the relationship we had,
because I really loved her.

"Aww, Cuba, how many times I gotta tell you that
you're family? Family sticks together. No matter what
everyone believes and how they went about the situation, I always knew better."

"Well, I had Khi take me to get my stuff this morning," I
said and let out a deep breath.

"Why didn't you tell me?" she asked with a look of
concern mixed with hurt on her face.

"Look, I ain't know how to tell you. Part of me was
scared to tell you, and shit, being that I needed a place
to lay my head, I didn't know how you would take it. I've
just been living in fear. Camp has been trying to fuck
me since about the second week I've been at your damn
house. I have to sleep with a chair on the door every night,
and just the other day, he popped me in the face with
the door trying to get in the room. I had to do everything
to keep Khi from beating his ass this morning. I didn't
wanna disrespect your house like that. I even got him on
video if you don't believe me," I told her all in one breath.

Tangie sat there stone-faced before tears suddenly leaked from her eyes. I felt so bad for her, because she obviously loved that nigga, but I felt she needed to know. That monster was gonna do the shit to somebody else one of these days, if he already hadn't. I wanted to save her the misery of being affiliated with a nigga like that, just in case he got himself caught up.

"I'm sorry. I know I should've told you sooner—"

"Yeah, you should've, but I should've known. Camp ain't shit; ain't gonna ever be shit. That muthafucka can't even keep a damn job long enough with his whack, little-dick-having ass. Fuck him. I wish you would've let Khi beat his ass. Matter of fact, let me call my bro up right now," Tangie said and pulled her phone from her apron.

I let out a deep breath. I was happy as hell that she didn't flip out on me and that she didn't take that nigga's side. Man, you never knew with females these days, and I was glad to see that Tangie was a true Lance girl for real. I didn't know why I even doubted her.

"Aye, what up?" I heard Khi say through the speaker after Tangie called him up.

"Cuba told me about that bitch-ass nigga of mine. I swear, I wish she would've told me sooner, 'cause I wouldn't have tried to save that nigga," Tangie told Khi.

"Aye, sis, you know me. I went back and fucked that nigga up as soon as I dropped Cuba off. That's a sick-ass dude, sis. You need to be careful who you lay down with. That nigga was in that bitch jacking off to some child porn and shit. I ain't never seen no shit like that in my life. I promise you if you didn't live in that apartment complex, I would've murked that bitch. He gonna fuck around and hurt somebody's child."

"Oh my God, are you serious, Khi?" Tangie asked in disbelief.

"Dead-ass. You might wanna get your locks changed, or shit, better yet, you just need to move."

"A'ight. Thanks, bro."

"Aye, where my baby at?" Khi asked, and a smile broke across my face. I felt myself blushing so hard that I covered my face in embarrassment as if he could see me.

"She's . . . she's up front. I came back to my office to call you."

"Damn, I wish you would've told me about her years ago before I went through all this fuckin' misery," Khi said.

"Aww, shit, don't tell me the li'l cuz already got a nigga smitten," Tangie said, and I had to keep myself from laughing out loud.

"Hell yeah, got me out here looking for places and shit for her ass. I don't know why she can't just move in. She must don't know how I am. I'ma let her have that space, though, for a minute."

"Well, you know after fucking with a nigga like Rue—"

Ahhh, fuck! I thought as I shook my head repeatedly. I knew it was too late, though, because the line grew quiet, and all I could hear was the sound of the wind in the background and the low music that played on Khi's stereo.

I'm sorry, Tangie mouthed.

"Aye, I'll talk to you later," Khi told Tangie, and the line went dead.

"I am so sorry, Cuba."

"It's okay. I was going to tell him. I just didn't want to mention it just yet. After seeing how him and Rue got into it my first day here, and then him coming up here all the time, I just knew it would be a problem. But look, he's calling me, so I'ma go outside and talk real quick."

"Okay, and I'm sorry again."

I nodded my head as I walked out of Tangie's office, and then answered Khi's call. I didn't even get a chance to say anything before he was going in on me about all the lying I had been doing. I shook my head, because I hadn't lied to him about shit. It wasn't like he asked me, and hell, it was my business to tell when I was ready to. I listened to him go on and on about how we had to be truthful with one another. I was about to agree with him as I headed to walk out of the shop, but once Rue stepped inside with a little boy by his side, all that shit went out the window.

"I'ma call you back in a few," I told Khi and hung up the phone before he could answer. "Oh my God. How did you pull this off?"

"I just talked to your pops, and he talked to your mama."

"He is so beautiful," I said, getting teary-eyed. "Hi, Bryson."

I held my arms out in front of me, and he ran for me while wearing the biggest and most beautiful smile I had ever seen. I couldn't believe that he came to me like he'd been knowing me all of his life, and it made me feel so good. I tried not to cry in fear that I would scare him, but I couldn't just hold it in. I pulled him back and stared at him. He looked so much like Alaska that it almost scared me to stare at him too long. I guess that I had been around Skylarr for too long, because he looked so much like her to me, too. They had the same chocolate skin and hazel eyes.

"Hey, Little Bry," Anastasia said, and I rolled my eyes and stood up. "Hey, baby."

"What's up, mama? I'm about to get ready to take Bryson down the block to get some breakfast. Cuba, ask Tangie if she mind if you take an early lunch. I mean, that's if you wanna go."

"Of course I wanna go. I'll send her a text and let her know I'll be back in a few. Let me grab my purse," I told Rue as I began to walk to my work station.

"Girl, you sure Khi gonna be cool with that? Bae, you know Cuba fucks with Khi now, right?" I heard this messy-ass broad say, and I had to stop, count to ten, and take a deep breath before letting it out and doing it all over again. After I grabbed my purse, I turned around with a big, fake-ass smile plastered on my face. I knew that me and this bird was gonna have our day real soon.

I followed Rue out of the shop, and me, him, and Little Bryson went to his car and drove down to the IHOP that was only a couple of blocks over. As soon as we walked inside and got settled into a booth, I just sat there and stared at Little Bryson. He was so grown to be only two years old. I watched as he stood up in the booth and pointed down at an item on the kids' menu.

"I want this, Daddy," he said to Rue, and that made me cock my head to the side.

"He calls you Daddy?" I asked just as my phone vibrated against the table.

"I ain't tell him to. I just been spending time with the li'l nigga since he was about six months. I feel like that was the least I could do since his daddy couldn't be here for him."

"Yeah." I nodded, not sure why I was feeling a way about that. I guess I still didn't know if Rue and Alaska had really slept together. It was not like Little Bryson looked anything like Bryson, and hell, truth be told, he didn't look anything like Rue's yellow ass either.

I looked down at my phone once it vibrated against the table again. It was Khi, and I picked it up to text him back.

Khi: Why you hang up on me like that?

Khi: Where are you?

Khi: Aye . . . man, where the fuck are you?

I went to text Khi back when I felt a tap on my shoulder. I looked up to see this crazy muthafucka standing over me. I exhaled, feeling like I had been busted when I was about to tell him the deal anyway. It wasn't like anything was going on between Rue and me, and the only reason I was here with Rue was because of my nephew.

"Let's go," Khi said.

"No," I looked up at him and said.

I could see his jaw twitching and could feel Rue's leg shaking under the table. I shook my head, feeling like this situation was going to take a turn for the worse. For the sake of my nephew, and to keep him from being hurt, I decided that it was best for me to leave. I exhaled and stood up from the table. I looked over at Little Bryson and held my hands out to him. Rue picked him up and handed him over to me.

"I am so glad that I got to meet and hug you. I know you don't know me, but I love you so much," I told him and kissed him on the jaw. He pushed me away and wiped my kiss off, but I kissed him again and caused him to laugh. "Remember, Aunt Cuba loves you, okay."

He shook his head, and I handed him back to Rue before turning around storming past Khi. I was so fucking pissed and hurt. He didn't know how long I had been waiting for a moment like that, and he just came and took it away from me before I really had a chance to enjoy it. I could feel my hands shaking as I walked out of IHOP and allowed the tears I was holding back to fall down my face.

"Aye, looka here, you gonna lose that fuckin' attitude. I'm not that nigga, a'ight. That shit was cute in the beginning, but you starting to piss me off with it."

"You just ruined probably the only chance I had of seeing my nephew! Do you know how long I have been waiting for this shit? My fucking parents wouldn't even allow me to see him because of Rue's bitch ass . . . but they allowed him to see him! That's my dead sister's baby, and you just took that away from me," I cried.

"How the fuck am I supposed to know that shit, Cuba? It seems like all you doing is giving me piece by piece to your life and expect me to just put that shit together. You should've fuckin' told me what the hell you was doing and not let me have to find out by Anastasia's ass that you down here eating with your ex nigga that I just fuckin' found out about. You know how that shit look to me?"

"I don't care how it looks. I don't want Rue!"

"I don't give a fuck if you want him or not. That nigga obviously wants your ass, and he's using your nephew to get to you."

"He's not using him. He knows how much I wanted to see him, so he got my parents to allow it."

"Bullshit. He ain't get your parents to do shit. And if he did, why the hell he didn't just drop him off with you? I ain't stupid. You tell that nigga the next time he come at you about your nephew that you don't need his ass to come with y'all. Let me find out you can't do that shit."

"Yeah, whatever." I sighed and shook my head. I crossed my arms over my chest and stared at Khi with so much hatred in my heart for him, but I hated that he looked so damn good to me right now. He was dressed down, rocking a white True Religion fit and a pair of black-and-white retro Jordans on his feet. The scent of his Gold cologne tickled my nostrils and forced me to exhale as I thought about all the places he'd had his tongue last night.

"The fuck you over there smiling about?" Khi asked, and I shook my head. "Yeah, a'ight. Let me find out. Take your ass back down there to that damn shop. Tangie supposed to hook your nappy-ass head up, because we got somewhere to be tonight."

"You wasn't going to ask me if I wanted to go, and you can't take me back to the shop?"

"Hell no, I'm not gonna ask you. Fuck I look like, man? And did I bring your ass down here? Shit, walk," Khi said, looking like I had offended him before he walked off.

"This nigga really gonna make me walk," I said under my breath.

I peeked inside the windows of the IHOP to see Rue staring directly at me. As much as I wanted to go back inside and hug on my nephew some more, I knew it would cause trouble. I looked over and didn't see Khi anymore, so I held my phone for Rue to see and walked off, heading back to the shop.

Chapter 19

Khian

As soon as I pulled up to the gate of my crib and spotted Briana sitting in front of it, I placed the car in park and hopped out. My heart was beating hard as fuck against my chest as I ran over to her, picked her up, and carried her to the car. I placed her in the back seat before I got back inside and pressed the button to open the gate. I glanced over at Cuba, and she didn't say anything, but I could tell that she had questions. She had never met Briana before, and I had only briefly spoken about her. Cuba knew that she was having issues with drugs, but for the most part, she didn't know how bad.

Once we got up to the house, I placed the car in park and went around to open Cuba's door. She stepped out, and I bit down on my bottom lip, just looking at how gorgeous Tangie had done her hair up. She had it long and in big-ass curls that fell down her back. I wanted to make sure she kept it like this at all times, especially while she was fucking with me.

"I left you a dress on the bed. I'll be there in a few," I told Cuba as I handed her the key to the house, and then went to pull Briana out of the car.

I carried Briana inside to one of the guest rooms downstairs and laid her across the bed. Seeing her in the condition she was in reminded me of the night I picked up Skylarr. She was the same damn way. I walked over, cut the light on, and shook my head as I stared down at Briana. I could only imagine the type of shit she had been out there doing to get high, and I didn't know why it fuckin' bothered me.

"Aye, Bri," I called out to her. "Bri!"

"Hmm," she mumbled.

"What's up? Where you been, man?"

"Not like you care, Khi. Where's Sky?" she slurred.

"She's with her grandma, and if she wasn't, you damn sure wouldn't see her looking like this."

"I need your help, Khi. I tried to do it on my own, and I couldn't," Briana cried and exhaled.

I nodded my head and crossed my arms over my chest. I damn sure wasn't about to turn her down this time. I was too in my feelings that last time, and that shit left me scared and worried every damn minute that I didn't hear from her.

"Who is that skinny-ass girl you with? And where's Selena dog ass?"

I chuckled and shook my head. It didn't matter what the hell Briana was going through. Her jealous ass was always gonna find a moment to question me about what the hell I was doing.

"Man, look, I got somewhere to be. Get your ass in the shower, and don't leave, a'ight," I told her.

"I'ma have Cuba bring you some clothes down here, but promise me you won't leave, Briana."

"I'm not gonna leave. I'm ready to get clean. I'ma do it this time for good. I promise you. I just wish you wouldn't have sent that dude to my house to bring me that money . . . but I should've never slept with him, though," Briana said, and my brow furrowed in confusion.

"Fuck you mean? I ain't send no dude to your house to bring you no money."

"Yes, you did. He brought money by there and said that you told him to. He came several times, and that's how we started fucking around and this shit happened. I woke up to him the last time sticking a needle in my arm, and I hadn't seen him since, until he came back and beat my ass that night you got Skylarr. He did this shit to me, Khi. I didn't do it on my own," Briana cried, and I sucked my teeth.

"What did he look like? Who is he?"

"I don't remember, Khi. You don't know who you got working for you. He was outside watching the house one day you came to pick up Sky. He said that you told him to watch your back, so he sat outside and waited a while. His name was Rob . . . or T . . . Jackson."

"Why you just now telling me this shit, Briana?"

"Because I didn't think you cared. You saw some nigga whooped on me and you didn't care!"

"'Cause I thought the dude that was laid up in your bed did the shit and you let him."

"What dude was that?"

"Aghh, fuck!" I yelled and turned around and punched the wall behind me. I walked out of the room and headed up the stairs to get dressed. I didn't have time for this shit. The meeting at Tamar's the day before was to let everyone know that he would be having a black tie party for the street lieutenants and bosses from all over the Metroplex. The location wouldn't be announced until an hour before everything started, just to keep out muthafuckas who wanted to try some slick shit.

I was glad that Briana was there and safe, but I couldn't miss that night. It was all about making connections and possible opportunities for growth that could expand beyond what we were already doing. I stayed hungry for the top, and I couldn't let an opportunity like this pass me by, not knowing when and if it would come around again. I just hoped that leaving Briana there alone wasn't a bad idea after what she'd told me.

She really fucked me up with that one, but I had to wonder if she was just running off at the mouth. I would never send another nigga to take my daughter's money when I was able to do the shit myself, especially not someone that wasn't fam. Even though my goonies knew where Briana laid her head, they ain't bother her like that, and neither did anyone from the hood. If what she was saying had any truth to it, I was starting to feel like maybe it could've had something to do with my spot being hit that night.

It was real funny how it seemed like everything came at me all at once on the one night I had to make the biggest pickup, which was around the fifth of every month. Only ones that knew that much info, though, was the goonies that worked the factory, my brothers, and Selena's ass. I knew it couldn't have been none of the factory workers, because all of them died that night, and Tramell had barely made it out. My brothers, not even Dae's ass, would stoop that low, and I was for sure about that. That only left that slick, crazy-ass, Spanish-talking bitch Selena. Now that I thought about shit and put it all into perspective, it was crazy how she went from blowing my ass up, crying and begging to come back up, to damn near nothing at all.

Let me find out, I thought.

Once we made it to the black tie affair, I couldn't even think from my mind being all over the place. I hadn't said two words to Cuba, not even to mention how good she looked in the tight-fitting Giuseppe dress that gave her curves I didn't even know she had. I licked my lips as I eyed her up and down, but just that quickly, my mood shifted again. I was pissed and reeling in my thoughts. I wondered if my baby mama had really been that shady to have me robbed and my goonies killed. I swea' I wouldn't be surprised, because she fuckin' hated Briana. She was always questioning me about her and accusing us of fucking every time I went to pick up my daughter. She did tell me one time . . .

"Are you okay?" Cuba asked, pulling me from my thoughts.

"Yeah, I'm cool. Why you say that?" I asked.

"Because you've been quiet since finding your baby mama at the house."

"I'm straight. Look, there's Dae, and I want you to meet the goonie Tramell," I told Cuba as I pulled her in the direction of my people. "Where KaeDee at?"

"How the fuck would I know where that nigga at? I don't fuck with him," Dae said, and I shook my head.

"I wish y'all would get over that shit," I said and looked around for my brother. "But aye, looka here. Tramell, I want you to meet Cuba. Cuba, this is the goonie Tramell, or Mell-Mell."

"Yeah, I think I know you. You had a sister name Alaska, right?" Tramell asked, and I spotted the sadness in Cuba's eyes as she nodded her head.

"Oh, yeah?" Dae said and sucked his teeth as he eyed Cuba and crossed his arms over his chest.

Fuck wrong with this nigga now? I thought as I looked around again for KaeDee. "Aye, I need to talk to y'all outside for a minute. Let's go out back," I told Tramell and Dae. "Be right back, bae. Get you a drink."

I walked out back on the upper level deck of the mansion with Tramell and Dae right behind me. I noticed how Dae kept looking at my girl, and I was about ready to call him out on it, until shorty walked up and tugged on Dae's shoulder. I threw my hands into my pockets, and my jaw twitched as I looked down at her. She had her hair pinned up and was rocking a black Versace dress with some open-toe pumps. I could see why Dae had went for her, 'cause she was a bad little biddie with a small waist and thick hips, but she wasn't the baddest there was. Not bad enough to fuck up my money.

"Aye, ma. I think I seen your brother over there somewhere," I told her as I stepped closer to her.

"I need to talk to Dae," she said and looked around nervously.

"Nah, see we about to discuss some shit, so I'ma need you to move around, shorty," I told her, getting frustrated as I gritted down on my teeth.

"Look, unless you want me to go and find my brother and let him know that Dae and I have been fucking behind his back, even in his bathroom during y'all's little meeting, then I suggest you let us have a minute," she told me.

I eyed Dae before sucking my teeth and turning around to walk away. I adjusted my tie and took a deep breath before I let it out and went to find Cuba. That was it. Good thing I had brought Tramell, 'cause he was for sure about to take his boy's place.

Chapter 20

Daelan

I was so fucking annoyed as I stood on the back deck with Taylana in my ear, whining about why I wouldn't answer my phone or come to the home that I made with her. I placed my hands in my pockets as my body rocked back and forth from the anger that was building inside of me. I could feel Taylana touching my arm, but I blocked her out and placed my attention on Cuba. I knew something was up with that chick. Khi was always hollering about it was something in a bitch's eyes, yet he couldn't tell when he was fucking with a snake bitch. Had it not been for my boy Tramell pointing out why there was so much familiarity in the air, Cuba's ass would've came and conquered what she had set out to do, and I would've never seen it coming.

"Aye, bro, so that's Alaska's sister?" I asked Tramell, and we both looked over at Khi and Cuba as the two became touchy feely, like they were in love and shit. "Sucka-ass nigga. What you think she up to?"

"Probably nothing, nigga. Sit your paranoid ass down somewhere," Tramell said.

"You said the bitch was in jail, nigga," I told Tramell as I looked at him and frowned.

"And I guess she not now. The fuck is you flipping out for? Now is not the time."

"So you don't think—"

"Dae, you don't hear—"

"Bitch, hold the fuck up!" I snapped, causing a few people to shoot their attention in our direction. I sucked my teeth as I looked over at Cuba and Khi again. My forehead started to sweat when the two of them looked my way. I took in a deep breath and looked down at Taylana as she stood by my side. "Man, look. I don't fuck with you no more. You think that shit you just did was fuckin' funny to me or something? Fuck outta here, yo. We're done. I have a family. Me and you were just something that happened that I allowed to go too far."

"Something that happened that you allowed to go too far? We moved in together. I'm pregnant. How do you . . . What do you mean you have a family?" Taylana responded as she looked up at me. Her hands shook as she held onto the handbag that she carried, and I could see her trembling as she tried to hold back the tears that were building in the corners of her eyes. "I'm just gonna tell my brother the truth. I can't believe—"

"Look," I said and grabbed Taylana's hand. I brought it up to my lips and kissed it. "You know a nigga love you, and I don't want shit to end like this. Just meet me back at the crib in a few hours so we can talk in a calm environment. All these muthafuckas around, and I feel like your brother gonna send his goonies over here any minute at a nigga. I'll see you later, a'ight?"

"You promise?" she asked and used the back of her hand to wipe the tears away.

I nodded my head as I looked up to see Cuba walking away from Khi and heading to what I assumed was the restroom. I leaned over and kissed Taylana on the forehead before walking away to catch up to Cuba. Once I had caught up to her, I slowed down and checked over my shoulder before I rushed up and snuck into the restroom behind her. I closed and locked the door and placed my hands into my pockets.

"What the fuck you lie for?" I asked Cuba as she stared at me through the mirror.

"What the hell are you doing in here? Where's Khi?" she asked as she walked over to the sink. "And lie about what?"

"So, you still gonna act like you don't know me?" I told her as I walked over and stood closely behind her. I sucked my teeth as I removed my hands from my pockets and ran one hand across her back. She arched her back as she continued to stare at me through the mirror. "I don't scare you?"

"No, but your brother does, and we both know he scares you too. Your face is proof," she shot back, and I gritted my teeth before wrapping my arm around her throat.

I pulled her roughly into my chest and squeezed her tighter. "Now that I think about it, you and Alaska really do look alike. What she tell you about me?" I asked her, and she shook her head. I squeezed her tighter, but the knock at the door forced me to release her. I backed away from her and continued to stare her down through the mirror. "You ain't slick. I got you now. You'll see me later."

I turned around and unlocked the door, and when I pulled it open, Tramell stood on the other side. I could see in his eyes that he knew I was up to something, and he had come to look out for me. When I looked to my left, Khi was coming around the corner in search of his bitch.

"Y'all seen Cuba?" Khi asked, and I bumped him as I walked past him. I loosened my tie before I pulled it off and threw it on the floor. Before rounding the corner, I glanced back at Khi and sucked my teeth when I saw that nigga kissing the bitch in her mouth. Placing my hands in my pockets, I knew I was gonna have to handle Khi's bitch sooner rather than later.

***

I pulled into the apartment building where I had lived with Taylana and saw her pink Maserati parked in its usual spot. I pulled my car on the side of hers and placed it in park. Before going inside, I sat back in my seat and rolled up a blunt. I was starting to feel like *fuck everything*. I didn't have shit to lose. The only reason why I kept going anyway after all the shit I had been through was because of my li'l dude, but the more and more reality set in that he wasn't mine, the less I felt like fighting. It wasn't like nobody was gonna miss me any damn way. My brothers hated me, and I hated them niggas too. Fuck 'em! I treated Amber so bad when she was the only bitch that would put up with my shit, but she had finally given up on me. Shit, fuck her too! I ain't have nobody, a muthafuckin' loner out here, and I hoped that none of them bitches that turned their backs on me showed up to my funeral with no fake-ass tears. They wasn't concerned about me while I was here, so they bet not be concerned when I was gone. I just really ain't care about shit no more.

I shook my head as I puffed on the hay and looked up toward the ceiling of my car. Somehow, I allowed all this shit to happen to me. I allowed things to spiral out of control. I fucked up everything I touched, and I damaged every person that tried to help me and love me. I really loved what I had with Taylana, but emotions always fucked up a good situation. It had always been that way. Muthafuckas could never just let shit flow and let the pieces fall where they may. Emotions would always get involved and rock the boat. It was something that Khi had always tried to teach me, and I had never really understood that shit until just recently. Now that I looked back on everything, emotions had always been the cause of every fucked-up situation I caused. Shit, I had to admit that I was one emotional-ass nigga, but it was too late to correct shit now. I just ain't care anymore.

I hopped out the car and threw the blunt down on the ground. I headed up to the apartment, took my key out, and unlocked the door. Once I walked inside, I shook my head and took a deep breath. Taylana had slow music playing on the stereo and had walked out of the room dressed in a sexy-ass negligee. I placed my hands into my pockets, and my jaw twitched as I watched her sexily walk over to me like she hadn't just snitched on a nigga earlier. I looked down at her when she wrapped her arms around me and smiled.

"I almost got scared that you wasn't going to come," Taylana said, and I frowned at her. "What's wrong?"

"What the fuck are you doing? I'm not about to fuck you. I came here so we can talk and get an understanding."

She dropped her hands to her sides and let out a deep breath. I was waiting on her to say the wrong mutha-fuckin' thing to me. I had already reached the point of no return with shorty. All that running off at the mouth, stepping out of pocket, and using her brother as a power card was really pissing me the fuck off. This ho had really thought she had a nigga wrapped around her finger and scared, but I wasn't Khi or KaeDee. Them niggas was willing to play bitch about losing that money, but I wasn't gonna do it. Fuck that and fuck her.

"Talk. I'm listening," Taylana said with attitude.

"Yeah, I hope you are listening. Take your ass back to Miami, get rid of that baby, and leave me the fuck alone. I don't fuck with you. I got a family already, and I don't want one with you, okay? Stop calling me from all these different numbers, stop texting me, and go the fuck away and leave me alone," I said, doing my best to keep my hands in my pockets as I rocked back and forth.

"So, you just gonna play me like that? Fuck me? Fuck our baby? You never really loved me, did you, Dae?"

"I told your dumb ass that I didn't, and you wanted to believe otherwise. You let all that shit that was reeling in your head bring us to this point. You should've left well enough alone. Now, it is what it is."

"No, because I knew you was a lying-ass, no-good-ass nigga. I knew you was lying about that bitch. That's why I sent her that message. That's who you got the family with, huh? I knew she wasn't telling you to come home if you all really didn't share a home together. Does she know that I'm pregnant?"

"No, and she's not going to know, because you're gonna take your ass on and get rid of it."

"I'm gonna tell her. I'm gonna tell Tamar. I'm gonna tell every muthafuckin' body that will listen to how fucked up you did me. You could've been straight up with me, but no, you wanted to lead me on. So, since you think it's funny to come along and fuck with me, fuck with my head and my heart, then I'm gonna do you the same," Taylana said.

I quickly pulled my hands out of my pockets and punched her in the face. She flew backward onto the floor and threw her hands up to catch her leaking nose. I slowly walked over to her and began to kick her over and over again. She was able to roll over onto her stomach, and she tried to crawl away, but I got down on the floor with her and wrapped an arm around her neck. Blood dripped from her nose and onto my hand as I covered her nose and mouth. She grunted and squirmed underneath me as I held on, trying to suffocate this bitch.

"Talk too fuckin' much. Look like I'm scared of your brother, bitch, huh? I let you use that shit against me long enough because of my fam and for the sake of my pockets, but fuck all that shit, and fuck you!" I yelled and could feel my veins protruding through my skin as I held on until she no longer moved underneath me. I dropped her, and her face bounced against the carpet as I stood to my feet and pulled the pistol from my back. I took a silencer from my pocket and screwed it onto the tip of my gun. I wanted to make sure her ass was dead, so I aimed for her head, ready to pull the trigger, when a knock at the door and twisting of the doorknob stopped me.

"Lana! Lana! It's Rozalyn. Tamar sent me over here to check on you. Open up, girl," I heard Rozalyn, who I knew to be Tamar's wife, yell from the outside.

I glanced over my shoulder and then back down at Taylana's lifeless body as I tucked my pistol and headed to the back of the apartment. I entered the bedroom I'd once shared with Taylana and grabbed anything that could tie back to me. Once I was done, I pulled up the bedroom window, climbed out, and crept to my car. I watched as Rozalyn pulled out her phone and looked around, until her eyes fell on me. I didn't think she recognized me, but I guess I would know sooner or later if she did. Fuck it.

Chapter 21

KaeDee

I sat inside of my office, downing a glass of Cognac, when my little brother Khi walked in. Stress lines were all over his face, as I was sure they were on mine as well. I slid a glass across my desk, and he grabbed it and walked over to the mini bar. It was nine o'clock in the morning, and I had been there all night. I skipped out on the black tie affair, and I was sure that was why Khi was there, to see what was going with his boy. I wasn't answering my phone or messages and had let the shit go dead after so long. I just got tired of everybody. Deonna had been reaching out to me every few minutes, begging me to hear her out, and Khi was constantly on my shit with bullshit from Dae.

I didn't wanna hear from nobody until I got my head together. I wasn't the type to lose my cool for nothing or nobody, but lately, I had really been showing my ass. Luckily, Tyrin Walker wanted me to defend him more than he wanted to press charges against me, so that shit was dead, but that nigga was still alive. Every minute he was breathing was another minute I sat and wondered if he was fucking my wife. I was too arrogant and stubborn to allow her to come back home no matter how much she begged and claimed that she was done fucking him. I didn't like the fact that she crushed my ego, making me feel like I was just a choice, and once she realized that she'd made the wrong one, she was ready to come home and be a family again. What type of bullshit was that?

"You heard from Dae?" Khi asked as he sat down in front of me.

I sat back in my chair and stared at him in silence while he downed the alcohol. He shook off the burn before he noticed the look I was giving him.

"Man, come on with the bullshit, KaeDee! We fuckin' brothers. Tramell told me that he snapped on Tamar's sister last night at the party, and Cuba said that nigga hemmed her up in the bathroom, questioning her about her sister. I need to find this nigga before he does something stupid."

"Well, find the nigga. He's not here, and I'm sure his dumb ass has already done something stupid. I can't believe you would bring Dae in that man's home knowing that nigga was fucking his sister. When you gonna stop excusing the shit he does and do something about it?" I said and snatched up the bottle of Cognac. I poured myself another glass, got up from my chair, and walked over to the window. I leaned against the window and tried to find peace in the beautiful view.

"Do what? You act like you want me to kill the nigga or something."

"Shit, why not? He ain't doing shit but fucking up his life and everybody else's too. You tap that nigga on his ass and he go harder. Fuck that nigga. I don't have time to worry about Dae and the shit he's in. Whatever happens to that nigga happens. He obviously doesn't care, so I wish the fuck you'd stop if you ain't gonna do shit about it," I said, and Khi sighed.

"Something is wrong with Dae, nigga. Can't you see that shit?"

"Well, get him some help then, Khi. Stop worrying me with that shit."

"I made a couple of moves last night that'll have us getting some money out of Atlanta. Tamar said that he'll put me in contact with the right people, and that is some for-sure paper. I've been thinking about just teaching Tramell to run Dae's spot, and since Cass about to come home, he can take over for me while I head toward Atlanta for a little bit."

"You just gonna pick up and go to Atlanta by yourself? You don't know nobody out there," I told Khi as I turned to face him.

"I'ma get down there and see what's what, but I'm thinking about taking a few of the goonies with me. I'm just trying to live up to my full potential, baby. You know that."

"You definitely gonna do that. I ain't never been worried about that."

"Just got so much shit going on, and I feel like I need to get away for a minute. Briana came to the house last night asking me for help, and when I got back for the party, she was gone, after I told her not to move. What the fuck, man? Then Selena . . ."

"Briana is gone, bruh. That shit gets harder and harder each time, so I don't even know why you stressing yourself over shorty. She's no good. Take care of Skylarr and move on. But what's up with this shit you was texting me about with Selena?" I said as I walked over to my seat just as my door flew open.

I looked up to see Tyrin Walker walk in like he was ready for war. Khi pulled his pistol and stood up.

"The fuck is going on?" Khi questioned, and I smirked.

"Sorry, Mr. Prince, I tried to stop him. The police are on their way," my secretary Lisa told me, and I nodded my head.

"This that nigga Tyrin I was telling you about, bruh," I told him as I stood beside him.

"Where's Deonna?" Tyrin asked, and I looked at this nigga like he had lost his mind.

"Man, you got a lot of fuckin' nerve coming through this bitch looking for somebody's wife. The fuck is you on?" Khi spoke, and I could see his jaw twitching as he stood next to me, his pistol idle by his side. We all had that shit in common: twitching of the jaws, gritting of the teeth, and pocketing of the hands when we felt shit was about to get crazy. My father had always told us to stay cool and never react unless there was no other choice. He said keep our hands in our pockets if we felt like we wouldn't be able to control them, and never pull a pistol on a nigga unless you was gonna use it. Khi was for sure ready to use it.

"Nah, he good. It's not his fault the wifey been dick-hopping, but she home now where she supposed to be. You still hanging around town, though. You must be waiting on these hollow tips."

Tyrin gritted and stepped forward, causing Khi to pop the safety and put the gun to his head.

"Tell your goonie to stand down, nigga. You can't handle your own problems. You see I'm *outchea* by myself. You caught me last time, but give me a fair one," Tyrin said, and I scoffed.

"Goonie? Try *brother*, nigga, and you keep talking that slick shit and watch how quick your body drop. He don't handle shit but that muthafuckin' courtroom, and I promise you, nigga, he'll get me off for murking your ass. Now, fall the fuck back and get Deonna off your mind. Let me find out you couldn't do that," Khi told him and stepped back. He tucked his pistol and crossed his arms over his chest just as the police stepped inside.

"He was just leaving, officers," I told them as I walked behind my desk and grabbed my drink. I took a seat and could see that Khi was reeling in anger. His hands shook as he crossed them behind his back and waited for Tyrin to leave my office.

"Yeah, you'll see me later, KaeDee," Tyrin said, and I nodded.

"Guarantee you'll see me first," Khi shot back. "Don't come to regret your decisions, nigga."

"Khi," I called out, and I watched as he released a breath and stepped back.

As soon as Tyrin left my office, the officers stood behind to make sure everything was cool, and then left Khi and me alone again.

"Aye, I'm out. I'ma handle that, though. Don't even worry about it." Khi nodded as he slammed his glass down on my desk after finishing his drink. It broke into pieces as he turned around and then exited my office.

Me: Why the fuck is this nigga coming up here looking for you, Deonna?

Send

Deonna: I told you that he crazy and won't leave me alone. I haven't talked to him, but he still keeps bothering. He keeps saying that he's not going to let me get away this time. Idk what to do. I'm scared to leave my hotel room. Tyrin has always been crazy but never anything like this. I know I'm not your problem anymore, but maybe you can send some men to where I'm staying. I'm at the Westin downtown.

Me: Just meet me at the house. We need to talk. Be there after grabbing Chanel from my mom's.

Send.

Deonna: Okay. See you soon . . . love you☺

***

Ding dong! Ding dong!

I pulled the door open to see Deonna standing on the other side wearing a navy blazer, a low-cut, cream-colored bloused underneath that showed off her cleavage, and tight-fitting skinny jeans, with Gucci pumps on her feet. I hadn't really paid her much mind since parting ways with her, but looking at her now had me loving the thickness the baby was already giving to her. I couldn't stop the lust I felt as I stepped to the side and allowed her to come inside. After sitting in my office overnight and reeling in my thoughts, I felt like maybe Deonna deserved that second chance she was asking for. Truthfully, I missed her, and I didn't want her out there running around too long thinking a nigga wasn't going to take her back and then another nigga grabbed her up.

I was mad as hell still and hurting behind this shit, but my mind was made up that I wanted my family, so I would I have to get over my hurt and anger with Deonna back at home where she belonged. I walked over to the bar area with Deonna following behind me. I grabbed a glass and a bottle of white and poured her some. I then grabbed me a shot glass and filled it partway with some Cognac.

"Have you had any since being pregnant?" I asked Deonna.

"I've had a glass. I don't wanna be like I was with Chanel and relying on it more often than I should when I was stressed. I had one glass. It was too good, and I had to pull myself away to keep from getting another one," Deonna said with a laugh.

"Is this thing really over with that you and that nigga, Deonna?" I asked her.

She looked at me and desperately shook her head yes. She took a sip of her drink, and I watched as tears fell from her eyes and hit the rim of the glass.

"I'm sorry. I was stupid. Really fuckin' stupid. For some reason, I told myself that because I left Tyrin because of what he did for a living, and then I got with you and you were doing the same thing, maybe I wasn't fair to him. Maybe I should try to see if he and I could continue from where we left off and see if that was something that I wanted to do . . . and then make a choice on who I really wanted to be with. I made you a choice when you are so much more than that. I never loved that man. I only loved the fun that I had with him and the fact that I was able to feel free, but when I think about what I have with you, I know that I never really knew what love was until I met you."

"I forgive you," I told her as I reached out and pulled her to me. I ran my hand over her face then leaned over and kissed her lips. Deonna looked up at me, surprised, before tossing her head into my chest and breaking down into tears.

I scooped her up from the floor into my arms and carried her to the stairs. I took them one at a time while Deonna wrapped one arm around my neck. I carried her into our bathroom and placed her down on the floor.

"You know what to do. I'll be right back," I told her as I went back downstairs to grab the liquor and her wine. Once I made it back up, Deonna had started the water in our Jacuzzi tub and stripped out of her clothes. I helped her inside, handed her the glass of wine, and then came out of my clothes. She poured a small amount of vanilla-scented Bath and Body Works inside the water, and then looked at me and laughed. She knew I hated that shit, but her ass loved everything that was vanil-la-scented.

I walked over to the Jacuzzi tub, and she held her hand up to stop me from getting inside. She leaned over the side of the tub and grabbed my erection. She pulled it into her mouth, causing it to grow inside of her. I groaned and bit down on my bottom lip as my hand went to her head.

"Shit, shit. Suck that dick," I said, moving my hips as my dick slid in and out of Deonna's mouth.

I couldn't take it any longer and pushed Deonna back and climbed in the tub. I had it custom made to make sure that a nigga as big as me would fit right inside without being all scrunched up and uncomfortable.

"Bring your ass here," I told Deonna and reached out for her hand.

She came over and straddled me before sliding down on my dick. The heat of the water, the bubbles that roared between us, and her hot box had a nigga curling his toes. I gripped Deonna's ass and looked into her eyes. She stared back into mine as she rode me like she had never done before.

"Ohhh, baby, shit!" Deonna crooned as I threw my hips into her each time she slammed down on me.

"Damn, you feel so fuckin' good. Come for me, baby! Come for daddy," I yelled before clasping Deonna's breasts together and sucking her nipples.

"Aghhh!" Deonna screamed, seeming to go wilder as she became tighter and wetter. "I'm gonna come!"

"Make that pussy come for me. Arghhh," I grunted as I sucked harder and harder on Deonna's nipples, feeling her walls sucking me inside of her like a vacuum. I could feel her muscles tightly contracting on my dick. I pumped in and out of her like crazy until I shot my load inside of her at the same time she rained all over my dick.

"Don't tell me that wasn't the best ever," Deonna said as her head collapsed into my chest.

"Got damn, that was the best ever," I agreed before I tossed my head back on the tub and closed my eyes. I just hoped Deonna really was done with that nigga and not about to make me regret taking her back. One thing I knew I couldn't take was looking like a fool again.

"Love you, baby," Deonna said.

"I love you too."

Chapter 22

Amber

"Little Dae, go get in the bed! I'm not going to tell you again," I called out and went into the kitchen to fix myself a drink. After Dae's ass was acting a fool in front of Deonna the other day and talking about Little Dae not being his, he texted me and told me that I didn't have to worry about leaving, because he would just move out. I knew that was another one his ploys to get me to stick around and not leave, and it worked, but only temporarily.

Khi had been looking for an apartment for his new girlfriend and said that while he was at it, he was going to find something for me and Little Dae too. He felt like me having my own place would be better. He said it was the only way that I was going to build my independence and stop relying on Dae or any other people to take care of me, and I had to admit that he was right. I had been living with Dae since I was fourteen, and six years later, at the age of twenty, I realized that I didn't know how to take care of myself. Of course, I knew how to cook, clean, and take care of other household duties, but I didn't know anything about surviving. The little time I spent hustling with Dae didn't last long, because as soon as we found out I was pregnant, he sent me home and told me to be a mother.

I had to drop out of school my sophomore year to take care of my child, and I had never even attempted to go back. And since talking to Khi, I felt like going back to school to get my GED was something that I should focus on. Khi agreed that he would pay my bills for me while I attended school and picked up some kind of trade. I had always dreamed of being a pharmacist when I was a young girl, and I was really thinking of becoming a pharmacy technician now and being a pharmacist later. I was still young and still had time to take charge of my life. I knew that no matter what happened with Dae and me, I could always count on Khi, KaeDee, and Deonna to look out for me and Little Dae. We were gonna be fine, and I was looking forward to claiming my happiness. For too long, I had loved Dae without it getting me anywhere in life but beat, walked all over, and cheated on, and I was done. I had finally reached my breaking point.

"Mama! I heard something," Little Dae said as he walked into the kitchen. I placed my hands on my hips and cocked my head to the side. I swear whenever it was time for bed, this little boy had every excuse in the book on why he either couldn't sleep or why he needed to get up.

"Um, look, little boy. I'm about to prop my feet up and relax, and you're about to go to bed. I've been taking care of you all day, and now it's Mommy's time. There isn't going to be any eating, any unnecessary trips to the bathroom, no boogie man under the bed or in the closet, and yes, Mama is okay, so I don't need you getting up to come and check on me."

"But, Mama, I heard something."

"Daelan, what did—Oh my God! Daelan, get down!" I screamed as I grabbed him and threw him to the floor. I rushed and crawled to him, covering him with my body as bullets flew through my home. "Don't move, baby. Stay down."

"I want Daddy," Daelan cried as he squirmed underneath me, and at that moment, I wanted him too. I had never been so scared in my life. It was times like this that I knew getting away from this man should've been my first priority a long time ago. He should've been there with us. He should've been there to protect our boy, but I could only wonder what woman he had caused problems with now.

It sounded like we were in the middle of a war as bullet after bullet continued to rip through the walls and windows. They were loud, they were fast, and they were destroying everything that they hit.

"Hmmm!" I moaned as I felt a fiery feeling burning through my back. I didn't want to scare Daelan as he continued to lie underneath me, so I bit down on my bottom lip to mask the pain that I felt.

"Mommy!" he cried, and I did my best to rock him back and forth and keep him calm. It seemed like the gunfire was never going to stop. Blood dripped from my mouth as tears fell from my eyes.

"Mommy, are you okay?" Daelan asked when the gunfire finally ceased.

"Don't move. Don't move, baby," I told him once I heard the sounds of glass crunching and footsteps coming our way. "Shhhh."

"Check the back," I heard someone say, but I tried to lay as still as possible.

I heard a group of footsteps run through our home and the sound of someone coming toward Little Dae and me. I was suddenly grabbed by my hair and pulled away from my son.

"Ahhhh! Dae!" I screamed.

"Is that nigga here?" he asked me.

I stared into his brown eyes, and he stared back into mine. I had never seen him before, but I could tell that

Dae had finally fucked with the right one. He knelt down in front of me and grazed his eyes over me before he locked them on little Daelan and then back on me.

"It's empty," a dark-skinned guy said as he came and stood behind the guy that was in front of me.

"Where is he?" he asked me again.

I felt myself getting weak. More blood dripped from my mouth as Little Dae scooted toward me and wrapped his arm around mine. "I . . . I don't know," I answered truthfully.

"You don't know? Or you don't wanna tell me?"

"I don't know. I promise you . . . I don't know."

"The bitch fucked my sister, got her pregnant, and then tried to kill her. That nigga gonna have to see me, ya feel me? You can protect that nigga if you want to, but I'ma keep coming back until I get him. I don't care who I hit in the process."

"Please," I cried. "I don't know. You can check my phone. It's over there. I haven't talked to Daelan in a couple of days. I need an ambulance. Please, I can't leave my baby here alone. Please don't let me die."

"Don't let you die? You mean like how he left my sister to die? Bitch, fuck you and that ho-ass nigga. I'ma hand you this phone, though, so you can hit that li'l bitch up and tell him Tamar said he gunning for him. And hard," he told me as he stood to his feet. The dark-skinned guy that was with him handed Tamar my cell phone, and Tamar dropped it on the floor in front of me. "Tell that nigga don't hide now. Me and the goon squad on that ass."

As soon as Tamar and his men left, I grabbed my cell phone and called 911. I told them that I had been shot and that I needed them to send help quick. I could feel my body shaking, and I felt so cold, but I refused to give up. I held onto Little Dae, and he held onto me, and we sat and waited.

Only minutes had gone by before I heard glass crunching in the distance. I pulled Little Dae as close to me as I could, thinking that they had come back. Little Dae started to cry again, and I rubbed his arm to try to calm him down.

"Amber! D.J.!"

Just like this nigga to show up in the aftermath of the fury he had caused. I released more tears and more blood as Daelan stepped in the kitchen with a pistol in his hand. Looking up at him, I saw the tears that stained his cheeks as he removed the hoodie from his head. He pulled his dreads from his face and knelt down and held his arms out for Little Daelan to come to him.

"Oh, fuck, Amber," Daelan said as he scooped his son into his arms and came to me. "You hurt?"

"This is your fault, Dae. Your fuckin' fault. Our son could've been killed," I cried, losing more blood.

"Who did this shit to you? Let me get you to the hospital."

"No! Get the fuck away from us! Put him down and get the fuck out! I swear, even if I don't make it, I don't want you coming anywhere near him! Get the fuck out before they come back looking for your ass."

Daelan dropped our son and stood to his feet. He used the back of his hand to dry his tears as he coldly stared down at me.

"Fuck you then, bitch! Not like the nigga is mine anyway. I hope your dumb ass lay there and die for always judging a nigga after the fucked-up shit you did to me!"

"What the fuck are you talking about?" I cried as Daelan ran to me and wrapped his little arms around me. His little body shook, and I did my best to bring him comfort as I ran my hand across his back. I brought my hand to cover my mouth as I began to cough uncontrollably. I had yet to hear any sirens and hoped that they would get there fast. I didn't know how much time I had left, but I felt myself fading away with every minute that ticked by.

"You know what the fuck I'm talking about, Amber. You fucked him. I saw you! And then you gave birth to that nigga's baby and tried to put that shit on me!"

"I've never had sex with anybody but you, Daelan. Why do you do that? Why do you put all your shit back on me when you fuck up?"

"Because you fucked him. You was in his bed, and I saw what you did with him. Don't lie to me, Amber. He looks just like that nigga, and I have to live with that shit every day when I look at him. I think of the shit I seen you do with that man, and every time I look at that little boy, that's all I see. That's why I'm never home. That's why I can't stand to fuckin' touch you or look at you. That's all the fuck I see, and that shit is killing me. It already has, and this is the result of a nigga that's dead inside, man." Daelan cried as he broke down like I had never seen before.

"I don't know what you're talking about," I said as I covered my mouth with my hand again and cried uncontrollably.

"He looks just like my uncle Lee! Admit it! Fuckin' admit it, Amber."

I looked at Little Daelan, and my heart broke into pieces. 'Til this day, I thought that no one knew what happened to me that night when I was left alone at home with Daelan's grandmother and her son, LeeRoy. The boys were taken to visit their father at the jail that morning, and because the drive there was six hours long, they weren't expected to be back until late that night.

I lay on the floor, asleep in my usual spot, when LeeRoy came into the room to wake me up. He told me that Daelan was in his room and that he needed me to come and help him with something. I didn't think anything of it and went to see what was up. As soon as I was in the room and noticed that Daelan wasn't there, LeeRoy had closed the door behind him and blocked me from leaving. I was only fourteen years old at the time and scared to death, and the moment I went to scream, LeeRoy told me that he would kill me, and I believed him. He was a big man, standing over six feet tall and weighing at least 220 pounds.

He asked me to undress, and when I refused to do so, he told me that he was going to hurt Daelan—hurt him again, the way he used to hurt him all the time when he was just a little boy. At first, I didn't know what he was talking about, but when I figured it out, I did what I had to do for Daelan. I took off my clothes and lay down in that bed with that grown-ass man. I allowed him to have his way with me, because as long as it meant that he would never have his way with Daelan again, I did that.

After he was done with me, I left his room, took a shower, and went back to lay on the floor in my usual spot. I cried that night, but not for myself. I cried for Daelan, because I could only imagine the pain he felt after being violated by a man that was supposed to protect him. No one was there for him, but I felt great knowing that I was going to be there for him. I was willing to protect Daelan every chance I got, as long as he wouldn't have to endure no shit like that again. When Daelan came and laid beside me that night, I never mentioned it to him, and he never said anything to me.

The following day, LeeRoy left the house and never returned. Each day that passed, I pushed what happened further and further into the back of my mind. I wanted to forget that it had ever happened. I had never told Daelan that I knew what LeeRoy did to him. It was a part of my life that I thought I had deleted.

Looking at my son, I knew that he looked different, but I just thought that one day he would begin to look like his father. That time with LeeRoy happened one time, and as a child becoming pregnant with a child, I would've never thought this was even possible. I didn't mean to deceive Dae. As much as I loved my son, I would have never brought him into this world if I had known that he was a product of rape from a man that had caused so much misery in the hearts of me and Dae.

"Admit it, Amber!" Dae yelled, breaking me from my thoughts.

"He told me that if I didn't sleep with him that he was going to do it you . . . again," I finally admitted aloud. "I did it for you. I did it to protect you."

"Shut the fuck up! That nigga never touched me! Shut the fuck up! Don't you ever tell nobody no shit like that! He never touched me! You fucked him because you wanted to, you lying, trifling bitch!" Dae yelled as he backed away from me. He shook his head dejectedly before he turned around and ran out of the house.

I shook my head and cried so hard. I guess we had both been ignoring our demons and the source that they had come from for our own selfish reasons. I felt so bad for Daelan, though. I never once considered how much what happened to him affected him, but now that I sat back and thought about everything he'd done, it started to all make sense.

Chapter 23

Daelan

The Next Day . . .

I looked around before I pulled my car to the gas station and pulled up to the pump. I had been hiding out in a motel out by the airport before catching my flight that would leave in the next few hours. I was headed out of the country to muthafuckin' Dubai to lay up and get my got-damn mind right. Wasn't shit nobody could do to help me. This shit was all on me, and I wasn't gonna get right until I accepted some shit and decided that I was gonna stop denying my past. I had fought with it since I was six years old, and no amount of women that I ran through was ever gonna erase what the fuck happened to me. I just wish I hadn't denied it for so fucking long. I had ruined the lives of many because I was always on the path of destruction, tearing down any and everything that ever got in my way.

"Shit!" I sighed and shook my head. All I could think about was the shit that Amber had said to me and how she had allowed herself to go through some ho-ass shit for her nigga. Tears came to my eyes just thinking about how bad I had treated that girl. I had walked all over her, abused her, neglected her for plenty of women, threw the shit in her face most times just to hurt her, and did everything in my power to break her down. I wanted to destroy her because of what I had witnessed that night when I saw my uncle enjoying my girlfriend. She wasn't crying, she wasn't fighting him, or none of that shit! They looked like they was enjoying each other, and that shit fucked me up. I made sure I dropped that nigga in the back of the liquor store for the shit he had done to me years prior, and then, for the shit I saw him doing with my girl. I tried my hardest to move on from it and act like none of it had ever happened, because I really loved Amber, but seeing Little Daelan look more and more like that man turned me into the man I was today.

I wiped the water from my face, and then took in a deep breath. I wanted to check on Amber, but I knew she was right. Going near her could cause her—or even worse, Little Dae—to get hurt, and that would kill me if something happened to them. Even though the kid wasn't mine, I still loved him like he was, and I would never stop loving him. I just had to get myself together so that I could love him and his mother the way they were supposed to be loved. I just hoped that I would have another chance to do so.

I got out to quickly pump my gas so that I could hurry up and make my way to the airport. It didn't take me long to find out that Tamar was the one that had shot up my house like that. Khi had been texting me nonstop, asking me for my location, talking about he was trying to help, but I didn't know who to trust. He said that Taylana was in the hospital and had suffered several broken bones, but she was expected to pull through. She told her brother the moment that she woke up that it was me that had done her like that, and that nigga didn't hesitate to come for me. I didn't wanna pull Khi into my mess like I had already done with Amber, so I didn't want him helping me. Soon as I got to the airport, I was throwing my phone out, and I'd get in touch when I felt it was safe for everybody. I knew that with me gone, Khi could handle it like always. He always cleaned up my mess, and I was sure that this time would be no different.

Khi: Come on, Dae. Bruh, answer me. You got me sick out here looking for you. I heard they got them goonies at the airport looking for you. Where are you, bruh?

"Fuck!" I said to myself after reading Khi's message. I got back inside the car and just sat there for a minute. I looked around and spotted a familiar white BMW pulling up in front of the store. I noticed the tags read: RUE-187. I knew exactly who it was. Yeah, I was about to jack the jack-boy for his ride.

I had just pulled my pistol from the center console and went to open the door when the passenger's side flew open and Cuba's ass stepped up. I chuckled and shook my head. This shit was getting more and more interesting by the moment. Funny, her being with this nigga, but I knew Khi wouldn't find it funny. I grabbed my phone and snapped a few quick pictures of Cuba as she pulled the back door open. I made sure I caught the license plate, too, before I looked down at my phone and quickly forwarded the pictures to Khi.

I pulled my hoodie over my head and was ready to reach for the door again, until a little boy hopped out of the back seat. He jumped up and down and then ran around to back of the car, with Cuba having to chase after him. My whole body froze as I caught a glimpse of his face. He looked so much like my nieces Sklyarr and Chanel, and like how I imagined Little Dae would look like.

Khi: Where the fuck are you at?
Me: I'ma follow this little ho for you and get back to you. Send.

Khi: Man, this heat is getting serious, nigga. Where are you? Fuck her! I'll handle her later. I need to know that my brother is gonna be okay.

I tossed the phone to the passenger's side and figured that I would put my plans on getting out of town on hold. I had some other shit I needed to figure out real quick.

Chapter 24

Cuba

I walked into Tangie's shop and spoke to a few customers as I passed them on my way to my work station. I took a deep breath, ready to take a seat, when it seemed like the entire front glass of the shop came crashing in. My heart seemed to leap out of my chest, and my mouth dropped open. The customers began to scatter around the shop as they did their best to get out of the way of two men that wrestled around on the floor, throwing blows at each other. One of the men was able to get loose and up off the ground. He took his foot and slammed it into the guy's face, and it was then that I recognized who they both were. I backed away and threw my hand over my chest once Khi took his foot and slammed it into the side of Rue's face again.

"Khi!" I screamed once he pulled his gun out and shoved it into Rue's face. I ran to him and grabbed his arm, but he turned around and backhanded me in my face.

"Get the fuck off of me!" he yelled.

My eyes bucked wide, and I jumped back and brought my hand up to my mouth. He stared at me, breathing heavily, with his chest rising and falling hard. I had never seen him so angry before, and it scared the fuck out of me. His eyes grew dark, and I was scared to move or say anything, in fear that he would hit me again. Tears ran from my eyes, and it seemed like it was then that Khi realized what he had done.

"Go get in the car."

I shook my head no, and he tucked his pistol behind his back before he walked over to me. My body began to shake, and I looked around the room and spotted Tangie, Anastasia, and Tameka all looking in my direction. Rue lay on the floor, bleeding, while the rest of the shop cleared out, except for the few that chose to straggle by the door to be nosey.

I brought my eyes back to Khi when he reached for me. I threw my hands up in defense, and he took a step back.

"I'm not gonna hit you. Just go get in the car."

"I'm not going anywhere with you," I told him, and I could see his jaw twitching, something I noticed he did whenever he was angry.

"I need to talk to you, Cuba. Go get in the car like I said."

"No, get away from me!" I screamed. "Get the fuck away from me, or I will call the police on you, Khi!"

Khi nodded his head and turned around. He kicked Rue again, and then left the shop. Anastasia ran to Rue, and I walked over to grab my purse and cell phone from my work station.

"I'm so sorry, Tangie," I told her as I looked around at all the damage Khi and Rue had caused.

"I'm not worried about that, because I know Khi will fix all this shit, but what I am worried about is you. I try not to dip into your business, but you didn't learn anything the last time, Cuba? Khi don't play, okay? He's not a nigga that you wanna mess with."

"I just wanted to see my nephew. I don't even know how he even knew that I was with him. I had Rue meet me at your house, thinking that nobody would see us. We took Little Bryson to a Chuck E. Cheese damn near all the way in Irving, and then I had Rue take me back to your apartment because I had left my damn cell phone there."

"Oh, that's why your ass wanted my key. And how the hell do you leave your cell phone, girl? I'm pretty sure he flipped the fuck out with you not answering your phone. God only knows what was going through that man's head. If you wanna be with Khi, you better figure out another way to see your nephew, because Rue is gonna get you in a world of trouble and end up dead himself."

"You think I'm gonna be with that nigga after what the fuck he just did? Look at my face," I said to Tangie, and she rolled her eyes and walked way.

"I'm just letting you know. Rue is using that little boy to get to you, and Khi knows that shit just like we all do. I wish somebody would hurry up and come get this nigga off my floor, too."

Khi: I'm sorry. Come talk to me please.

I looked down at the message that Khi sent and rolled my eyes. I was done with him. I didn't give a fuck what Rue was doing. If he was trying to use my nephew against me, then that was his dumb ass. It wasn't working, nor would it ever. Rue had his time with me, and he'd fucked it up when I did time for him. The way I looked at it, I was using Rue to get to my nephew. That's all I cared about, and that was what Khi should've understood before he came down there acting an ass.

Khi: Bae, come here . . .

Khi: I'm outside.

I took in a deep breath and headed to the back of the shop, where Tangie had gone inside of her office. I knocked on the door before I walked in. She held her finger up to let me know to give her a second, and I nodded and began to pace the floor. Once Tangie was off the phone, she stood up and walked around to the front of her desk.

"Can I stay at your place tonight?" I asked, and she looked at me like I was crazy.

"What? How you gonna be mad at him for what he did? You don't think—"

"It doesn't matter. I don't give a damn about him beating Rue's ass, but putting his hands on me is another thing. I just need to stay there a couple of nights," I told her and let out a deep breath. I felt better being at her place now that Camp was gone, and I just needed to be somewhere where I could clear my head. I knew I was wrong for lying to Khi again, but shit, he just didn't understand. It had nothing to do with Rue; it was all about my nephew. I would never climb back in bed with a nigga like that. Khi didn't have anything to worry about, and I just wished he had realized that, because he and I would've been real good together.

"Go ahead," Tangie told me with a roll of her eyes.

I quickly hugged her and left out the back of the shop.

Chapter 25

Khian

"'Preciate that, Tangie," I said as I ended the call and slid it into my pocket. I couldn't fucking believe I hit Cuba like that, but she ran upon me in the heat of the moment, and I just reacted. Shit was real live crazy, and Cuba had chosen the wrong time to be running around with that nigga Rue again after I had already warned her the first time. I wasn't even thinking about her ass, to be honest, when Dae sent me that picture of her at the gas station.

My main concern was my brother and trying to find him before Tamar and his goonies did. Since I knew that he was following Cuba based off the pictures he kept snapping and sending to me, I came this way hoping that I would find him in the area. Instead, I saw Cuba and that nigga Rue trying to be on some sneaky shit. Bae had to be careful when it came to shit like that. I knew that nigga was just trying to take advantage of her, being she was in a desperate state of mind, and seeing him with my baby and knowing what he was doing, I just snapped. Still, this shit could've waited. I had planned to take care of Cuba later, after I got my brother safe, not doing the shit right now when I could be out looking for Dae.

I knocked on Tangie's door and waited for Cuba to answer. Tangie told me that Cuba planned to stay at her house that night, and I was finna drag her ass back to the crib with me. I ain't want her over there with too much time to think and convince herself that I was just some fucked-up nigga that liked to hit on women. Cuba was what I needed in my life. I just felt that shit. Being with her was perfect for me, and I could really see myself falling in love with the girl. I wasn't about to let this one mistake destroy us before we really got a chance to see how great we could be together.

"Who is it?" Cuba said from the other side of the door.

"Come on, babe. Open the door. I know you saw it was me out here," I said and tapped on the door a few more times.

KaeDee: This nigga Tamar just left my house looking for your brother. Handle that, because if not, I will.

I looked down at KaeDee's message and slid the phone back into my pocket. My annoyance level was at an all-time high with this nigga KaeDee acting like he couldn't drop his fucking beef with Dae and see that our fuckin' brother needed our help. I ain't have time for that ego bullshit right about now. We were supposed to have each other's back through it all, no matter what the fuck we was going through. I knew this shit was Dae's fault, and it was without a doubt that he fucked up. I was mad as shit that he did and had jeopardized my business and my money in the process, but at the end of the day, he was my brother. He was our brother. I knew whatever the fuck he was struggling with had to be something serious. That nigga had walked out on his girl after she was shot in the back, and I knew my brother wasn't that damn cold. He loved Amber, and I was glad that she didn't die in that bitch the night before 'cause I knew that would've definitely sent him even further over the edge that he was barely hanging onto. I just needed to get to him, wherever he was.

"Cuba, I got shit to handle. Open the door and let's go," I said through gritted teeth.

"I'm staying here, Khi. Leave me alone."

"Cuba . . ." I paused and took a deep breath. I sucked my teeth and stepped back for a second. All this shit going on had me hostile as a muthafucka. My attitude wasn't shit to be fucked with right now. I was gonna have to learn how to tone that shit down when dealing with Cuba. The look in her eyes when I saw how scared she was of me had messed me up. "Babe, open the door. I'm sorry for putting my hands on you. It was a reflex thang. You caught me when I was in the middle of beating that nigga's ass. . . . Cuba, open the door."

"I'm done, Khi. Just leave me alone, okay?"

"Aye, man—"

I pulled my phone out of my pocket as it vibrated again. This time it was Tamar calling me. I pressed the *end* button, slid it in my pocket, and backed away from the door.

"I'ma be back, Cuba. Get that shit out your head, man. I'll be back."

I pulled up to my crib to see six cars posted in front of the gate. I spotted that nigga Tamar sitting on top of a Wraith while puffing on a blunt. He was surrounded by a bunch of his goonies, and they were all holding onto some serious-ass firepower. I patted myself to make sure I still had the hammer, but I knew that it didn't really make a difference. I stepped out of my car and made my way over to where they stood.

"Where your brother at, Khian?" Tamar asked, and I shrugged my shoulders.

"Trying to find him myself."

"You know what he did to my little sister was real fucked up, my nigga. Broke six bones in her fuckin' face. That nigga gotta see me about that. He can't hide forever, and it ain't nowhere he can go that I can't reach him. I'm a global-ass nigga, ya feel me?"

"I hear you," I told him and sucked my teeth.

"Did you know he was fucking with my shorty like that?"

"Nah, I ain't know," I lied.

"A'ight. Bet that. I gotta lot of respect for you, Khian, because I know, like myself, that you about your money. I know you hate for muthafuckas to fuck wit' your paper. You told me that, and I can sense it. Which one means more to you, though? Your brother or that dope, nigga?" Tamar asked and laughed like something was fuckin' funny.

I knew what he was trying to say. He was about to cut me off, and if I didn't have anything to supply the traps with, my goonies would be going elsewhere, and niggas was gonna for sure come through and try to take my territory. I shook my head and placed my hands in my pockets. Tamar's little goon squad got a little antsy at that move and started aiming their weapons in my direction. Shit, one thing about me was that I wasn't a bitch-ass nigga. Guns and niggas with them didn't bother me. I had guns and niggas, too, but I stayed out there by myself. This little whole scenario and them parked out front my house didn't fuckin' bother me. It was a respect type thing more than anything, and the fact that Tamar pulled up at my crib on this Mafia-type shit was disrespectful as fuck.

I understood, though, 'cause the same way he was going hard for his sister, I was gonna go the same way for my brother, right or wrong. I'd be damned if I let another nigga gun him down. If anything was gonna happen to Dae, I was gonna be the muthafucka to do it. Bet not no nigga that wasn't his blood ever lay a hand on him without having to see me about it.

"I'ma find that nigga, but I'll take care of him. You know I can't just hand him over to be killed. If you find him, you find him. And I understand that you gotta do what you gotta do. I mean, 'cause if a nigga was to touch one muthafuckin' hair on my fam, I would do what I have to do, too."

Tamar laughed and jumped down off the Wraith. He came closer to me, and we stood toe-to-toe. He was about the same height as me, maybe an inch taller. He nodded before he sucked his teeth. I could see his veins popping through his neck, so I knew I had pushed a button.

"That's what's up. I can't even do nothing but resp-ect that. My brothers never really did look out for me like that. One of them, anyway . . . but they both gone now. One of them betrayed me, and then the other one, I couldn't even save. I know if I could've, I would have," Tamar said and took a couple of steps back. "He just bet-ter hope that you find him before I do."

Tamar turned around and walked away, and I stood and waited as they all got into their cars and peeled off. As soon as I saw that they were out of sight, I pulled my phone from my pocket and saw that I had missed calls and text messages from Dae. I opened up my text messages app and read the messages that he'd sent to me.

Dae: Damn, I really fucked up this time.

Dae: These niggas is really on me.

Dae: Bruh, I just had to ditch my car. Money, gun, everything. Look out for me, bruh.

Dae: Answer the phone, Khi. Nigga, I'm out here on feet.

Dae: At North Park Mall. Come through for me, bruh.

Dae: Just help me get out of town please. I know I been fucking up. I need you. Love you, bro.

Dae: I don't know why I called KaeDee. I knew he wasn't gonna answer. I'm at North Park Mall if you can make it. I just needed to get to where it was crowded and figure out my next move. Let me know something. Love you, bro.

Me: On my way. Fall the fuck back and stay out of sight. Send.

I got inside of my car, cranked it, and pulled off, heading toward North Park Mall. I really ain't see how I was gonna get Dae out of this situation, but I wasn't gonna give up on the kid. Tamar was known all over and had niggas for days that would put in that work for him, so it was almost impossible that I was gonna get him up out of Texas and somewhere he couldn't be touched, but I was gonna try.

Me: Bruh, meet me at North Park Mall . . . right now! Send.

I shot Tramell a text to meet me at the mall, because I knew that these niggas was following me. Dae needed a car, and I was gonna get Tramell to hand over the keys to his ride, knowing nobody was sitting on his shit. At least, I hoped not.

I sat back in my seat and pushed out a deep breath as I rode through the city as quickly as I could, trying to get to Dae. My thoughts traveled back to Cuba, and all I could hear was her telling me she was done. I respected her for that shit, because a man should never put his hands on a woman, and she was letting a nigga know that she wasn't going to tolerate no bullshit. I made mistakes, though, and Cuba was either gonna ride with me or she wasn't. I had chased her enough, and I wasn't about to keep doing the shit.

Me: Man, when all this shit over and done with, I'ma need a fat-ass nut.

Send

Me: I know I don't really talk to you much about what's going on out here, but it's real, man. I'm stressed out, baby. These niggas trying to kill my brother, and I need to find him, and I'm out here just trying to save him. Somewhere along the lines, we fucked up when bringing him up. Don't nobody else wanna look out for that nigga 'cause he always messing up, but I feel like I have to. Who else gonna do it? That's my brother, you know . . .

Send

Me: I need to be able to come home to you and Skylarr at night. Get them thoughts about being done with me out your head

Send.

After I sent Cuba a few text messages, I pulled up into the parking lot of the North Park Mall and got out of the car. I knew that I was being followed after I seen three of the same cars that was just parked out front at my house pull in and park as well. I had sent Dae a text message, letting him know to meet me in one of the dressing rooms at Neiman Marcus. I had also told Tramell to drop his keys off to the lost and found and let them know that Dae was going to be picking them up.

Heading inside of Neiman Marcus, I looked around at the suits and ties, checking out a few of my favorites before I decided on a three-piece set that was a light blue color. I found an associate and had her point me in the direction of the dressing room. I thanked the lady, and once she left, I made sure I wasn't being watched before I searched the stalls for Dae. I found him with his head resting against the mirror and his eyes closed. He was rocking a hood that hid his dreadlocks and damn near covered his face.

"What's up? You good?" I asked him as I locked the door and stood over him.

"How is Amber and Little Dae?" Daelan asked me, and I nodded.

"They're good. Amber is gonna pull through. Fucked up you left her hanging like that."

"My bad," was all he said, and I shook my head.

I pulled a few bands of money from the inside of my jacket and dropped them in Dae's lap. I then took my pistol and handed it over to him.

"'Preciate it."

"Them niggas is around. Tamar just left my house looking for your ass, and they followed me here. I need you to do your best, though, to get the fuck out of dodge."

"Where's Cuba?"

"She's at Tangie's. Why?" I frowned.

"You trust her?"

"I'm still getting to know her, but I'm hoping that I will be able to grow to trust her."

"I think I have a son. My son."

"What the fuck is you talking about?"

"I'm tired, bro. My mind has been going nonstop since I've been six years old, and I just can't seem to slow it down. I'm so fucking tired," Dae said, and I sighed.

"I wish you had talked to me and told me what's going on with you. I know something is up."

"Something has been up since forever, but niggas just now trying to take the time to notice, so I'm good now."

Dae stood up and was face-to-face with me. I pulled him in for a hug, and he let out a deep sigh. Part of me wished that I could take on his struggles and live that shit out for him so he didn't have to. My brothers meant the world to me, and seeing any of them in fucked-up situations did something to a nigga.

"I love you, bro," I told him, and he nodded.

"I know. I'm sorry," he said as he broke down crying.

Chapter 26

Daelan

I waited and waited in the dressing room after Khi left, until I knew the sun had gone down, before trying to get out and leave. I had gotten jammed up earlier that day after trying to take a piss at a gas station. My dumb ass was so fuckin' tired and out of it that I left my money and my pistol, thinking because I wasn't gonna be gone long that everything would be good. I came out to find a few of the goonies that be rocking with Tamar sniffing around my car like some damn animals. I ended up hopping over a gate that was behind the gas station and running until I was blocks away. It took me to walk a few more blocks before I was able to find a bus stop that took me to the mall.

I didn't know where I was going to end up, but there was something that I had to do before I figured it out. I couldn't get that little boy that I had seen with Cuba out of my mind. I had thought about him all night and had even followed Rue and Cuba out to a nice little neighborhood in Oak Cliff, where they dropped him off. I didn't know what the fuck Rue was doing with that little boy, but I knew I wasn't crazy. I knew what I felt in my heart for him, and I had never even met him. It was what I tried for years to feel with Little Daelan, but I could never get that type of connection with him. I knew I would never be able to move on and leave without figuring this shit out. I had to see if that little boy belonged to me.

I tapped on the door where I had seen Rue take Cuba to, and I placed my hand over the peephole. I could hear light footsteps from the inside, and then, I heard the blinds moving in the window. I kept my head down, knowing that if she knew it was me, she wasn't going to open the door.

"Who is it?" she asked.

"Ma'am, was this your ID sitting out here on the ground? It was sitting in front of your door," I said, doing my best to disguise my voice. "It says Cuba. . . . It's so dark out here I can't even see the last name."

It took a few long-ass seconds, and I was thinking I was just gonna have to kick this bitch down to get the answers I needed, but the locks unlatched, and the door cracked open. Soon as Cuba looked me in the face, she tried to close the door, but I pushed it back and maneuvered my way inside. She backed away from me as I closed and locked the door behind me.

"You can't tell me that it's a coincidence that you just start talking to my brother. What, you come thinking you was gonna use him to get back at me or something?" I asked her.

She stared up at me before her eyes began to wander around the room. "I don't know what the fuck you talking about, Dae. You need to leave. Tangie will be here any minute. She just went out to get food."

"I don't give a damn about no Tangie, and you know what the fuck I'm talking about. You was there that night! Don't fuckin' lie to me! You using my brother to get to me! You trying to pay me back for killing your trifling-ass sister that night, huh? What the fuck was you gonna do, rat me out to the police, kill me? What the fuck was you gonna do? What, you and that nigga Rue plotting on some payback-type shit or something? Everything that happened to Alaska that night, that bitch deserved it. I knew I should've killed your ass too," I yelled.

Cuba's eyes bucked as tears began to fall down her face. "You did that to her?" she asked as she broke down.

I was beginning to wonder if she really didn't know who the fuck I was. The shock that displayed on her face was evident, and I didn't give a damn; there wasn't an actor alive that could act out the way she was reacting to what I'd just said. That shit was real. Shorty had real live tears. I scratched my head and sighed. I leaned back against the front door and pulled a blunt from behind my ear and lit it up.

Alaska, Alaska, I thought.

"Is the kid mine?"

"What?" Cuba's head popped up, and she looked at me as if it was the first time seeing me. She shook her head and covered her mouth. "You was the one she kept trying to tell me about. It was your baby?"

"How? She told me she was pregnant the same day I killed that bitch. How the fuck was she able to give birth to my seed?"

"How could you do that shit to her if you knew she was carrying your baby? Why would you take my sister away from me? Alaska didn't die that night! She didn't die until months later, after she gave birth to Bryson Jr. Why would you do that to her?"

"The fuck you mean Bryson Jr.? She named my kid after that fuck nigga? After the nigga she told me was beating her ass and that she needed my help to get away from him? Had me really believing that she loved a nigga when the whole time, that bitch was setting me up to be robbed. I was gonna let her make it that night, too. I figured she was a rider for her nigga, and I couldn't do shit but respect that shit. I had a bitch at home and couldn't even be mad that I got played by that ho, but it really fucked me up to see that ho crying over that nigga like that, 'cause that manipulating-ass ho really had me thinking that she was in love with me. Told my goonies that I couldn't leave without putting them hollow points in her head. I wanted her to feel my pain." I chuckled.

"Something is really wrong with you," Cuba said as she took off running to the back of the apartment. I chased after her, but she was able to close the door to the bedroom and lock it before I could get to her. I pushed on the door a little before taking my shoulder and popping it open.

"Your brother is here—" she was able to get out before I snatched the phone from her.

I punched her in the face and sent her flying across the bed.

"What the fuck you go and do that shit for? I wasn't even gonna hurt you! All I wanted to know is if that was my kid, and you gotta go call my brother and put him in this shit!"

"Get away from me, Dae," Cuba cried as blood shot from her nose. "I don't know whose baby it is. Alaska never got the chance to tell me, because you killed her! I didn't see my nephew until three years later when I got out of jail because of the mess you all created. I don't know shit about what my sister was doing and who she was doing it with. All I know is that she didn't have to die. . . . You didn't have to do her like that. And what if he is your son? You could've killed him too!"

"Take me to see my son," I told her and reached over and grabbed her by the hair. I turned around, ready to walk out of the room when I was punched in the face. I pointed my gun and tried to pull the trigger, but it was knocked out of my hand right before a bullet went smashing into the wall. I backed up and noticed that it was Khian. He wrapped his hands around my throat and squeezed.

Looking into his eyes, I could see that he was really fed up with me. I should've just left, but damn.

Alaska, Alaska, I thought as I felt myself slipping out of consciousness.

She was a vulture for real. I had just turned eighteen years old when I'd met her, and I finally thought I'd met the one that could make me leave Amber. Alaska had me doing any and everything she asked. I was wrapped around her finger, always taking her shopping and buying her expensive-ass gifts, knowing damn well my pockets wasn't sitting like that just yet.

We were always laid up in some hotel, sucking and fucking on each other until we would just pass out. It was too many times when I would sit up on the phone with this chick for hours at a fuckin' time, man, just talking about our future together. I knew she had her little situation with a nigga, but I just didn't know who he was. She also knew I had a little situation with Amber, but the love and chemistry between us was undeniable. We always talked about making shit official and leaving what we had at home to be together.

So many times, Alaska claimed to be getting her ass beat and needing a place to run to, and I would always be there. I had seen the bruises on various parts of her body and had never had a reason not to believe her, until Bryson and Rue kicked in the door to the Telly, stuck a gun in my face, and Alaska handed them the keychain to my car that held two keys I was supposed to have dropped off hours earlier.

I was sick as fuck, knowing my brother was gonna have a fit about that loss. I called up the goonies, Tramell and a nigga named Anston, and we bled every block, looking for them niggas. Word was they had the nerve to stop by the fair like they hadn't just been on no jackboy shit and riding around with them birds. We waited for their asses, rode them all the way through the South, until we felt like it was the perfect time to pop them. Shit went crazy so fast that I didn't even get a chance to get my shit back, and I still took an L that night. Me and Amber suffered for three months straight after I had to take every bit of what I saved to replace them bricks.

Alaska, Alaska, I thought again. She was love, even if it hadn't been real. She'd given me a son, and it was fucked up that I would never even get a chance to meet him. When I looked back up at my brother, I didn't see shit. I knew, then, that I was past the point of no return.

Chapter 27

Cuba

Six Weeks Later . . .

"Hmmm," I yawned as I rolled over onto my side. I looked at the digital clock next to the bed to see that it was only three in the morning. I had been asleep since around eight o'clock p.m. the previous day. I threw the blanket from my body when Khian grabbed me from behind and pulled me close to him. He kissed on my ear and then rubbed his hand between my legs.

"Where you think you going?" he asked as he turned me over onto my back and climbed on top of me.

"Khi, no. I don't think I can take anymore. Shit, we been going at it since four o'clock yesterday afternoon."

"So, who's keeping up with the time and shit?" Khian joked as he slid himself inside of me.

"I am, nigga, since I'm the one with the sore pussy. Damn, let a bitch breathe," I said as Khian slowly stroked in and out of me. I felt myself about to come already, and I threw my head back. "Shit."

"Why you about to come if you so tired?" Khian asked, and I closed my eyes and held my breath. "You should have never tried to take my pussy away, and now I can't get enough of it."

"But we been going at it . . . nonstop for two weeks, babe. I'm not going anywhere," I moaned and wrapped my arms around Khi.

I had done everything I could to fight this man off, but every minute of the day that I was without him, I found myself having a thought about him. That day at the shop where he hit me, and then finding out that his brother was responsible for killing Alaska, had really put me in a shell where I didn't want to be bothered with anyone. I wanted to blame Khian as more of a reason to stay away from him. I kept telling myself that it was no way possible that he didn't know about what Dae had done and that he was probably one of the ones that was in the car, but I knew that wasn't true.

Khian had been nonstop with flowers, gifts, showing up to the shop and Tangie's all the time, and even dropping a set of keys to a new BMW in my lap just to get me to come back to him. I had held out for as long as I could, but I just couldn't take it anymore. We had so much fun when we were together, whether it was just joking around and kicking back on some food and drinks, taking Skylarr out, or just on some Netflix-and-chill-type shit. I couldn't quite deter what I felt for Khi just yet, but I knew that what I was feeling for him was something I had never experienced before, not even with Rue. It was like a part of me knew that he would one day be my husband and that we were gonna spend a lifetime together.

I had really hoped so, too, because I found out that I was pregnant about a week ago with Khi's baby, and I didn't even know how to tell him. Every time I thought it was a good time, something would always pop up, making me have to hold off until the next time. His family life was still in an uproar, and Dae was still out there causing problems.

The night Dae confessed to me that he had killed Alaska and that Bryson Jr. may be his, Khi had almost killed his brother, but he had only choked him long enough for him to pass out. He had Tramell and a few other guys come through, and they were able to get Dae out of town safely. But Dae could never leave well enough alone.

After him being gone for three weeks, Khi found out that Tamar's sister ended up leaving and that she was somewhere hiding out with Dae. Tamar was looking high and low for his sister, and Khi for his brother. Business was never the same for Khi, and I could tell that he had finally, finally reached his breaking point with Daelan. I heard him telling someone over the phone that as soon as he got a location on Daelan, he was going to put an end to everything once and for all, like he should've done a long time ago. I didn't know what that meant, but I knew, whatever it was, it wasn't going to be good for Dae. I could tell that the shit was really stressing Khi out, and I just didn't want to be the one that added to it. For now, my news could wait until it was the right time.

"Is there a time limit on when you can fall in love?" I asked Khian after we finished having another round of passion-filled sex. I was laid out on his chest, and he was lighting up a blunt as usual after sex. He said the high he felt after busting a nut, combined with some good hay, had him feeling like all life's problems had been solved, even if only for a minute.

"Shit, I don't know. Why you ask that?" Khi asked, placing the blunt to the tip of his lips.

"Just wondering if what I feel for you is what I believe it to be."

"What you saying? You love a nigga?" Khi asked.

I shrugged my shoulders. "I feel like I'm living in one of those urban fiction books. Rich dope boy saves poor girl, they fall in love within two weeks, have a bunch of babies, baby mama drama, and a bunch of other shit I be reading about all the time."

Khi chuckled. "Yeah, your ass reads all the fuckin' time, but ain't shit wrong with that. And ain't nothing wrong with falling in love quick. If you feel it, you feel it. It's nothing that you can stop. Look how long you avoided me before you finally let a nigga in. Stop doing that shit and just live, babe. And as far as us having a bunch of babies, that's gonna happen for sure. I want us to be married first, though. I don't want what we got to be ruined because we rushed into anything. I know what I feel for you is real, but I'm just trying to learn from past mistakes. I just want us to take our time and let this shit flow. You know."

"Yeah . . . I understand," I said and sighed.

"You good?"

"Yeah, I'm okay. Just got a lot on my mind, that's all."

"You just need some rest. I guess I'll leave you alone and let you sleep. Get you some rest," Khi said and climbed out of bed. "I got something I want you to see in the morning."

"You leaving?" I asked, and he shook his head.

He walked to his closet and grabbed something to wear before walking back and standing next to the bed. "You know I don't talk too much about this dope shit, but I just gotta keep grinding. Just trying to keep my shit going. I worked too hard to let it go. I just feel like I can't sleep. Soon as I even allow myself to close my eyes, I'm back up feeling I'm getting too comfortable. I gotta keep going."

"Okay," was all I said before I rolled over onto my side.

"What's up? Talk to me," Khi said as he climbed onto the bed and turned me onto my back.

I looked up into his hazel eyes and rubbed my hand across the side of his face. "I'm good. Just tired. You just be careful and come back home to us," I told him absentmindedly, speaking of our unborn child.

"I'll be back. I got something I want both you and Sky to see," Khian said, and I nodded as he walked off and headed to the shower.

Morning had rolled around quick after Khian left the house that night, and he hadn't been back since. I had gotten up around nine to fix Skylarr and I some breakfast, but the smell of the eggs and sausage had me huddled over the toilet for the past few hours. I had whipped up something quick for Skylarr and put a movie in while I laid out on the couch, hardly able to keep my eyes open. I didn't know how much longer I was going to be able to hide this pregnancy from Khi, because with each passing day, I'd become sicker and sicker.

After the talk we'd had the night before, I wasn't even sure if I wanted to keep my baby. This was my first child, and I refused to carry a baby for a man that didn't want it. I wasn't one of those type of chicks that felt like a baby would keep a man around, and I didn't have a problem with taking care of it until I felt the time was right. But I won't lie and say that it didn't make me feel bad. I agreed with Khian that we should be married and more stable in our relationship, but it wasn't like I had planned this pregnancy. Coming home from prison, the only thing on my mind was working and getting on my feet. I had sworn off men, making them the last thing on my mind, which meant that birth control was not something I thought about either. I should've been more careful, though, and should've run to the clinic after having sex with Khian the first time. I was careless, and now I was here.

"Daddy," Skylarr said once the door chimed, alerting us that someone had come in. I sat up on the couch and yawned. I then brought my hand up to my head, feeling dizzy and like I had to throw up again. I decided to lay back down because my skin felt so clammy and just hot to touch.

"Mama!" I heard Skylarr say, and I was ready to answer her, until I spotted Khi's baby mama standing a few feet away. For some reason, I started to feel a whole lot of damn jealousy. Skylarr had been up under me ever since I first started my little "job" for Khi, and I had developed a relationship with her. She had started calling me Mama, and I felt like she was my daughter. I remembered the last time when we found Briana half-dead and waiting for Khi outside of his gate. I had felt a way about her returning then. I hated to admit it, but I was happy when we came back and saw that she had disappeared. I saw the love he had in his eyes for that girl, and it scared me to think that she could take something from me that I had just begun to get to know and love.

I sat up on the couch slowly and folded my arms across my chest. I watched her hugging all on Skylarr and was hoping that my dismay wasn't evident on my face. It didn't matter, though, because when Khi showed his face, my face lit up and tears instantly sprang from my eyes.

"Oh my God. Where did you get him from?" I squealed as I stood up to my feet on wobbly legs.

"I got him from your parents," Khi said like it was nothing.

"My parents?" I questioned in disbelief. "They let you take him?"

"Hell, yeah. The fuck you mean? Didn't you tell me that this little nigga was probably Dae's? Shit, I had him tested against some shit Dae had lying around his house, and yeah, he's a Prince. I wasn't about to be letting Rue's punk ass raise nothing with my blood in it. I'm gonna take care of him, and your parents can't do shit about it. They know they ain't trying to see me in court, so we worked some shit out. Here," Khi said and handed Little

Bryson to me. "Briana, go take your stuff and put it up. I got some shit that I gotta handle, but I'll be back in a while."

I looked over at Briana, and for the first time, I noticed the two bags that sat at her feet. I bit down on my bottom lip as I watched her retrieve them and walk away with Skylarr trailing behind her.

"She's staying here?" I asked Khi, and he nodded his head.

"Just for a little while. Why? Is it a problem?"

"Wish you would have told me. I could've stayed at Tangie's." I told him.

He sighed as he looked down at me. He sucked his teeth and touched my face with his hand. "I don't want her, a'ight? What me and her had is over with, and it has been for a while. But I just wanna make sure she's good before I let her get away again. She just got out of rehab, and I just want to watch her for a bit. That's all. You ain't got nothing to worry about." Khi leaned over and kissed me on my lips. "What day was that you said your sister got killed?"

"October third, two thousand nine. Why?"

"Just asking. Go lay down. You seem like you coming down with the flu or something. Put his big ass down and let him and Skylarr play. They got a lot of catching up to do," Khi said as he headed to leave.

"See you later, Khi," Briana said, causing me to look over my shoulder at her as she stood there with a big-ass smirk on her face. I tried not to roll my eyes, but I wasn't feeling this shit at all.

Chapter 28

Deonna

"Chanel, go get your backpack so that we can go. I swear, if you be late for school again, you gonna have them people at that school and your daddy after me," I yelled as I went to open the refrigerator to grab some fruit for the two lunch bags that sat on the counter.

"Damn right. Women always late for shit, even school that's only five minutes away," KaeDee said as he popped me on my ass and kissed me on the tip of my earlobe.

"Shut up," I laughed.

"Shit, it's true." KaeDee opened the refrigerator and pulled out a bottle of his favorite juice, Naked. He twisted the cap off and leaned against the island as he looked down at me. I smiled and continued to fill up the bags.

"What?" I said to him.

"You look good pregnant."

"Thank you, Mr. Prince. You wear it well, too. This must be our boy."

"I really hope so. Shit."

"How are you feeling?" I asked him, noticing that he was little down.

"Just wish I wasn't so hard on Dae after what you told me that Amber said."

I sighed, thinking back to the conversation I'd had with Amber a few weeks ago after she'd gotten out of the hospital. She and Little Daelan had come here upon her release, and I had assisted the home health nurses with her care. She was paralyzed from the waist down and required around-the-clock care, so KaeDee and Khi made sure she got the top-of-the-line doctors, nurses, and therapists caring for her. I would sit with her for a couple of hours in the afternoon after work, and one evening she just broke down. She waited and waited for Daelan to contact her after he got settled, but he never did, and after finding out that he may be hiding out with the girl that was partly responsible for her condition, it had really broken her spirits.

She told me everything that had happened with the boys' uncle LeeRoy, and how she had unknowingly gotten pregnant by him. That was the reason Daelan hated her so much. I thought that had been the worst of it, until she told me that she did it so that LeeRoy wouldn't rape Dae again. Amber begged me not to tell anyone, but secrets between my husband and me were a thing of the past. Plus, I felt like he needed to know what happened to his brother and the reasons for his troubles. I made KaeDee promise me that he wouldn't tell Khi or anyone else, but I could see that holding it in for all this time was eating at him. He felt guilty that he had turned his back on him when Khi had been begging him to help with Dae. Now, he and Khi were barely talking, and their whole business was hanging by the wayside.

"Maybe you should go ahead and tell Khi. I know that I said not to, but I think that Amber would understand if she knew that you all just want to help Dae."

"Tell Khi so that he can rub it in my face about how right he was about something going on with Dae?"

"He's not going to throw it in your face, baby. Everyone handles their anger differently, and Khi knows that you're just a stubborn asshole sometimes."

"Damn, it's like that?" KaeDee laughed.

"Go talk to him. Don't let too much time go by, and definitely don't let this small little beef you have boil over like it did with Dae. You gotta be the bigger man sometimes, and I know that you can definitely be the bigger man after what you did for me."

"What you mean what I did for you?"

"You—" I turned to around to face him. I shook my head as tears fell from my eyes. I had done my husband so wrong, and he had forgiven me and given me a clean slate and loved me like it had never happened. I was so foolish to think that there was something better out there than the man that I had spent the last four years of my life with. I didn't deserve him. I didn't deserve to wake up next to him every morning, and I damn sure didn't deserve to be able to be wearing his ring on my finger, carrying his last name, and carrying what I knew would be our little son. If anyone knew my husband, then they would know that he wasn't much of a forgiving person, so for him to forgive me for the way that I had damn near ruined our family said a lot. I would spend the rest of my life making it up to him. "You gave me another chance at life. I don't know where I would be if you wouldn't have forgiven me, and I know I've said it before, KaeDee, but I am so sorry for the way I did you. I am so sorry. I don't know what—"

"Babe," KaeDee said as he stood in my space. He lifted my chin and forced me to look at him. "I don't want you apologizing for that shit anymore. I just want you to make sure that nothing like that ever happens again, because I know—"

"It never will. You don't even have to think about that, because it will never ever happen again. I know what I have in you, and I love my family. I will never ever do anything to jeopardize what we have again."

"Then stop worrying. We're gonna be fine," KaeDee told me as he dried my tears and wrapped his arms around me.

"I'm ready now," Chanel said from behind me. I turned around to look at her and laughed at what she'd decided to wear that day. She was tacky as shit, but KaeDee and I agreed that we would start letting her dress herself. She was only three years old, so I didn't expect much, but it was pretty bad. She was rocking a pair of pink leggings, a gold bodysuit that had different-colored teddy bears, and she had strapped the bodysuit on the outside instead of the inside. I was guessing she couldn't decide on which of her favorite boots to wear, because she wore one of each, a green one and a brown one.

"She get that shit from you," KaeDee said, and I looked up at him and frowned. "Shit, you know we stay fly in my family. Ain't no way in hell she learned that type of style from me. That's all you."

"Whatever. My little baby looks cute," I said and fastened her bodysuit the right way.

"Daelan!" KaeDee called out before kissing Chanel and then kissing me goodbye. "I'll see you at the office. Hurry the hell up."

"Okay, see you soon. Babe," I called after him.

"Yeah." He turned around to face me.

"I love you."

"Yeah, show me how much when you get to the office," KaeDee said as he again turned around to leave.

I made sure that I had everything before I gave Daelan and Chanel their lunch bags. We headed to the garage, and I strapped them inside and left as quickly as I could. Daelan had been transferred to the same school that Chanel attended for Head Start to make it easier on me each morning when I dropped them off. The school was only five minutes from our house and about twenty minutes from the firm.

Each morning, I had to get out of the car to walk Chanel in, because they required that parents sign them in and out for the day. I said goodbye to Daelan, and he took off running in the direction of his class. He didn't say much these days, and I hoped that everything that had happened over the past couple of months hadn't traumatized him too much. He went from watching his daddy beat on his mom to her being shot while trying to protect him, and now his mom barely being able to care for him. KaeDee and I tried to show him as much love as we could by showering him with affection, and shamefully, even gifts, but not much would put a smile on his face. He often asked about his father and when he would be home, but KaeDee would always tell him soon.

After signing in Chanel, I walked out of the school and headed in the direction of my car, which was parked in the lot across the street. I waited for the cars to pass and jogged at the first chance I got. Pulling my keys from my pocket, I got inside and closed the car door behind me. Sticking the key in the ignition, I cranked the car and went to place the car in drive, but I was grabbed from behind.

"Babe, what's up?" I heard Tyrin say. I glanced at him through my rearview mirror as he held his hand over my mouth to keep me from screaming. "How you been?"

I nodded my head, unable to speak, and I could hear him sighing behind me. I hadn't heard from Tyrin in almost two months, since I told him that I was going to work things out with my husband. Even after I told him and he went up to the firm to confront KaeDee, he had still continued to harass me. He was constantly calling my cell from different numbers, until I had finally gotten it changed. He would send flowers to the firm, along with a note attached that always ended up being a threat to KaeDee. I was scared as shit knowing that Tyrin's ass was crazy, until he just went away and all the harassment had stopped.

"Can't believe you left me again like that, Deonna. Then you got these niggas thinking they bossing up on a nigga and shit. Your punk-ass husband and his brother sent them goonies my way, thinking that shit was gonna scare me. I got hit a couple of times, and I'm fine. Niggas couldn't even kill me, but they killed a few of my partnas, and they didn't have to do that to my fam like that. I want revenge, and I won't stop until I feel better," Tyrin said.

All this was news to my ears. KaeDee had never mentioned that, but I wasn't surprised. I had warned Tyrin to leave him alone, but he wouldn't, and this was what happened when you fucked with the Prince brothers.

"They gotta pay for that shit." Tyrin removed his hand from my mouth finally, and I let out a deep breath.

Shit, I thought as I turned to look at him just as he shoved a pistol in my face. I couldn't even open my mouth to say anything before he pulled the trigger, taking the life that I had just gotten back.

Chapter 29

KaeDee

"Mr. Prince, I just thought you should know that the news was reported that Chanel's school and a few other buildings in the area were closed due to someone reporting gunshots in the area," my secretary Lisa said as she stepped into my office.

"Damn, have you heard from Deonna? She should've been here by now, and she's not answering the phone."

"No, sir. She had a nine o'clock appointment that I ended up having to reschedule."

"A'ight, cool. Thank you. Call the school and make sure everything is okay with Chanel and Daelan. Keep calling until you get confirmation."

"Yes, sir."

She closed my door, and I pulled out my cell phone to call Deonna again. It took a lot in me to forgive my wife after fucking off with that nigga, Tyrin, but after that nigga stormed into my office that day, I realized that I had something that another nigga wanted badly. That shit did wonders for my already crushed ego, but it made me realize that I had a treasure in Deonna. We all make mistakes, and I forgave her, because I was far from a perfect man. I had stepped out on Deonna a few times when she was in D.C. and I was in Dallas waiting for her to move. She didn't know anything about it, and it wasn't no emotional cheating either. I fucked a few bitches and left them alone, but see, women couldn't do that. They associate sex with love, which is why a man can never take it when a woman does him the same way he's done her. Deonna's affair fucked me up, but for the sake of the love I had for her and the daughter we shared together, I swallowed my pride and got my wife back.

Things had been dope as fuck, too. I felt like I had to go ten times harder in the bedroom, and I guess she felt the same way, because we'd been having some of the greatest sex imaginable. Not only that,but we were back to the nights where we stayed up talking and laughing, just doing shit to enjoy each other's company. Things were rocky as hell, but if what happened was what it took to have forever, then I was all for it. I knew that Deonna was the one that I wanted to spend the rest of my life with. That was why I had married her.

"Mr. Prince, I finally got through, and the kids are okay. They also lifted the lockdown after not finding anything suspicious in the area," Lisa said, snapping me out of my thoughts.

I looked up and realized that another hour had gone by. I had been sitting there staring out of the window at the view and waiting for Deonna to show her ass up. It never failed. There was hardly ever a day that went by that she wasn't late, but she had never been this late, and never without calling. I was beginning to worry . . . and wonder if she was out doing something she had no business doing.

I decided to try to call her again, and when she didn't answer, I pulled up the Find my iPhone app and typed in my password. I waited for what felt like forever as it located her device. I recognized the streets that surrounded where it was picking up, but not necessarily the exact address. I walked over to the computer and sat behind my desk. I typed in the address that showed up on the screen, and Chanel's school popped up.

My forehead wrinkled in confusion as I hopped up, grabbed my keys and my phone, and headed out of the office. I stopped by Lisa's desk and told her that I was thinking—that Deonna was probably stuck at the school and was unable to answer her phone. Once I made it to the parking garage and got inside of my car, I dialed Deonna's number again, but I still didn't get an answer.

I drove out of the garage and headed toward Chanel's school. I was thinking about calling up Khi and sitting down with him to talk about what Deonna had told me. I did need to swallow my pride on that one and let Khi know that he was right. Our brother did need our help, and somehow, we had failed him. I thought back to the many times when this shit could've happened and realized that it was plenty of times that Uncle LeeRoy could've violated Dae in the way that was being said. Our mama and daddy would drop us off plenty of times with our grandmother for her to babysit while they ran the streets. LeeRoy's ass had always been a drunk and had never really worked a job long enough to amount to shit. He had stayed with his mama damn near forever, and I had never heard her bitch one word about it.

When our father got locked up and we moved in, he was always there and always getting drunk. He would sit out on the porch with us some nights, smoking weed and shit like that, and now that I really thought about it, he was a quiet, weird-ass nigga. I never knew why somebody wanted to kill him when they found him in the alley of the liquor store, because he never bothered nobody, but now I knew that shit all fell back on Dae.

I couldn't help but wonder about the li'l one, our youngest, Emon. I didn't give a fuck how he felt about it. I was asking Emon on my next visit to see him. I needed to know if anything had happened to him as well.

As soon as I turned down the street where Chanel's school was, my phone vibrated in my lap, and I quickly scooped it up, thinking it was Deonna. I noticed it was an unknown number. Hesitantly, I answered, because I didn't know if it could be Deonna calling because something had happened to her phone.

"Hello," I said.

"Aye." It was Dae. "That nigga set me up, man!"

"Who set you up?"

"Your bitch-ass brother. That ho poisoned a nigga, bruh. Man, twelve all around my front door, and I swear, nigga, I'm on some suicide-type shit right now," Dae cried. "My brother did that shit. I know he did, KaeDee. Call him, man. Call him. He won't even answer for a nigga, 'cause he know what he did."

"What the hell is you talking about, Dae, and where are you? We've been waiting on you to get in contact. Nigga, you got that girl with you? Is she straight?" I questioned as I pulled up to Chanel's school and parked out front. I got out of the car and looked around, but I didn't see Deonna's car.

"Man, the girl carrying my seed, and I called to check up on her and tell her I was sorry for how I did her. I felt bad for fucking her up like that, and shit, I thought about the last bitch that led me on the way I led her on, and I knew exactly why she was acting the way she was. I had to reach out. She begged me to come down here where I was at, and we cool. She good. I promise, I'm taking care of her. But look, man, tell Khi I'm sorry, man. Tell him to call these dogs off. I promise I'm getting my life together. I can't be a part of no chain gang, man. I'm scared of that shit, man," Dae cried, and I sighed.

"Look, they probably there because they trying to get ol' girl and send her back home. Just calm down and see what they want," I told him.

I could hear him breathing heavily over the phone as I looked across the street to the lot that was used for the school's parking overflow. I spotted Deonna's BMW still parked in the lot and made my way across the street as soon as a few cars had passed.

"Nah, I sent her out there already, because I didn't want her getting hurt. They here 'cause that bitch got in Khi's head and told them that I murdered her sister Alaska. They out there yelling for me to come out and be arrested for that shit or they coming in. I ain't going out like that, nigga. I can't let them take me in, KaeDee! Just tell Khi even though he chose that bitch over me, I love him. And tell Emon and Cass I love them too. And, KaeDee—"

"Come on, Dae, don't be like—" I froze when I spotted Deonna slouched over in her car.

Boom! Boom! Boom!

I could hear the loud banging through the speaker of the phone, but it fell from my hand and shattered against the pavement as I took off running and pulled Deonna's car door open. A gun rested in her hand, and there was a hole in the side of her head.

"Oh, fuck!" I cried as I pulled her out of the car. "Deonna, Deonna, why would you do this, baby? I forgave you! I forgave you, ma."

I carried Deonna's limp body in my arms as I walked through the parking lot and headed back to my car. People started appearing from different directions and trying to help me, but I just wanted to get her in the car and get her to the hospital. I didn't understand this shit. I had told her that morning that she didn't have to worry about nothing, and she told me she loved me. Why would she do this? Why would she kill herself knowing we have a daughter and she was carrying my seed? Something wasn't right, and I refused to believe that this was what she resorted to. She just thanked me for giving her her life back, so why would she take it from me?

Chapter 30

Khian

"Tell that nigga Tamar to get at me, man, for real. I did my part; now I need him to fuck with me," I said desperately into the phone.

"He ain't trying to hear that. The nigga ain't dead, so for him, you ain't did shit," Tamar's goonie Black said, and I sucked my teeth. "He knows your brother is a lawyer, and y'all ain't gonna do nothing but defend that nigga and he'll be home."

"Bruh, I just snitched on my li'l youngin', nigga. I turned that nigga in for murder, and that nigga Tamar's sister should be home in a day or two, and you telling me that's still not enough for this dude? He should've fuckin' found him then! I wasn't about to pop my brother for him. Fuck I look like?"

"But, nigga, who the fuck you yelling at, though?" Black said.

I pulled the phone away from my ear and tapped the end button. I punched my fist into the steering wheel and gritted down on my teeth. I had dug up everything I could on Cuba's sister Alaska and her boyfriend Bryson's murder after verifying the date it happened with Cuba. I knew, after finding out that Dae had Taylana with him, that nigga was never going to change, and I wasn't about to keep putting myself out there. I didn't have it in me to put a bullet in the nigga, but shit, after the way I was feeling right now, if that nigga was there in front of me, I would empty the clip in his ass. Ho-ass nigga.

I ain't know what the fuck I was gonna do about this dope shit, because didn't nobody have that fish scale like Tamar, and I refused to go through some low-level niggas just so they could tax my ass. I just had to tough this shit out and wait for that nigga to come around.

"You couldn't get your ass out to greet a nigga?" my big bro Cassidy said as he opened the driver's side door.

I had been so deep in my thoughts that I halfway forgot that I was out there waiting for this nigga. I stepped out of the car and slapped hands with him twice before he pulled me into a hug. It had been a few months since I had been down there to see him, because I knew he would be coming home soon anyway. Since then, either I had gotten small, or that nigga had gotten big as fuck. Either way, I was happy to see my brother finally standing on the other side of them walls.

"Bruh, what the fuck you been in this bitch doing? Man, it ain't been that long since I been down here," I told him as I looked him up at down. Cassidy was about six foot two, looking like he weighed at least 240 pounds. He had the same skin tone as the rest of us, but Cassidy had some weird-ass eyes—one dark brown, and the other a light hazel brown. He had been born that way, and Mama always said he was the special one because of it. He had some long-ass hair that he mostly kept wild and unkempt, but them hoes loved his dog ass.

"What, nigga? I had to beef up for these hoes. It's been four years since I had some pussy, and I had to make sure my stamina was up. No more FiFis, nigga," Cassidy said as he dropped a ball into my hand that looked like rubber gloves that had been blown up and tied together.

He walked around to the other side of the car to get in, and I stared down at it, with my face suddenly turning into a frown. I looked across the hood of the Mazi at him. "Cass, what's a FiFi?" I asked him, and he laughed.

"That's my bitch Jessica. I ain't been fucking her that long now. Probably about two weeks now," he said.

Once I realized what he was saying, I dropped the shit out of my hands and kicked it across the ground. I wiped my hands across my shirt before I pulled it over my head and tossed it at Cassidy.

"Ho-ass nigga. I see your ass ain't changed, you bitch."

I shook my head, got in the car, and cranked it up. Pulling away from the jail, I wished this would be the last time I would have to see that place, but Emon was still there for another year, and it was about to be Dae's home. He had been hiding out in Colorado with that damn girl, but I knew that as soon as they got his ass, they were sending him back to Texas to face his charges.

The way I felt about what I did toyed with me. In a way, I felt like he deserved it, but after picking up Cass that day and knowing I would be back soon to get Emon, I didn't want that for Dae. I just wished that nigga would've gotten right. I really fuckin' tried, and that shit just frustrated the hell out of me that I couldn't get it right.

"So, what's up? Where Dae and KaeDee at? I was expecting to see all y'all niggas."

"I ain't really been talking to KaeDee. Think it's been a couple of weeks since we last spoke," I told him, and I could see him turn to look at me out the corner of my eye.

"What? Why, nigga?" He pulled his hair out of his face and frowned.

"Just a bunch of shit that happened with Dae, and that nigga acting like he didn't give a fuck really pissed me off. I mean, shit, it's a lot of stuff going on, Cass, and with it being your first day being back, I don't really wanna put that burden on your shoulders like that."

"Is everybody all right? I should've known something was up when none of y'all had been down here to see a nigga in a while."

"Just been trying to set shit up for you for when you came home, and then shit just seemed to spiral out of control all of a sudden. Like, all at once. If you hadn't called me a few days ago, nigga, I would've honestly forgot all about picking you up today. That's how bad it got, bruh."

"I don't understand. What Dae still fucking up? I mean, you ain't saying shit, nigga. Tell me what's up."

I sighed and filled Cassidy in on everything that had been going on. By the time I finished telling him—of course, leaving out the part where I had snitched on Dae for Alaska's murder—we were back in the city and pulling into a gas station.

"So, you got two bricks left and no plug?" Cassidy asked, sounding as depressed as I felt. "And Dae hiding out somewhere with a bitch that he damn near beat to death that just so happens to be the plug's sister?

"Hell, yeah, only two left. And that nigga won't be out there too long before something or somebody catches up with him. I tried my best with him," I told him and got out of the car to pump the gas.

"Hey, here. Somebody named Cuba calling you," Cassidy said through the window as he handed me the phone.

"Hello? What's up, baby? You good?" I said after pumping the gas and getting back in the car.

"Look, you need to tell me what I need to know so that I can change the code to your gate. Somebody just walked up to the door and dropped another yellow envelope on your doorstep just like the last one that was left. I walked over to put it where the other one had been sitting all this time and realized you didn't even open it. So, I opened it for you, 'cause I felt kind of strange after seeing that man walk away from here like that. Anyway, it's just a bunch of photos of your crazy-ass baby mama and pictures of some little dope baggies that got the word *Allah* marked across it. I don't know what that they trying to say, but I figured maybe you would understand."

"Pictures of which baby mama?" I asked as I cranked the car and frowned.

"Of Sele—"

"Aye, bruh, what the fuck?" Cassidy yelled as I dropped the phone from my hand and reached for my pistol.

"Get down, get down!" I yelled as a barrage of bullets came flying our way. All I could think about was Dae was still fuckin' shit up for me. I had been so busy with trying to straighten out the mess that he created that I had forgotten about checking into Selena and finding out if she had something to do with us being hit that night. Not only that, but them muthafuckin' Arabs had finally come for their payback for the shit that Dae had caused.

I should've just killed that nigga, I thought as I kept my head down, put the car in reverse, and smashed on the gas.

Scrreeechhh!

To Be Continued in Addicted to a Dirty South Thug 2, coming soon!

ORDER FORM
URBAN BOOKS, LLC
300 Farmingdale Rd - Route 109
Farmingdale, NY 11735

Name (please print):_____

Address: _____

City/State: _____

Zip: _____

QTY	TITLES	PRICE

Shipping and handling-add $3.50 for 1st book, then $1.75 for each additional book.

Please send a check payable to:
Urban Books, LLC
Please allow 4–6 weeks for delivery